'I loved her.
        We all did ...'

BRIDGE TO ETERNITY

ROMOLA FARR

WILDMOOR
PRESS

First published 2019 by Wildmoor Press

ISBN 978-1-5272-3648-6

For Benita, Harry and Ollie, whose love and wisdom
I cherish more than they will ever know.

For my sister, Rowena, who inspired my lead character,
Audrey; and her husband, Chris, who is so much more than
my brother-in-law. For my paternal grandmother, Audrey,
whose name I took for my protagonist and whose grit
comes through in many of the actions she takes. For my
father, Guy and his wife Julie, who are shining examples of
what making the best of every situation can achieve. For my
brother, Ashley, who is my brother in every way and at all
times. For my paternal grandfather, The Reverend William
Longden Oakes, for playing an integral role in my life and
this story. For my Aunt Margot, whose love and intelligence
turned the course of my family's history.
For my dear mother, Jean, whose love, support and talent
imbues and inspires me every day.

For all my aunts and uncles, cousins, nieces and nephews,
Goddaughters and close friends who may not realise how
much they mean to me.

PROLOGUE

September

The legal speed limit for vehicles travelling along the Old Military Road was sixty miles an hour and he was breaking it. If a car rounded a corner in the opposite direction it would end up in a ditch because this driver was not in the mood to slow down for anyone.

The sound of cannon fire blasted from his top pocket and he reached for his phone. He took his eyes off the road to read the text, grunted, and handed the phone to the person seated beside him.

The passenger glanced at the short message, looked up and saw they were approaching a humpback bridge.

'You're going too fast.'

There was another round of cannon fire and both took their eyes off the road to look at the phone's screen. The message was clear and unequivocal. It was time to return home.

'Watch out!' yelled the passenger.

The driver lifted his eyes from the phone. Ahead, two people, holding hands, were blocking the mouth of the bridge.

He jammed on his brakes and skidded.

To regain control he took his foot off the pedal and steered the only course acceptable to him, hoping the inevitable impact would not cause too much damage to his van.

CHAPTER ONE

October – the previous year

Audrey Willatt crossed her legs and smoothed the skirt of her dress. The view out of the carriage window was exquisite but with every passing mile, the knot she felt in her gut grew tighter. She was leaving her home in the south of England and heading north to a Victorian pile she had bought a few months after her husband died, situated on the fringes of a bleak moor.

'*The next station is Hawksmead,*' stated the recorded voice from the train's speakers. Audrey stood and pulled down her folded coat from the rack above her seat and slipped it on. She picked up her handbag and followed a few passengers down the carriage to her two large and way too heavy suitcases. She felt the train slow as she lifted the heavier of the two from the rack and placed it down by the doors. She went to collect the second case and was momentarily taken aback to see it within the firm grip of a tall, well-dressed, elderly gentleman. She had spotted him when she had changed trains in Derby, and wondered whether there would be an opportunity to make his acquaintance. There was something about his posture, the way he carried himself, that appealed to her.

'May I help you get your bags off the train?' he asked.

'That's very kind of you. My mother drilled it into me never to pack more than I can easily carry. She would not have been impressed.'

The train slowed and came to a gentle stop. The door adjacent to the platform was opened by a fellow passenger pressing the illuminated button, and Audrey took her first breath of fresh moorland air.

'You get off and I'll carry the cases to the platform,' the Good Samaritan said.

Audrey didn't argue and stepped from the carriage. The stranger followed her and placed the first suitcase at her feet.

Towards the rear of the train, the guard blew his whistle. Audrey felt tense as she watched her helper climb back into the carriage to retrieve the second case. She knew this was the really heavy one.

The guard blew his whistle again.

The man held onto the door frame as he eased his way off the train and with some relief on his face placed the suitcase at her feet.

There was another long blast of the whistle and warning beeps as the door began to close. The stranger turned and almost leapt through the narrowing gap. The door slid shut and Audrey waited, expecting to see the man's face at the window, but the train moved, gathered speed and soon she was standing alone with her suitcases on the empty platform.

CHAPTER TWO

Tina Small hated carrying clients in her white VW Golf, but it was part of the job. She was usually good at relaxed chit-chat but on this occasion she had something to hide and the elegant woman sitting beside her as they drove through the former mill town was tugging at her usually immune, estate agent's conscience. How had she let this happen? She should have sent a taxi. She had broken her own golden rule and allowed Audrey Willatt to penetrate her tough enamelled veneer. *Never like a client*, her boss had warned her, and she never had, until now.

'Has the sale of the boarding house provoked much local interest?' Audrey asked, breaking the long silence.

Tina felt the blood rushing up her neck and spilling out across her cheeks. Thankfully, she had applied plenty of make-up so, with luck, her client wouldn't notice. Blushing was for losers and she had worked hard to train her brain not to do it. At one point she'd gone to a hypnotist but, ultimately, it was Tina's determination that had won through – until now. Her body felt hot as blood, pumped by guilt, flooded into surface veins, undoing years of hard work. She was a blusher and always would be. Fortunately, her hot ears were hidden by her blonde hair, but she could not hide her discordant breathing.

Her mother had suffered from panic attacks for years. Was this one? She had to get a grip. She knew she was smart, too smart to go to university.

'Why should I waste my life and money going to a school for grown-ups when I can get on with my career right now?' she had told her disappointed parents.

Now, twenty-one and with three years' working for what she had helped become the area's leading sales and lettings agency, she was experiencing her first major trauma.

It had seemed casual enough at the beginning when Trevor Harper, Tina's boss, dropped a huge bunch of keys, the largest she had ever seen, on her desk and beamed down at her. 'We got it! If we get an offer and it's accepted by the executors managing the estate, it's double commission for you, Tina, my girl.'

'Nice tie,' she responded as she scooped up the heavy bunch and pulled open a cupboard door to retrieve the agency's digital camera; its wide-angle lens giving properties a scale they often didn't deserve.

'So, what's the address?'

Trevor stopped thumbing a text on his phone, looked at the designer label on his tie and replied, 'Hugo Boss'.

'Not the tie. Where am I going?' She slipped into her new Ted Baker raincoat.

'You know, the old school boarding house, just off the High Street. The one that's been empty for years.'

Tina froze. She hadn't seen it coming. She'd been so busy selling new-build properties on an estate gracing former fields to the south of the River Hawk, she'd not heard about her boss going after the old school boarding house. If she had, she'd have ducked the job and made sure her lazy colleague, Max, had the pleasure; but now, standing with the keys in one hand and the camera in the other, she couldn't back down.

Somehow, she forced a cheery smile. She liked working for Trevor. He was happily married and never tried it on with her. He was also ambitious, and she hoped one day to be offered a partnership in what she expected would become a long chain of estate agents.

She walked to her VW Golf, worried about the task ahead but too proud to confess her fears. There was absolutely no way she could wriggle out of spending at least a couple of hours within the forbidding building and retain her pride.

She sighed as she slipped into the black leather driver's seat and clicked her belt. She checked her phone for messages before slotting it into its hands-free rest. And then she had a thought. She reached for her phone and searched online for Hawksmead and articles about the old school boarding house. Over lunch, one Sunday, her maternal grandmother had taken great delight in detailing the shocking goings-on that had led to the boarding house gaining its reputation for being haunted. To Tina's surprise, her father had got up from the table and, without a word of explanation, had walked to the end of the garden.

After much badgering, her mother had told her about her father's big brother. 'He should have been a day boy but, for some reason, your grandparents thought it would be less disruptive if he boarded. Every day, he rode his bike from the boarding house up to the main school on the moor. One morning, he was hit by a car and killed.'

'How come I've never heard of him?'

'There wasn't much child psychology in those days. Your dad was only five, and his parents thought it best if he forgot he ever had a brother. He was not taken to the funeral and all photos were hidden away.'

Frustratingly, Google could find nothing about the

events of fifty years ago. It didn't matter. Tina knew enough and it churned her perfectly flat stomach. She took a deep breath and fired up the car's engine. She told herself it was just an old building like any other. She'd be fine. When was anyone ever hurt by a…? She couldn't bear to even think the word.

She slipped the lever into first and released the handbrake. Her car always gave her a great sense of personal pride, but not today. She checked her side mirror and pulled away from the kerb with a feeling of dread she hadn't experienced for a long time. Despite photographing and measuring up numerous empty properties and never being bothered by mice and spiders, the history of the old school boarding house chilled her to the core.

Driving across the moor with its beautiful golden hues caressed by the September sun did not calm her troubled thoughts. The humpback bridge that was the northern gateway to Hawksmead came way too soon and within a further minute she was parked in a short drive that led to a porch with a tiled roof and a large oak door. She picked up the camera from the passenger seat, took a deep breath, and went around to the boot to retrieve a tripod.

She looked up at the imposing, former annexe to the abandoned school out on the moor, and decided to shoot the exterior once she'd photographed all the interiors.

Finding the right key amongst so many on the large bunch took time and Tina was all for giving up when the aged lock gave, and the door creaked open. She stepped inside and was almost overwhelmed by a sense of impending doom. The hallway was dark, despite the hour, and eerily silent. Wooden panels caked with dark brown varnish lined the walls. The floor was a mix of well-trodden terracotta tiles and patches of cement filler. Ahead was a wide oak wood staircase leading up to a half-landing, with a corridor to the left and a short flight off to the right.

Tina looked at her phone and selected one of her favourite play lists. If she was going to have to work in this miserable old building with its well-deserved reputation, she wanted to fill her head with Sam Smith, not with squeaking hinges. She inserted her ear buds and entered a world of silent tears, accompanied by the melodic pleading of *Stay With Me.*

The air in the cavernous hall had its own peculiar smell — not typical of an old house. It was pungent, and she feared it would linger in her nostrils long after she'd escaped. But that wouldn't be for several hours, even when using her super-fast ultrasonic measurer. She had no idea how many rooms there were but, judging from the exterior and the number of keys on the bunch, she was going to be alone in the house for way too long.

Determined to suppress her fears, she twisted the telescopic legs on her tripod and fixed the camera to the screw fitting. Looking at the screen on her phone, she terminated Sam Smith mid-song and welcomed Ed Sheeran's *Thinking Out Loud* into her head. After a few bars she terminated him, too. The music had to be more upbeat. She laughed at her choice and joined in the singing of One Direction's *Story of My Life,* a song she was too cool to like even when she was a teenager.

Nearly four hours of photography and measurements later, after jumping at her own shadow more times than she would admit to her boss, Tina felt boundless relief as she finally stepped out of the former boarding house. She closed the heavy front door, ensured it was locked and carried the camera across Hawksmead High Street to get a good angle on the entire structure, the last building before the High Street became the Old Military Road. It felt good to be outside, breathing in air that was sweet and fresh. Fortunately, whatever horrors lurked within the corridors had been quelled by a constant flow of her favourite music, piped into her ears.

It was early afternoon by the time Tina returned to the estate agency. Without saying a word, she hung up her raincoat and slumped down in her desk chair.

Trevor wandered over. 'Did you take all the measurements for the floor plan?'

She nodded. She'd never felt like this before as her mood was invariably buoyant.

'It's quite a place, isn't it?' he said.

She looked at him for the first time since getting back to the office. 'Nobody's going to buy it unless it's to knock down and they can't do that as it's Grade II, so it's going to stay empty.'

'You'll find some angle. There are people out there with more money than sense. And it's going for a bargain price. Of course it will sell.'

'I don't think so. It's the scariest and most depressing property I've ever been in. You do know its history?'

'Rumours and hearsay. It's just a building that needs revitalising. A little TLC. Anyway, I know you'll do your best. Get it online as soon as possible.'

Tina created the floor plan, which covered four storeys, and then turned to her camera. She transferred all the photos from the chip onto her computer's hard drive and set about selecting the best shots.

She was half-listening to Trevor's phone conversation when she saw it. She leapt up from her chair and backed away from the computer, her eyes fixed on the screen.

'I'll put it to the vendor.' Trevor ended his call and came over to her. 'What is it?' The swirling screensaver blocked the image. He moved the mouse and the image that had shocked Tina came back into view.

Trevor put his head close to the monitor. 'It's the Victorian glass. There's always a slight ripple and it's created an optical illusion.' He looked at Tina. 'Add in the clouds and you have another online hoax like the mystery ghost girl in Shropshire, or wherever it was.'

'Except, that wasn't a hoax.' Her voice caught in her throat.

'Every ghost picture online is either an elaborate scam or an optical illusion. You don't even believe in God, Tina. How can you believe in ghosts?'

'My grandmother is from Wern in Shropshire and that girl actually existed. They even know her name.' She knew she was starting to sound shrill.

'Really? Let's keep it real.'

She slumped back into her chair. 'Are you sure you want me to post this picture online, optical illusion and all?'

'Go back before the light fails and shoot the house from a different angle.' He took control of her mouse and deleted the image.

'Could you please delete it from my memory, too?' she asked.

CHAPTER THREE

Audrey Willatt opened the VW's passenger door as Tina hurried around to the boot to retrieve her cases.

'It's bigger than it looked in the photos,' Audrey said. And bigger than she remembered, aged fifteen, sitting in her parents' car waiting for them to return. She looked up at the imposing building and felt doubt creeping in as her bones caught the first chill of winter.

Tina hauled the two large suitcases out of the Golf's boot and placed them by the entrance to the driveway. 'I'll be off,' she said.

'Aren't you going to show me around?'

'It's bought and paid for, Mrs Willatt. It's all yours. My job is done.' Tina jumped into her car, but Audrey held the driver's door open.

'I think you're forgetting something.'

Tina dropped her head. 'Okay, I should've told you but it's not a legal requirement.'

Audrey waited for Tina to explain but the young woman seemed unable to find the right words.

'Relax,' Audrey said. 'It was up to me to have the building surveyed, but I chose not to. Unless the house is regularly flooded by the River Hawk or is about to be demolished by a new railway line or trunk road, I cannot imagine what it is you haven't told me.'

Tina licked her lips and looked beyond Audrey to the

red-bricked pile with its dark windows and neglected garden. She gasped.

Audrey turned around to see what had caught her attention.

'Can you see it?' Tina asked.

'See what?'

Tina looked away from the building. 'Nothing. It was just a passing cloud reflected in the Victorian window.'

Audrey waited for Tina to continue, her patience wearing thin with the increasing cold. 'I'm getting chilled. Either tell me what's bothering you or come inside and show me around.'

Tina took a deep breath and looked down at her immaculate nails.

'You're going to tell me,' Audrey continued, 'so, you may as well get on with it.'

Tina looked up, resignation written across her blushing face. 'It's haunted. I was going to mention it, but – '

'You didn't want to scare me away.' Audrey looked at the exceptionally pretty young woman sitting in the driver's seat and wanted to give her a hug. She liked the way Tina presented herself. The pride she took in her groomed appearance and pristine German car. She didn't blame her for keeping quiet about something that Audrey knew didn't exist. On a more realistic level, even if the property was riddled with wood rot and rising damp, the house was still a steal at the price Audrey had paid.

'Terrible things happened in that house a long time ago,' Tina said, in little more than a whisper. 'I should have been honest. I should have told you its history.'

'I see. Well, as it was a school boarding house, I expect there were plenty of crimes committed in the name of education.'

'I should have said something. I'm so sorry.'

'It's an old house with a sad past. That's all there is to it,' Audrey said. 'Nothing to feel bad about.'

'I've got to go.' Tina closed her door and fired up the engine. She slipped the gear lever into first and was about to pull away when Audrey banged on the roof.

Tina lowered her window. 'What's the matter?' She looked desperate.

'Excuse me, am I a ghost?'

Tina stared up at Audrey, doubt in her eyes. 'I don't understand.'

'Do you think I'm a ghost, too?'

Tina did not respond, puzzlement creasing her brow. Audrey held out her hand which Tina touched with her fingertips. 'You're not a ghost.'

'Correct. And, as I am not a ghost and cannot walk through walls, perhaps you would kindly give me the door keys?'

'I'm so sorry. I'm not thinking straight.' She scrambled for her bag and pulled out the large bunch of antiquated keys. 'There are quite a few internal doors and they all have locks.'

'Why don't you come in and show me?' Audrey felt the weight of the keys in her hand.

Tina looked up at the top window, and Audrey saw the fear in her eyes.

'It's okay, Tina. Your job is done.'

'Let me take you back to the station,' Tina blurted. 'I'll put the house back on the market. No commission. You don't want to live there, Mrs Willatt. Believe me, you don't.'

'Goodbye, Tina. Please call in whenever you're passing.'

Audrey watched Tina drive off, spinning her front wheels as she accelerated way too fast. For a few brief moments, she contemplated reaching for her phone and booking a taxi to take her back to the station. Now she was finally standing by her new home, the enormity of her situation hit her, coupled with an almost overwhelming wave of loneliness.

She was a widow, sixty-five, slim, stylish, awash with life insurance cash and shivering, not from the chill moorland breeze or the threatening clouds, but from the enormity of the task she had set herself. What had seemed a good idea at her home in Kent now felt entirely foolhardy as she stood alone, by the imposing house with its tragic past, missing her wonderful husband. But it had been her decision; her choice to rip up the inevitable future that had lain before her in Sevenoaks and strive to lure out the truth that lay within the walls of the old school boarding house.

~

September 1965

This is the secret diary of Robert Oakes
DO NOT READ UNTIL 2065

I am thirteen years old and frightened. I am not very bright. When stressed I cannot get the words out. My parents took me to a doctor. He recommended vigorous physical exercise in an outward-bound school. He said it would cure me of my stutter and help me with my school work.

It took five hours for my father to drive my mother, sister, and me to the fifteenth-century former monastery. As we drove onto the humpback bridge, which spans the River Hawk, I got my first glimpse of my uncertain future rising up out of the moor. Why do all boarding schools have to be so frightening? Why can't people be friendly?

My father parked our car near the front door. School had not officially started so there was lots of room. I wanted to fail the entrance exam but it was so easy, even I couldn't achieve that dream. A woman called Mrs Barry opened the door and guided us through the various corridors to the headmaster's study. On the way she told my parents that I wouldn't be entering the school through the main entrance once they had gone. Junior boys had their own entrance where they could change their shoes and take off muddy sports clothes. She didn't speak directly to me but to compensate my mother gave me reassuring smiles, except she wasn't really smiling. We were told by Mrs Barry that Mr Gibbs was a mountaineer and had climbed Everest or tried to. Frostbite had got the better of him and we were not to be surprised by his hands, which every boy has to shake after lunch.

Mrs Barry knocked on the headmaster's door and walked in without waiting for a reply. The room was large for an office. My first thought was that he needed the space to wield his cane – surprisingly, it was my mother's first question. Brilliant news!! There is no caning – they have many other punishments that Mr Gibbs said were much more effective.

Mrs Barry left, and Mr Gibbs invited us to have a guided tour. He went into the history of the school; how it was once an abbey and then a hospital for people with highly infectious diseases before being converted into a school in the 1920s. Being an outward-bound school, there are lots of activities apart from rugger, hockey and cricket, such as climbing the high ridge, canoeing on the River Hawk, camping on

the moor and at least half a day each week working on
the school farm that provides much of the food eaten
by the boys. My parents nodded politely. I shivered. All
I hope is that I survive until Christmas when I can go
home. Mr Gibbs took us back to our car, weighed down
at the rear by my heavy trunk. He held out his hand to
me and, for the second time, I had to shake his hard,
stubby claw. I felt sick.

My boarding house is a tall building a mile away
from the school, across the river in the local town. It
has many locked doors that Matron said once housed
workers for the local cotton mill. She showed my
parents and me up to my dormitory at the very top of
the house, which I share with three other boys. My
sister was forced to wait in the car as Matron said her
skirt was too short and would attract unwelcome
attention from older boys. It's freezing in the house
and it's not even fully-autumn yet! The cold truly bites
into my legs. Part of the school uniform is that we
have to wear corduroy shorts, whatever the
temperature outside. My father helped me lug my
heavy trunk up the stairs to the top room. My mother,
under Matron's guidance, helped me unpack, as
Matron says that all the trunks are stowed in the attic
until the end of term. Luckily, I can keep my tuck box
under my bed.

The moment came that I dreaded and feared almost
more than anything in my life. My mother pulled her
coat around her neck and I could tell that she wanted
to return to the car before she started crying. Matron
said that I could have a few minutes with my parents
to say goodbye and then I was to go and see her.
Outside the house, the cold gripped me – not the wind
off the moor, but the unwelcome chill that emanates

from every brick within the building.

Mummy gave me a hug and a kiss on the cheek and a pack of stamps so that I could write as often as I wanted, and she would write to me. My father gave my shoulder a squeeze and said, "Chin up old boy. You'll be fine. And remember, what I told you – think what you want to say and then say it – clearly. Don't stutter. If you do, other boys will pick on you and make fun." My sister hugged me and had to be prised off.

How could they leave me here? What have I done? Thirteen weeks lie ahead, but what sort of condition will I be in by the time I go home for Christmas?

I watched as the rear car lights disappeared into the rising moorland mist. I wanted to run, but there was nowhere to go. I have never felt so alone. I have no money as the school keeps my allowance and just gives me five shillings each week to spend on tuck. I went to Matron's private room. I knocked on her door, and she actually gave me a smile when I entered. She's quite old, at least forty. She told me about the bed sheets which I have to change once a week. We're allowed to change our shirts and underwear on Wednesdays, and on Sundays so that we look smart for chapel. Jockstraps are washed after every game. I hate the look of my jockstrap. It's so ugly and way too big. Matron said that she encourages showers to be taken as often as required, but each boy must shower every other day.

More new boys arrived, and Matron gave us jam sandwiches in the house kitchen. We sat there, silently eating, eight condemned boys thinking of home. The rest of the new boys coming to the school sleep within the main school building out on the moor – we're the lucky ones, Matron told us with a smile. I don't think any of us felt lucky.

After tea, we were allowed into the Common Room to watch television and to read a book. We watched The Man From UNCLE, but I couldn't follow the plot – my mind was hundreds of miles away.

Other boys arrived, older boys who turfed us out of our comfy chairs and called us names. We decided to go up the squeaky stairs to the loft room. In the dim light emitting from the bare bulb, we chatted and got to know each other. They all seem resigned to their fate, as though this experience is something that just comes with life. I know I'm here because it's my fault. If I were cleverer and didn't stutter, I wouldn't be here. This school is for boys whose parents are at their wits' end, or that's how it feels, although some of the boys seem to be really smart. I'm doing my best not to stutter and to avoid words that begin with 'W'. That's my worst letter. Sometimes my mouth goes into a spasm and my face contorts just trying to get out the word "where".

In the bed next to mine is a boy we have nicknamed 'Mini'. We're all small, but he's even smaller. I think we're going to be good friends. His real name is Small – that's funny. We all laughed – I hope he didn't mind. There's a boy called McGrath who's trying to take control of the dorm. I don't like him very much – I hope he doesn't read this. If he finds out how I really feel he'll probably give me a fat lip. The fourth boy is Phillips. His middle initial is 'L' but he won't tell us what it stands for. I don't have a middle name, but I already have a nickname – B.O. – short for body odour. They got the idea from the TV when a woman whispers into a man's ear telling him he has B.O. and that he needs deodorant. I shall write home and ask my mother to send me some. Mini told me that it's after my initials which are burned into my tuck box. But my initials are R. O. – Robert Oakes. Of course, Bobby, which my sister calls me, is short for Robert and Oakes is my surname. I've only been here a few hours and I'm B.O. – I expected a black eye but not that. I'll probably get used to it, but I'm still going to ask my mother to send me deodorant – just in case.

If you are reading this diary in a hundred years' time, ignore the printed dates. I want to be a writer and my English teacher at my prep school said that writing down thoughts and events helps to keep them in proportion – makes them more bearable. It helped Scott of the Antarctic to write down what was happening, especially as he knew in his heart that they were all doomed.

Am I doomed? I feel it.

CHAPTER FOUR

It took a while for Audrey to find the right key and a bit of
courage to push open the heavy oak door and enter the
dark, echoing hallway. She searched for a light switch and
was rewarded by the flickering of a neon strip, incongruous
within the Victorian setting. She dragged her suitcases into
the hall and pushed the front door to until she heard the
latch click in its keep. Immediately, she was subsumed by a
pervading silence and a biting chill.

She waited a few moments as her eyes adjusted to the
artificial lighting and to stiffen her resolve. Ahead, she knew
from the plans she had seen on the agency's website, was a
kitchen and laundry facility.

Leaving her bags in the hallway, Audrey went behind the
stairs and followed a dark corridor until she entered a large
kitchen which clearly had not seen much modernisation
since the Second World War. She found a Bakelite light
switch and sent power along old wiring. Neon tubes
hummed and flickered into life, illuminating a white tiled
room with an ancient cast-iron coal-burning range and a
separate hob with six gas rings.

On the far side of the kitchen, below high windows was a
deep, ceramic butler sink with separate hot and cold brass
taps. Audrey turned on the hot tap, and icy water ran over
her fingertips. Next, she checked the hob – there was gas,
but no spark to ignite it. She made a mental note to buy a

long-stemmed lighter. Prior to completion of the sale, she'd insisted the gas hob was checked by a heating engineer and was pleased to see a gas safety certificate left on the heavily marked, wooden worktop.

The lights flickered, and for a moment Audrey feared she would be spending her first night in darkness. She had not wasted money having the electrical wiring checked as she knew it would not pass muster and needed to be replaced in its entirety.

Off the kitchen in the laundry room, she discovered two 1980s Bendix washing machines. She remembered as a child, her mother had been particularly proud of her Bendix. Audrey tested them both for power and was pleased to see the glow from two dim red lights. She opened the doors and checked the drums. In one, she found a few blue-and-white rugby socks and some strange-looking under garments. Audrey held one up to the light.

'Interesting. A jockstrap. I think you've come to the end of your useful life.'

She emptied all the old clothes out of the drum and onto the floor, closed the door and set both machines to a rinse cycle.

Next, she turned her attention to the boiler. It was a vast oil-fired Paxman, at least fifty years old. Although it had been serviced prior to completion of the sale, the engineer stated in his report that it was not fit for the twenty-first century, and he could not supply a safety certificate. Audrey decided to wait until morning before trying to fire it up. She would definitely need heating when winter set in.

Leaving one suitcase in the hall, Audrey grabbed the lighter of the two and reached for the burnished handrail. Perhaps it was the additional weight of the heavy bag, but each step she took was accompanied by a creak of welcome – or warning – by the old wooden stairs. At the top of the first flight, she was presented with a wall-mounted sign with aged gilt letters stating that the lavatories were to the left. She turned right and headed up a short staircase that led to a long corridor. On her left was a closed, panelled door. She turned the knob and pushed, but the door held fast. In the gloom, Audrey found another light switch, and filaments within a dusty bare bulb hanging from a plaited flex, lit up to provide a dim glow. Out of her handbag, she withdrew the heavy bunch of keys and sighed at the quantity.

'We have the front door, and possibly the back door.' She inserted the third key on the bunch and gave it a twist.

'Well, thank you. Somebody has applied logic.' She turned the knob and swung the door open, its dust-encrusted hinges groaning.

Fading daylight, through sun-damaged, moth-eaten drapes, revealed a room that was clearly once the house's grand drawing room. A magnificent, marble fireplace, long since cold, stood against the left wall and was one of the room's few original features. Bare floorboards, bowed and worn by years of pounding by pupils, squeaked with surprise as Audrey crossed to the window. She attempted to pull open the perished curtains, but the frail material came away in her hands. With her back to the window, she examined the room, deciding whether to make it her base, her bedsitting room.

She looked up and admired the ornate ceiling, with its plaster rose and fancy cornicing, and wished she was sharing the experience with Duncan. Missing him came in waves, and it was at moments like this she felt the pain of loss the most. She yearned for his relaxed company, his wit, his wisdom and, most of all, his love and, she admitted, his love-making. Her sons would not wish to think about that aspect of her life, but Audrey was not prepared to say adieu to one of life's great pleasures quite yet, although many of her women friends seemed to relish the moment when they could shut down that particular department. Their loss of desire puzzled Audrey; hadn't they worn the same mini-skirts she had in the 1960s? Hadn't they stripped off their bras and danced through the summer of love smoking pot to Scott Mackenzie? Hadn't they spent Saturday afternoons in record shop listening booths swooning to The Beatles, The Stones, The Troggs and The Kinks? How could their tastes have changed so much? Was bridge really better than an enthusiastic husband, even one bolstered by Viagra? Audrey sighed. She loved her friends, but she didn't miss their endless talk about money, house prices, and ticking off the next item on their bucket list.

The low sun was casting angular shadows across the stark walls as Audrey stared at the fireplace. She could almost hear the chatter of boys, sent away by their parents to an outward-bound school, far from home and far away from anyone who really cared. She shivered at the thought and determined to get on with moving in. She felt the drawing room was too big for a bedroom but ideal for a sitting room which, of course, the original architect had designed it to be.

It took another hour and fifteen minutes of heaving her suitcase and examining various former dormitories before Audrey settled on a room at the top of the house that still had a working ceiling light. Bare floorboards led her eye to a tiled, cast-iron fireplace with a scorched grate. There were four narrow iron beds with thin stained mattresses and a sash window with flaking paint and panes coated with dirt. Although there were no curtains to speak of, Audrey was not concerned as only a passing falcon would be able to spy on her thin frame.

She opened her suitcase, pulled out fresh sheets and made up a bed nearest the door. She searched the room for blankets and found a pile in a high cupboard above a bookcase full of classic-looking dusty tomes, clearly overlooked by cleaners for decades.

She selected a blanket from the pile, and when shaking it out, she noticed a faded crest identifying the school: Hawksmead College. She placed the blanket on her top sheet but decided one was not going to be enough. She pulled down several more that she discarded as they had moth holes but found one in the middle of the pile that looked good enough for the time being, until she could buy a duvet. She was just unfolding it when she heard something drop on the floor. She looked down and, to her horror, saw her gold wedding ring roll along a floorboard towards the window. Unable to move fast enough, she watched it reach a gap between the boards and slip from sight.

She dropped the blanket and rushed to the spot where the ring had disappeared. She put her eye to the gap, but the light was too poor for her to see. She got back up and looked around for her handbag. In it, she retrieved her phone and went back to the spot where she had last seen her ring. She turned on the phone's torch and shone it between the boards. Light reflected from several sixpences, shillings and decimal coins that had obviously met the same fate as her ring. Although the narrow light beam did not pick out her ring, she was confident it would be safe until she could get the floorboards lifted.

~

This is the secret diary of Robert Oakes
DO NOT READ UNTIL 2065

The first morning, this morning, I got out of my warm bed into the chilly air and hastily put on my new school uniform. I took my new blue wash bag to the washroom and cleaned my teeth. I found my hat and gloves and made my way down to the bike shed where my father had deposited my second-hand bicycle, which he'd bought for twelve pounds and we'd transported on top of our car. I knew my way to the school because I could see it across the river, rising forbiddingly out of the sodden moor. A few new boys from my dorm and the dorm below, looking as fearful as I felt, also gathered their bicycles. In the dim, dawn light, we pedalled past the old cotton mill towards the humpback bridge and into a terrifying new world. My mother's last words to me were to keep my chin up and to make friends with the other boys. I'm trying.

Today involved finding our way to the various classrooms, including the science block and the biology lab. We were handed books and tools such as a slide rule which Mr MacIntosh, the maths master, said cost thirty shillings and would be charged to our parents' account. I like the mechanics of the slide rule with its clear-plastic cursor but the multitude of numbers makes my brain hurt. I was already floundering, and it was not even lunchtime.

Sorting out the pecking order seems to be what the bigger boys want. There's no real structure within each year, so who tells whom to do what is decided amongst the boys. Everything seems to be about toughening us up.

Lunch – hooray, we thought. We walked into the

great hall which is lined with long wooden tables and matching benches. Grace was said in Latin by the headmaster, who then clapped his fingerless hands and we all sat down. To welcome the new boys, the older boys ordered us to go and collect food for them and then they shouted at us for only carrying two plates, one in each hand. More experienced boys know how to carry two plates in one hand. I don't think my hand is big enough. By the time I sat down to eat, it was time for pudding. I was pushed off the end of the bench and ordered to get the gypsy tart and custard. I tried to carry three bowls, but I couldn't. When I got back to my seat to eat my first course, my plate had been taken away. I went to get pudding, but I was told I was too late – it was all gone. I shook my head and laughed to myself but kept my mouth shut. I could feel the stuttering coming on like a table lamp with a bad connection. At the end of the meal, the headmaster stood and clapped his stubby hands again.

"Today, we welcome new boys to our fraternity. There is much for them to take in and so I trust and expect older boys to offer friendly advice and a helping hand. Hawksmead College is more than a school – it is an institution where boys become men and we are unremitting in our pursuit of that aim."

Those were his words exactly as he spoke them. After lunch, I had to shake his hand again. I expected him to remember me, but I'm just another new boy.

This afternoon a trial was in store – games! Except, rugger is not a game. Games are fun, and rugger is not fun. We put on our sports kit and football boots and ran out to the rugby field. The sports master, Mr Tozer, gave us a brief rundown of the rules, which seem very confusing to me. I was placed at full-back, the last defence to stop someone scoring a try. A boy whose nickname is Elephant – he has size thirteen shoes – came running towards me. Mr Tozer told me to fall on the ball, but I knew that if I fell on the ball, Elephant would fall on me. I kicked the ball, and it spun off the field. Elephant gave me a push, which was better than being squashed. I don't like rugger. I much prefer football. Mini told me that I can get out of playing rugger by volunteering for extra work on the farm. I wasn't sure until I saw a boy called Kirby emerge from a scrum with a bleeding mouth and scratches on his cheek. Why am I here? *WHY?????*

On our second morning, the new boys in my house had to go to the sanatorium. We were told not to pee when we woke up, so all of us were bursting by the time we had cycled over the bridge and along the Old Military Road to the school some bright spark had placed in the middle of a damp moor. The school nurse gave us each a glass jar and we had to pee into it right in front of her. I filled mine to halfway but, Pearson, a big boy in the dorm below, kept on peeing until the jar was full and over-flowed. The nurse was not happy. I thought it was very funny until I was called into a room where there was an old man called Doctor Jefferies. He told me to drop my shorts and underpants and then he felt my balls. I have never been so embarrassed.

~

Audrey closed the front door of her new home and stepped out to find a place to eat. The bunch of keys given to her by

Tina weighed heavily in her handbag and she made a mental note to remove the ones she needed to open her front door.

Daylight was dwindling fast as she walked down her gravel drive. There was no gate at its mouth but Audrey saw the old steel fixings where a gate had once been positioned. She turned around and looked back at her new purchase. It was a detached, imposing residence, set in its own walled garden, and would once have been the home of a wealthy merchant before being turned into a boarding house for mill workers and then pupils attending the school out on the moor.

She decided to explore her garden while there was still enough twilight to see. The grass was high after a wet and warm summer, but excessive shrub growth had been cut back prior to sale. Audrey liked gardening, but the extent of the work to be done to restore her new garden to its former glory required the skills of a professional and, more importantly, professional equipment. She admired the old brick wall that bordered her property and the mature trees that gave her house privacy. Not that she wanted to exclude people; quite the opposite, she wanted to attract the curious and, possibly, the guilty.

The damp, long grass had soaked her shoes and feet, but Audrey was not worried as she stepped from her drive into Hawksmead High Street. To her right stretched the Old Military Road that cut through the moorland wilderness; to her left was a pavement leading to Hawksmead Methodist Chapel, an early Victorian construct in red brick and stone, with a modest spire. The church would, no doubt, have been built to provide a place of worship for mill workers; not too grand or beautiful, but a physical presence to remind hardworking weavers that God was all knowing, all powerful. Audrey liked visiting churches and looked forward to hearing its bells on Sunday morning. She may even attend a service, more for the communion of fellow parishioners than for kneeling in the presence of a constructed deity. Lying in on Sunday mornings was in her past. Sitting in bed with a cup of tea and sharing the Sunday Times with her husband, reading articles to each other, was one of the many joys from her marriage she missed.

She continued on down the High Street which was lit by Victorian lamp posts emitting sodium-coloured light. The air had a damp chill, and she made another mental note to buy some warmer clothes. Hawksmead was a small town, exhibiting enough human life to make it thrive and affording Audrey ample opportunity to say "Good evening". In many ways, walking alone made it easier for her to talk to strangers than if she'd been part of a couple; also, being of a certain vintage, passers-by were not as wary of her as they would usually be of a stranger in their midst with a distinctly southern accent.

The bow window of a news agency caught her eye, and she stopped to look at the goods on display; a mix of practical items for the office, including a variety of hole punchers, plastic folders, treasury tags and a wide selection of staplers. There were also a few plastic toys for young children, including hideous masks for Halloween. What attracted Audrey was a selection of handwritten postcards stuck in the window. She was not looking for anything in particular, but she always enjoyed reading cards advertising products and services. She opened her bag, removed her spectacles and used her phone's torch to read some of the messages. One in particular interested her and she sent a short text to herself, noting the phone number.

She went into the shop and purchased a gas-powered candle lighter, which she popped into her handbag as she carried on down the High Street. Across the road, she was pleased to see Merlin's Hardware Store. On the sign was a drawing of a bearded man holding a long staff above a marketing slogan: *A Wizard Way to Work*. Was this the one corner of the world where Harry Potter had yet to reach? Audrey laughed and continued on. Apart from a few awkward exchanges, her approaches to passers-by were rewarded with plenty of welcomes and good lucks.

'I hope you'll be very happy here,' said a tall Irishman, with a crooked back and a walking stick. 'Have you bought on the Hawk estate?'

'No,' Audrey replied.

'I hear the sound-proofing is non-existent and owners are already complaining about mould. My firm tendered for the construction, but we were undercut by a Russian outfit with an Olde English-sounding name that fooled the council. Or, perhaps it was cash in brown envelopes that swung the deal in their favour. Affordable homes? That's a joke. I protested, got a campaign together, and then had an accident. You go figure.'

Audrey was momentarily taken aback by the onslaught but regained her composure. 'My new home is the old school boarding house at the top of the town.'

The Irishman's mouth fell open, and Audrey waited for him to comment. What came out was a mirthless cackle followed by a loose cough. Struggling for breath, he carried on making his observations.

'So, you own the old school boarding house? I thought the Russians had it. Well, you do surprise me. We considered turning it into flats, but it's not really viable for conversion. I expect the Russians planned to burn it down, but you trumped them. Anyway, I wish you all the best, but be careful walking down the stairs. The floorboards are very uneven.'

'Is that how you hurt yourself?' She was beginning to regret starting the conversation.

'The executors for Hawksmead College invited a number of contractors to take a look around and bid for the property – including the Dryomov brothers. I tripped at the top of the stairs that go down into the main hall, but I could've sworn I felt a Russian paw push me from behind.' He lifted his walking stick, which was made of aged oak with a rounded end that fitted into the palm of his hand, and held it out to Audrey. 'Take this.'

She made no move to take the stick.

'Those Russkies don't give up easily. Keep this near you when alone in the house, and use it if those vodka swilling bastards ever cause you any trouble. And, believe you me, they will.'

'I think your need is greater than mine, but thank you for the insight – very much appreciated. It's been a pleasure to meet you Mr – ?'

'Hyde.'

She offered her hand. 'Audrey Willatt.'

'My advice to you, Mrs Willatt, is sell to the Russians and get the hell out.' He left her hand outstretched and hobbled away.

~

A few days have passed since my last entry and I'm beginning to get used to the way things are done. My father was in the army during the war. He said that being in the ranks with thugs was more dangerous than fighting the Japanese. He got away from them by joining the Military Police. I don't want to join anything. I just want to go home.

Each morning, I wake up in our freezing dorm, quickly pull on my clothes and go down to clean my teeth. My toothpaste is all used up. Other boys steal it. I went into town and bought Eucryl tooth powder. They don't like that. Nobody steals it. I'm learning.

Mini and I are becoming good friends. We cycle to school together and generally try to watch out for each other. People like him. They don't like me so much. I still don't know how to use a slide rule, and that is really bothering me. Mr MacIntosh is not friendly. He doesn't hit us, but to be called a numbskull is not nice – but, it could be worse.

Today, I went to a woodworking class and met some older boys. I always try to sit to one side of a class and near the front. Bad boys always sit at the back, and my theory is that the master will look over me to the trouble-makers at the rear. But woodworking is different as it's a room with loads of workbenches that we have to share.

Our first task was to practise using the tools, such as the vice, the lathe and various chisels. I could hear whispering behind me. At first, I thought they were joking, but it started to get a bit heated. Mr Cooper, the master, seemed preoccupied at the front, using a lathe to carve a candlestick-type of lamp. He was making a lot of noise but even he turned when he heard a high-pitched scream. I looked around and saw a boy with his cheek slashed open – blood was pouring down his chin and onto his shirt. The room went quiet. A boy holding a chisel tossed it onto the bench and claimed it was an accident.

Mr Cooper told me to get help. I ran out of the room and into the corridor. I saw some older boys and ran up to them, but they pushed me away before I could stutter a word. I ran out of the building and across an open area towards the headmaster's study. I tried to open a door, but it was bolted on the inside. I thought about the boy bleeding to death because I couldn't get help. I ran around the whole building, searching for a way in. The only door I knew for sure that would be open was the main entrance. I could hardly breathe when I pushed open the heavy front door. I tried to remember the way to the headmaster's study.

I was running down a corridor when my English master shouted at me to stop running. I was so relieved, I went up to him and tried to find the right words. All that would come out was 'Help!'. The master gripped my arms and looked into my face. I think he could see how worried I was. I managed to tell him what had happened. He hurried off, and I sat on a bench. I didn't know what to do. I thought rugger was bad enough, but this was serious. When I was eight, I got attacked by a dog and needed stitches. I looked at the scar on my wrist and knew that the boy would have a very long scar on his face. What would they do with the other boy? I haven't seen him since. I don't think it was an accident.

The woodworking class was the last of the day. I was too scared to go back and see all the blood. I met Mini for tea in the main dining room, or refectory as the school calls it. He told me that Mr Cooper had been in a panic. He tried to stop the blood and was cursing me for taking so long to get help.

Mini told me that some boys in the school are not normal. They've done something bad and their parents had a choice of their sons either going to a government approved school called Borstal or an outward-bound school, if the parents could afford the fees. The judges think that exercise will sort out the boys; reduce their anger and violence. I don't think my parents realised this when they agreed to send me here. Now, it really is a matter of getting through to Christmas.

CHAPTER FIVE

The Falcon had no pretensions of being a gastro-pub, but Audrey liked the look of the sandwiches and put in an order. Ted and Heather, who were the licensees for the popular chain, had managed to create a personalised environment. Although the decor clearly followed the brewery's company lines, extra little touches were distinctly Hawksmead, especially the old framed photographs taken of the local cricket team, the rugby club, and summer fetes held in the grounds of Hawksmead College. Audrey was particularly drawn to a monochrome photo of a school play and asked Ted why he had it in his pub.

'Ah, well, I wasn't always a publican,' he confessed with a smile. 'Believe it or not, when I was a boy at Hawksmead College, I did not plan to spend my days pulling pints and rolling out the barrels.'

Audrey slipped on her spectacles and examined the photo more closely, which was entitled: *Cyrano de Bergerac*. She looked at the tall, imposing publican.

'I know what you're, thinking,' Ted said. 'You're wondering how a slim, handsome, young actor became a florid, stout-of-girth landlord. Well – ' he indicated the pub, 'this is now my stage and my customers are all my players, bit parts, one and all.' He laughed at his own joke.

'Tell her who you played,' called out Heather, Ted's wife, as she carried used glasses back to the bar. She was the exact opposite of Ted: slim, petite and blonde.

'I'm sure the lady can determine simply by looking at my handsome visage,' Ted responded.

Audrey turned and examined the black-and-white print more closely; the name of each character was printed below the teenage actor playing the role. 'I don't think you were Cyrano – you don't have the nose. I don't see you as Comte de Guiche or Le Bret. And you're much too commanding to have played one of the pastry chefs.' She moved her head closer to the photograph and looked into the eyes of Roxane, the focus of Cyrano's passion. After a few moments, she put away her spectacles and approached the bar. 'You'll have to tell me.'

Ted slid a gin and tonic across the polished rosewood counter. 'It's a G & T to welcome you to our fair town.'

'Thank you.' Audrey picked up the glass and only put it back down when it contained nothing more than crushed ice and a slice of lemon. She patted her chest. 'That was a surprise – but very good.'

'Here's another surprise.'

Audrey looked across at a man sitting on a bar stool, his face red and bloated.

'Most people think Roxane was played by a girl. After all, she was very beautiful – but *he* lacked the necessary.' The man used his artisan hands to outline a pair of breasts.

Ted looked at the large clock on the wall with Roman numerals. 'Isn't it your bedtime, Vincent?'

'Have you not heard? They closed the mill more than a quarter of a century ago. There is no longer a morning horn calling workers to the looms. These days, I wake up to the gentle sounds of Ken Bruce on Radio 2.'

'Barman!' Audrey called, with a laugh in her voice. 'The same again for my friend.'

Ted grunted and exchanged a look with his wife as he pulled another pint of The Edge.

'What happened to Roxane? The boy who played her?' Audrey asked, moving closer to the old soak. 'You appear to know a lot about him.'

'Where are you from, lady?'

Audrey hesitated for a moment. 'Kent. Sevenoaks to be precise.'

'Been here long?'

'A few hours. I've bought the old school boarding house at the end of the High Street.'

Ted placed the pint of ale in front of Vincent and removed his empty glass.

'To you, good lady,' Vincent said, lifting his tankard. 'May your time in our fair town be pleasant.' He put the glass to his lips and opened his gullet. After three long pulls, the pint was gone, and he slammed the empty tankard back on the counter. He controlled a rising belch then through red-rimmed eyes he focused on Audrey. 'The old school boarding house – if only walls could talk.' He almost slipped off his stool, but regained his balance as he stood to give a mock bow.

'Madame. Before you stands – ' This time he failed to suppress the belch and grimaced as beer mixed with stomach acid surfaced into his mouth. Audrey waited for him to swallow and recover. 'Madame. Before you stands Cyrano de Bergerac – poet, musician, philosopher, swordsman – and Roxane's one true love.' He wiped away an escaping tear and sniffed, hard.

'It's fifty years, Vincent. It's time you came out of character,' Ted said from behind the bar.

'How can I? I loved her. We all did. None of us will ever forget what happened.' He meandered to the door.

'He's too smart for his own good,' Ted commented to Audrey. 'Clever, gifted, but he's allowed an unfortunate incident to cloud his entire life. Real shame.'

Audrey watched Vincent pull open the door and stagger into the chilly night. She turned to Ted and ordered a half pint of The Edge. With her drink for company, she selected an oak booth and settled back into the old, red leather padded bench. A few moments later, Heather delivered a plate of pork and applesauce sandwiches.

'Is that going to be enough?' Heather asked.

'I'm not a big eater.'

'Unlike me. What's the secret?'

'Fear. Fear of putting on weight at my ballet school and fear of putting on weight as a photographic model.'

'Then you've got a bit of catching up to do. Let me make you another round. Or, I've a lovely Bakewell pudding aching to be eaten. It looks like a squashed cowpat but it's delicious. I'll save you a slice.' Heather winked and headed for the kitchen.

Audrey took a sip of The Edge and thought about where she was at the age of sixty-five. In story terms, she was at the beginning of her third act of a life she regarded as very fortunate. She considered the many forks in the road and the decisions she had made along the way and wondered what her story would have been if she had taken another route. More and more these days, especially since the death of her dear husband, Audrey would reflect upon her life.

'Last orders,' called Ted, which Audrey took as her cue to set off for her new home. Before taking her leave, she returned to the cast photograph from *Cyrano de Bergerac*, hanging on the wall.

'Christian. You played Christian.'

'Handsome but thick!' laughed Ted, as he loaded glasses into an automatic washer.

Audrey said goodnight and, a little reluctantly, left the warmth of the friendly pub. The walk up the High Street was chilly, dark and, much to Audrey's relief, uneventful. By the time she got back to the old school boarding house, there was light rain. She wondered how a building, on the edge of a small, pretty town could look so remote and desolate.

Snapping on the dim lights, Audrey paused in the large entrance hall and looked up the flight of wide stairs ahead of her. The air was still. What was she hoping to achieve? She closed the door, and the bang echoed around the hall. Any noise felt better than the silence. She walked through the hall to the rear corridor and on to the old kitchen where she made herself a hot milk drink, courtesy of her newly purchased gas lighter and a travel-sized milk pan. It was one of a few practical items she had brought with her, together with a travel-sized kettle, an old Philips FM transistor radio, and essential supplies including teabags, a pack of Rich Tea biscuits, a small tin of cocoa, and a pint of milk. Fortunately, the giant-sized refrigerator still worked, albeit without an interior light.

In the laundry room, she took another look at the boiler and was tempted to try and fire it up. Chilled air emanated from the tiled walls, and Audrey was in no doubt she was in for a long, cold, draughty winter. But she needed daylight and a mind refreshed with sleep before attempting to get the boiler going.

Standing in the kitchen, sipping her hot drink and looking at the faded white wall tiles and terracotta floor with its old fitments for appliances long since removed, Audrey felt a strange kind of contentment. She had come to

Hawksmead on a mission and was determined to see it through, but she knew even the best-laid plan could take her in a new, unforeseen, direction. Keeping her mind open to fresh possibilities had helped to make her life interesting. She'd enjoyed her first evening in The Falcon and was intrigued by Ted. He had a wonderful, positive outlook that could only come from someone who had the imagination to enjoy the very best that life brings. He had been an actor but, like so many in that profession, he'd had to branch out. Ballet would always be Audrey's first love. She had often gone up to London by train from Sevenoaks to watch the wonderful prima ballerina, Darcey Bussell, perform, loving her stunning technique and effortless grace. Sometimes, Audrey's husband had joined her but he'd not been a theatre lover and often a long day in the office was followed by a long snooze in a very expensive Royal Opera House seat.

At the bottom of the stairs, steaming mug of cocoa in hand, Audrey looked up into the dark above and thought about the man she had met with the injured back. In the belief that houses reflect the spirit of the owner, she put on a brave smile and placed her foot on the first step, which groaned in protest under her weight. Very soon, she would appreciate that the old house creaked and howled at any excuse, whether it was from her weight on the stairs or from the wind that would often cut across the moor and whip the angular building on its way through the town.

Despite switching on all the lights, the impregnable shadows conspired to play tricks with her mind, helped by the accompanying creak of the floorboards. She wanted to hurry up the stairs to the cosy refuge of the top dormitory room, but she didn't want to spill her hot drink, so the climb was eerily creepy and slow. The house was cold, and although at this time of night, since the death of her husband, she always felt alone, she also felt a kind of presence that almost gave her comfort. Her rational mind laughed at herself, and she was smiling as she entered the top dormitory. Maybe she had been mad choosing a room so far from the nearest lavatory, but it was easily the cosiest. In time, she would move to another, larger room but, for now, this one suited her best.

She slipped out of her clothes and took masochistic pleasure in the cold biting into her thin flesh. She kept her vest on and slipped her nightdress over the top. Her phone was her link with the outside world, and she looked around for a plug socket for her charger. She found a Bakelite socket that was on the lighting circuit, designed for turning on table lamps from a wall switch, but her modern plug was the wrong size for the small, rounded holes. She moved a couple of beds and located a single, wall-mounted socket that had the contemporary rectangular holes. She plugged in her phone, turned off the centre light and climbed into the narrow bed with its strangely comforting lumpy mattress. She took a deep breath and laughed at her situation; she was lying on an old iron bed in a freezing room in a creaky house in an unfamiliar town and had not a clue what was going to transpire over the coming weeks.

With her eyes closed and the room lit only by a full moon, Audrey wrapped the thin blankets around her frame and drifted off to sleep. A cloud blotted out the moon, and the dormitory became almost pitch black.

A few minutes later, she stirred and opened her eyes but couldn't see a thing. She rolled onto her side and let sleep envelop her once again.

The moon reappeared from behind the cloud and cast a

small, human shadow on the far wall.

~

She was standing outside the prefects' room, quaking in her buckled, patent-leather shoes. The door opened, and Diana's piercing blue eyes stared down at her. Diana was head of house and not someone Audrey had ever warmed to despite her popularity with the other girls – her prowess at lacrosse having secured the winning goal in the inter-house competition.

'Come in,' Diana said, holding the door open.

Audrey had heard what happened to girls who were called to the prefects' room and felt the tears spring to her eyes. Somehow, she made her twig-like legs carry her body into a room she had never seen before. Through her blurry vision, she saw worn armchairs, an old oak coffee table with stains going back years, black-and-white framed photographs of winning lacrosse teams, and exquisite photos of the school's prima ballerinas. The door closed behind Audrey, and she heard the key being turned in the lock. Now there was no escape.

There were four prefects in the room including Diana; Sarah Woody, known as Swoody, who Audrey knew was brilliant at tennis; Elizabeth, the school's current prima ballerina since playing the lead role in *Coppelia;* and Victoria, a wonderful singer, who had melted the hearts of many of the girls' fathers when she took the role of Maria in *West Side Story*. Audrey was in awe of them all and terrified in equal measure.

Diana pulled a wooden box to the centre of the room and stared at Audrey who was trying not to wet her knickers.

'Step on the box.'

Audrey looked at the box and wished that she'd told the truth. But she'd had to protect her friend. Marjorie was on a strict diet. She was banned from eating sweets. Fat dancers were not allowed at the school where girls often went on to perform with the Royal Ballet.

'Step on the box,' snapped Diana.

Audrey moved her feet and felt wee trickle down her leg. Not much – she'd already been to the lavatory – but enough to make her feel even more self-conscious.

She climbed onto the box and stood there, not knowing where to look.

'Sing your name, girl,' Victoria barked.

'I don't understand,' Audrey said.

'Sing – Your – Name.' Diana repeated Victoria's command.

Audrey tried to sing her name, but it came out as a croak. All the girls laughed. It was a fake laugh to humiliate her.

'First position!' Elizabeth demanded. Audrey looked blank. 'She doesn't know the first position. Ha, ha, ha.'

Audrey shuffled her feet to create a hundred and seventy-degree angle – ballet's first position.

'Third position!' Elizabeth ordered.

Audrey moved her feet to second position.

'The girl's a fool. She really is dim. How long have you been here, Audrey?' Elizabeth asked.

'Nearly two terms,' Audrey said in a quavering voice.

'Fourth position.'

Audrey shuffled her feet and received a mocking round of applause. She could not believe her face could get any redder.

'Why have we summoned you, Audrey?' Diana demanded.

'Because I told a fib.'

'No! Because you lied to a prefect,' Swoody snarled. 'Do you know what happens to liars, Audrey?'

Audrey shook her head.

'Well, you're going to find out.' Swoody leapt out of her chair and reached for a heavy book which she held out to Audrey. 'Put this on your head.'

Audrey took the tome and carefully balanced it on her head. The dense pages made it very heavy. She had to stand completely still to stop the book from falling. But she managed it. Diana checked her watch.

'Now sing a song from Oklahoma,' Victoria commanded.

Audrey croaked out the first verse from the opening number, and all the girls laughed. The book fell from Audrey's head.

'Oh dear. You were so close, Audrey,' Diana said. 'Now you have to do it all over again.' She handed the book to Audrey who placed it back on her head.

'Fifth position,' ordered Elizabeth. Audrey tried to move her feet without the book sliding off her head.

'If the book falls off your head again, you'll be punished much more severely,' Diana said with glee.

Audrey felt the book sliding down the back of her head.

CHAPTER SIX

Tina arrived at the estate agency early in the morning. Magdalena and her cleaners were just leaving so she was relieved not to have to punch in the alarm code as her nail extensions had caused her to set off the alarm on more than one occasion.

She was early because she couldn't sleep. Her usually impervious conscience was bothering her. She liked Audrey; there was something good about the older woman that had cut through to Tina's heart, and she didn't feel happy leaving her alone in a house that had such an awful history.

She headed for her desk and to her surprise saw two keys she recognised attached to the agency's identification tag. Trevor must have found them in the locked key cupboard and decided that they should be given to the new owner. She checked her watch. She had time.

The VW Golf came to a quiet halt in Audrey's short drive. Tina turned off the engine and sat for a moment, not wanting to leave the warmth and safety of her comfy car for the creaks, groans and worse that lurked within the old house. She opened her bag and looked at the two house keys. She could simply post them through the letter box but that would not put her mind at rest. Of course, there was an alternative solution: Tina had Audrey's mobile number. It was 7:45 a.m. so Audrey should be awake. She tapped her screen and waited to be connected but it went straight to voicemail. Audrey must be one of those rare people who actually turned off their phone at night.

Tina opened her car door, eased herself out, and closed it quietly. She walked to the front porch, took a deep breath of cold morning air, and pushed the old porcelain button. From inside, she heard the bell ring. She waited. She imagined Audrey hearing the bell, getting out of bed, and hurrying down the stairs into the hallway.

She listened for any sounds. The door remained shut.

Tina imagined Audrey waking, taking her time and being very slow as she walked down the stairs.

Still the door remained shut.

After more than four minutes, Tina rang the bell again. She was getting cold standing on the doorstep, and even the scary house was becoming a little more inviting. She gave the bell a long push and then slid one of the keys in the lock and opened the door. Immediately, she was overwhelmed by the gloom of the hallway.

'Mrs Willatt? Audrey? It's Tina, from Harper Dennis.'

She listened.

Nothing.

She walked towards the base of the stairs and called again. No response. She looked back at the open front door and thought about the safety of her little car.

'Audrey!'

Tina knew the house well from having measured it up and decided to head for the kitchen as that was on the ground floor. The sun had not made much of an impact on the day so she dug in her bag for her small, rubber torch of which she had quite a few stashed in her car. Many houses had unlit areas and hidden hazards, so a strong, lightweight torch was an estate agent's essential tool of the trade.

Tina opened the door to the kitchen and saw the jar of cocoa sitting on the worktop. As she stood there, holding the door, pondering, she heard the piercing scream of a child, cut off by the crack of a rifle or the snapping of wood. It was an ugly sound, one that she'd never heard before, and it chilled her blood.

She slammed the kitchen door and leant against it. Her hand shook as she opened her bag and took out her phone. She had a signal, not a great one but good enough. Should she call the police or her boss, Trevor? The police would take at least ten minutes to arrive and Trevor even longer. She put her ear to the kitchen door and heard the front door slam shut. Was she trapped? In her chest she felt her heart, pounding. She took a deep breath and pulled open the door. The corridor looked long and dark.

'Hello?' She tried to instil confidence in her voice. 'Audrey?'

She hurried along the corridor into the hallway.

The front door was shut. It must've been a draught. The temptation to escape into the safety of her car was almost overwhelming. She looked up the stairs to the first landing.

'Is anyone there?'

She climbed the stairs, each step creaking under her weight. Nothing about the house felt right. She was desperate for the loo and hurried down the corridor to the washroom. She pushed open the door and looked at the long line of closed cubicle doors. A ripple went up her spine and she shivered. She could wait. She wasn't that desperate.

She returned to the top of the stairs and looked down the long corridor that led to the dormitories.

'Audrey?'

She climbed the few steps and ran to the stairs at the far end.

She called again. She looked back down the long corridor and decided climbing the stairs was her only choice. She hurried to the second floor and was halfway up the flight to the top floor when a voice stopped her dead.

'Who is that?' it called.

Relief flooded through every vein in her body.

'Audrey. Mrs Willatt. It's Tina. May I come up?' She did not wait for a response but hurried up the stairs to the top landing where Audrey was waiting, wearing slippers and a dressing gown.

'Good morning, Tina. What a surprise.'

Tina did her best to control her breathing and held out her manicured hand. In her sweaty palm were the two front door keys on a ring with the estate agency's tag.

'I found these in the office, Mrs Willatt. I rang the doorbell but when there was no reply, I was concerned.'

'For *my* safety? You look scared witless.'

'I wanted to make sure you were all right.' Tina felt far from all right herself.

'That's very kind of you, Tina. As you can see, I have survived my first night.'

Audrey took the door keys out of Tina's hand. 'I'll carry these rather than the heavy bunch you gave me. Would you like a cup of tea?'

Tina was desperate for a cup of tea, desperate for the loo, but even more desperate to leave the house.

'I would love to, but I have an early viewing.'

'Perhaps another time. I'll see you out.'

Tina walked back down the stairs, ahead of Audrey. 'May I ask a question?' she said.

'Of course.'

'Why did you pay so much for this house?'

'I put in what I thought to be a derisory offer.'

'You could have gone in much lower,' Tina said, taking care not to trip in her heels.

'I wanted the house. I didn't want to lose it. Does that surprise you?'

'I can think of a couple of people it did surprise.' She walked down the long corridor, followed by Audrey and stopped at the top of the final flight of stairs.

The front door was wide open.

Audrey shivered. 'A chilly morning. I'm surprised you left the door open.' She walked down the stairs to the entrance.

Tina stared at the open door, then followed her down.

'Thank you for bringing the keys.' Audrey smiled at the young estate agent.

'No problem. I hope you'll be happy here.'

'So far, I've been made to feel very welcome.'

'By whom?' Tina looked back into the cavernous hallway.

'By the house. I think it's happy to see me.'

'I must go.'

'Please come again. My door's always open.'

Tina gave Audrey a tight smile and walked, as quickly as her heels would allow, to her car. She pressed her fob and the alarm beeped.

'I'm planning a housewarming tea party,' Audrey called from the porch. 'You must come – bring your beau.'

'I will. I promise,' Tina replied. She gave Audrey a cheerful wave and then her situation went from desperate to critical. She really needed a pee.

'Audrey? Sorry to bother you, but can I use your loo? It's the cold air.'

'Of course.'

Tina almost ran back to the front door.

'I'll come with you,' Audrey said.

'Thank you. I didn't want to go alone.'

Audrey laughed and closed the front door. Tina followed her up the stairs and down the corridor to the washroom.

'Audrey, are you just putting on a brave face, or does this house really not bother you?'

'It doesn't bother me one jot.' Audrey opened the door to the washroom and held it for Tina, who stopped dead.

'What is it?'

Tina couldn't move. Every cubicle door was wide open. If she hadn't been bursting, she'd have run screaming from the house.

CHAPTER SEVEN

Audrey watched Tina back out of the drive and then hurried to the lavatories; the cold air was affecting her, too. She selected a cubicle and sat down, leaving the door open. Although the old wooden walls were scrawled with insults, rude words and even ruder drawings, Audrey came from tough enough stock not to be intimidated. When she pulled the chain with its decorative porcelain handle, the rush of water was a comforting sound.

She decided to test the showers, which were located around a corner from the lavatory cubicles and washbasins. They were in a large open area that had several shower heads and drains, affording no privacy. She imagined how vulnerable young boys must have felt when using them. Audrey kicked off her slippers and hung her dressing gown on one of many old iron hooks. She turned a knob and leapt back as icy water was forced out of the old brass showerhead. The boiler was off, and she was not in the mood for a cold drenching.

She wrapped her dressing gown around her shivering body and slid her feet back into her slippers. She pulled open the door and hurried down the corridor. The house felt especially bitter, so getting the old boiler going was now a priority. At the top of the stairs, the sole of her slipper caught on an uneven floorboard. Her foot came out and the vast void of the open staircase came to meet her. She flailed the air with her right hand searching for a purchase and her fingers found the burnished dome of a finial at the top of a newel post. Audrey swung round on her slender arm and slammed into the handrail and balusters. The weight of her upper body lifted her feet from the stair tread and she could feel herself going over the banister. She screamed.

No!

This could not be it. This was not why she had come to this desolate house.

Somehow, she managed to regain her balance and sat on the stairs, shaking with fear. She reached up for her slipper and made a mental note to fix the uneven floorboard. She knew she had been lucky, unlike Mr Hyde, whom she had met last night, hobbling along the High Street, condemned to back pain for the rest of his life.

The nameplate informed her it was a *Paxman Autonomic Oil-Fired Boiler.* In a stained and cracked plastic folder was an instruction manual, but Audrey did not have her glasses. In Sevenoaks, her father had installed an oil-fired boiler and she remembered watching him fire it up. She found the water stop-cock and aligned the handle to the pipe. The tap to the oil pipe was very stiff but, using the old jockstrap to protect her hand, she managed to twist it open. It took a further eight minutes of experimentation before she heard a frightening roar coming from the furnace. Toxic fumes caught in her throat, reminding her to open the exhaust flue. Satisfied with her handiwork, she looked through the thick glass viewer at the ferocious power of the flames.

The shower room was still freezing cold as she slipped off her slippers and hung her dressing gown on a hook. She turned on a tap and, surprisingly quickly, the room filled with steam.

Luxuriating in the warmth of the hot streams of water, she considered her situation. She had come to Hawksmead for a reason, but first, she must deal with practicalities, such as buying food from the local shops, and arnica for her recently acquired bruises.

She turned off the water and dried herself as quickly as she could in the rapidly cooling shower room. She shuffled into her slippers and pulled on her dressing gown as she walked back into the main washroom area. She noticed that the old mirrors were all steamed up, and was about to wipe a mirror clear when she changed her mind.

'Probably for the best,' she laughed, picking up a comb for her wet hair.

If she had wiped the mirror, she may have noticed the reflection of a young boy in corduroy shorts, standing by one of the lavatory cubicles.

~

This is the secret diary of Robert Oakes
DO NOT READ UNTIL 2065

It's over two weeks since I last made an entry on these pages. My mother writes to me all the time and manages to fill her letters with lots of news. I am at fault, not my parents. If I were half as good as they are I wouldn't be here. I look up to them in every way. I haven't mentioned the chisel fight as I know my mother would panic – but what can she do? It's down to me to find a way through.

Something bad has just happened. McGrath wanted to read my diary. I said it was just thoughts. He snatched the book away from me and looked at the front which says – 'diary'. He started to read this, and I threw myself on top of him. Mini helped me get back my book, which I've now got to hide to stop him from reading my private thoughts. Anyway, Matron came in to make sure that all was well and gave us five minutes before lights out. I pulled my diary out from under my pillow and was just about to write when a fist came out of nowhere. McGrath punched me in the eye for not allowing him to read my diary. He just punched me once, but it really hurt. Matron is coming so time to hide you, my friend.

When I woke up this morning my eye was still hurting. All today, boys have pointed and laughed at me. I don't look good. My actual eye is blood-shot, and there is swelling and purple bruising all around it. I'm not going to punch McGrath – he wants to be my friend. He said he's sorry, but I know he'll punch me again if I annoy him. Perhaps he is one of the violent boys that should be in an approved school? I don't know. I just try to ignore him.

I have some good news! I don't have to play rugger anymore. The farm has an abundant potato crop and needs extra hands. The work is cold, back-breaking and dirty, but at least I don't have Elephant landing on top of me. I'm also excited about the cows. I could get to work with them and learn how to milk. I wrote home to my parents, and Mummy said that Daddy had worked on a farm at the same age as me. She said that cows are big and heavy and to take care. Elephant is big and heavy – I'm not worried about the cows.

CHAPTER EIGHT

Word spread rapidly around the small town that the old school boarding house was now occupied by a widow. People who had avoided the building ventured to take a look, with some even bold enough to ring the doorbell, keen to meet the brave woman who'd taken on the place.

Audrey was surprised by her new celebrity and quite enjoyed being the focus of attention. Perhaps her showbiz inclination from her time as a dancer and model was bubbling to the surface.

Lying in the narrow bed, with its worn springs, she felt welcomed by the house, even comfortable. She had been dreaming of her husband. They were both in their twenties, and she wanted to hold onto the feeling. But, as with morning mist, it evaporated the more she was awake.

Audrey was making tea in the kitchen when the doorbell rang. She glanced at her watch and saw it was only a few minutes past eight o'clock. Smiling at the prospect of a visitor and hoping it would be Tina, not just the postman – with whom she'd already spent quite a while chatting on the doorstep – Audrey hurried to the front door. She pulled it open and was surprised by the size of the person blocking out the morning light.

'I'm here to make you offer.' His voice was gruff and distinctly unfriendly.

'And you are?' She knew full well that he must be the Russian property developer that Hyde had mentioned on her first night in Hawksmead.

'My name Spartak Dryomov. You heard of me?'

'By reputation. Currently, I am not in need of any services.'

Audrey was surprised. She had expected rough, peasant features but standing on her doorstep was a bulked-up Rudolf Nureyev, the famous Russian ballet dancer whose beautiful, chiselled face still made her heart beat a little faster.

'I buy house. Cash. Today, if you like. More than you pay.' His blue eyes and dirty blond hair perfectly complemented his cheekbones, and Audrey fought the urge to reach out and touch his face.

'Why now? You had plenty of time to buy it before?' she managed to ask, slightly more forcefully than she had intended.

'I wait for price to drop, then you steal it from me.'

'Now you're being ridiculous. I think you should be on your way.' She attempted to close the door but the weight of the Russian leaning against the aged oak was too great.

'You hear my offer. That is polite.' He fixed her with his blue eyes.

'I'll tell you what is polite. Not ringing my doorbell at eight o'clock in the morning without an appointment and not holding my door open in a threatening manner.'

Spartak lifted his hands and backed away.

'Sorry lady. I don't want to offend. My mistake. I am not yet used to English way.'

He strode down her drive to a white van parked at the end, opened the passenger door and climbed in. The engine revved.

Audrey waited for the van to leave before re-entering her house and slamming the door shut. She knew the Russian could be dangerous, but she did not feel in the least bit intimidated; just annoyed with herself for finding him attractive. He had sex appeal, there was no denying that. She hurried upstairs to the top dormitory room and selected practical clothes for the chill morning.

She returned to the washroom to sort out her hair and make-up. Her dear mother had taught her never to go out of the house without first applying her face. Of course, when she was young, a little mascara usually sufficed but now, skills she'd picked up as a fashion model received more and more employment. Another skill she had learned as a model was speed, and surprisingly quickly, she was smiling at passers-by as she walked down the High Street.

The little brass bell above the door tinkled as Audrey entered the front office of *The Hawksmead Chronicle*.

'Call me Mystic Meg, but I know exactly who you are, Mrs Willatt,' Andy Blake said, a tall man with sandy hair and a beaming smile. 'How may I help you today?'

Audrey slid a sheet of handwritten paper across the counter. 'I'm having a tea party to warm my new home and I would like to invite the whole town.'

Andy whistled through his crossed front teeth. 'Ooh, that could be risky. Hawksmead is a good town, but there are some unsavoury elements – not that I'm xenophobic. But, you have no idea who you may be inviting in to case the joint, so to speak.'

'They're welcome to case my joint. There is, literally, nothing to steal.'

'Interesting point of view,' Andy said. 'I'll put your advertisement in for free if you'll agree to *The Chronicle* writing an article about you. Perhaps a photo of you standing by your new home?'

'Are you sure that makes good economic sense?'

He laughed. 'If I had good economic sense, I would not have given up my chartered accountancy practice and followed my true love of journalism by saving *The Chronicle* from folding.'

Audrey held out her hand. 'You have a deal.'

Andy shook her hand. 'I'll be sending my son, Tony. He's the best journalist this side of the River Hawk. If you have time to do the photo this afternoon while it's still light, I could get the article in for the next edition, together with your invitation. Unless something actually happens in this town in the next day or so, you may well make the front page. I can see the headline now – *Haunted House Has New Resident.*' He laughed at his own joke. 'That should attract a few readers. I may have to increase the print supply to the library.'

So far, thought Audrey, as she walked back up the High Street, her simple plan seemed to be working out. Of course, it didn't mean she would achieve what she set out to do, but at least the ground was being prepared to give it a good go. And, if her plan failed, as was most likely, she would return to Sevenoaks and meet up with her old friends again for bridge, and swimming at *St Julian's Country Club*.

Giant-sized meringues in the bow window of the Olde Tea Shoppe caught her eye and, on impulse, she decided to go in. It was quite busy with customers but a table by the window came free. Whilst waiting to be served, she watched the small world of Hawksmead pass by. After a couple of minutes, she looked in her handbag and took out her phone. She wanted to give her new home a good going over before the housewarming tea party and searched online for a cleaning company.

The tea shop door banged open, and a young mother with a double buggy tried to push her way in. Audrey leapt up from her chair, leaving her phone on the table. She held the door open, as the young mother manoeuvred the buggy between the tables and chairs.

'Thank you so much. I thought, while he's asleep, I'd stop off for a coffee. I may even get to drink a hot one.'

Audrey looked at the sleeping baby and at a pretty toddler, wide awake, sitting in the buggy beside him.

'You've bought the old school boarding house, haven't you?' continued the mother.

'Is it that obvious?'

'I'm married to Tony Blake. His dad owns *The Chronicle*.'

'Then you must join me.' Audrey indicated her window table.

'If you're sure. By the way, my name's Eden – as in the famous garden.'

'Audrey Willatt.'

'And this is my little Princess Georgiana – after Prince George.'

Audrey parked the buggy whilst Georgiana was helped by her mother onto a chair. Out of her large holdall, Eden produced a book and a small pack of crayons.

Audrey sat down at the table and looked at the sleeping baby. 'What's his name?'

'Officially, it's Charles.'

'After the prince?' Audrey tried to keep the smile out of her voice.

'The prince? Oh, you mean William's dad? No, not at all. It's after Princess Charlotte. But we couldn't call him Charlotte, so Charles was the next best. Anyway, as soon as

I saw his little scrunched-up face, I knew it had to be Charlie.'

'He looks a little pale.'

'Yes, he's not himself at the moment. He had a restless night. I thought a walk out would do him good.'

Audrey looked around for someone to serve them and saw a handsome woman emerge from the kitchen, who waved and smiled. She approached the table, pad in hand. 'Hello Eden, how lovely to see you. How's your dad?'

Eden turned to Audrey. 'My dad and Eleanor dated in the seventies, but she dumped him when she went to London to sing with the English National Opera. He's never got over it.'

'I'm quite sure he has,' Eleanor said. She took Eden's order for cappuccino, and an apple drink and chocolate chip cookie for Georgiana.

'I would love a pot of tea,' Audrey added.

Eleanor peeked at the sleeping Charlie. 'He looks a bit pale.'

'He's not himself,' Eden responded.

'Back in a minute.' Eleanor headed for the kitchen and disappeared through the swing door.

'I love babies,' Audrey said. 'Would you mind if I held Charlie?'

'If he starts crying, don't blame me,' Eden said with a smile.

Audrey got up from her chair and gently eased Charlie out of his buggy seat. He slightly stirred when she held him in the crook of her arm. 'I think he may have a temperature.'

'It was up a bit when I took it this morning. I gave him Calpol. That usually works.'

Charlie's eyes opened, and he arched his back as though

trying to get away from the daylight. His little cry was dry and pained.

'He did that arching thing this morning.'

'Mummy, wee-wee,' Georgiana announced, wriggling in her seat.

'We've just got her out of nappies,' Eden declared.

Audrey touched the top of the baby's head with her fingertips and a great sense of foreboding shot through her body. 'His fontanelle is raised.' She looked at the baby's mother. 'Eden, listen to me. Call your father-in-law or your husband and get them to drive you and Charlie straight to hospital. Don't waste any time. Call now.' She saw the colour drain from Eden's face.

'Are you a doctor?'

Before Audrey could respond, Eleanor emerged from the kitchen carrying a carton of apple juice and a cappuccino, which she placed on the table, ensuring that the cup of hot coffee was away from Georgiana.

'Sorry to bother you, Eleanor, but would you mind taking Georgiana to the loo?' Eden asked getting up from her seat.

'Come on princess.' Eleanor lifted Georgiana from the wooden chair. 'You're getting heavy.' She looked at Audrey holding the baby then carried the little girl to a toilet at the back of the tea room.

Eden grabbed her bag, hanging by its straps on the back of a chair and searched in its deep recesses for her phone. Audrey noticed her shaking hands as she scrolled through contacts for a number.

'What do you think it is?' Eden asked, without looking at Audrey.

'I'm not a doctor, but he needs to be checked over.'

'It's meningitis, isn't it?' She wiped away an escaping tear and spoke for a few moments into her phone.

Audrey handed the stiff little body to his mother. Within a minute an Audi, driven by Eden's father-in-law, pulled to a halt outside the window. Audrey opened the tea room door, and Eden hurried across the pavement to the waiting car. There wasn't a child seat, but Audrey believed that the danger to Charlie from the bacteria coursing through his bloodstream was far greater than the risk of a car crash.

Or maybe she had overreacted and sent mother and baby off on a fool's journey? She hoped that was the case because the alternative was a parent's worst nightmare.

She returned to her chair and sipped the cappuccino Eleanor had made for Eden. Her thoughts had been tugged back many years to a Tuesday afternoon when she had taken her first-born son to the local GP surgery. Typical of many new mothers, Audrey had bought every baby book she could lay her hands on. From her own research and motherly instinct, she knew that something was wrong with her baby but she allowed the doctor to reassure her.

The following day, her husband, Duncan, stayed at home to nurse their son whilst Audrey read and reread her baby books. There was no internet and nobody else to talk to. By the evening, both Audrey and Duncan were convinced that their son was seriously ill. They called their local surgery and a young general practitioner came to their house. Dr Manson examined the sick child, especially his chest area.

'I'm not sure what it is but I think you should get him checked out,' she said, writing on a pad. 'Drive to Farnborough Hospital, now, and give them this note. I'll ring and let them know you're on your way, and then I'll let myself out.' She picked up their phone.

Duncan drove Audrey and their son to the hospital, where they were greeted by a junior doctor in his late twenties, who was accompanied by an older nurse.

Ten minutes later, they were approached by another doctor. 'Mr and Mrs Willatt, we believe your son has meningitis,' stated the registrar, not wasting time introducing himself. 'But, to be sure, we need to do a lumbar puncture. I recommend you wait here.'

Audrey and Duncan sat and waited, stood and paced – few words passed between them.

Another ten minutes dragged by and then the junior doctor emerged from the treatment room. 'We have sent the sample we took from your son to the lab for testing, but we are convinced he is very poorly with meningitis. We have given him antibiotics while we wait for the results of the test; they should come through before midnight.'

Pneumococcal meningitis was confirmed, and Audrey and her son were placed in an isolation ward, away from other babies. At about 3 a.m., "industrial strength" antibiotics arrived at the hospital, and a drip was set up to administer the medicine. Not being able to find a vein in the baby's arm, the drip went straight into his little head.

Saturday afternoon, Ms McFall, a consultant paediatrician, spoke to Audrey.

'Your son is very sick. The next twenty-four to thirty-six hours are critical. If he survives, he is at risk of losing most, if not all, of his hearing and vision.'

Audrey looked out of the Olde Tea Shoppe window to the pavement, where just a few minutes before she had seen the young mother holding her sick baby. She heard excited chatter as Georgiana, followed by Eleanor, rushed from the toilet, and picked up a napkin to dab her flooded eyes.

'Mummy! Mummy!'

Eleanor scooped Georgiana up into her arms. 'Mummy's had to pop out with your little brother. She wanted you to have fun, so she said we could play with you.'

Audrey saw the girl's lower lip tremble as she took in this bad news.

'But where is Mummy?' Georgiana was now fighting to free herself from Eleanor.

'Georgiana, come and have your apple juice and then I'll tell you a story about a very pretty little girl who became a princess,' Audrey said.

'And I'll get your cookie,' Eleanor added, hurrying to the kitchen.

'What's her name?' asked Georgiana, sucking up apple juice through her straw.

By the kitchen door, Eleanor sang in full operatic voice: '*Her name is Georgiaaaaaaaaana*.' The patrons in the tea room stared at Eleanor in amazement.

Georgiana's mouth dropped open. Audrey looked at the toddler and arched her eyebrows, questioningly. 'And what is the name of the little princess?'

Almost in unison, the whole room sang: '*Georgiaaaaaaaaana*.'

'Georgiana!' laughed Georgiana.

~

Hello reader in 2065. What is your world like? Have you heard of the Beatles? I like pop music. My mother likes Elvis – have you heard of him? My parents bought *Wooden Heart*. There's a lot of wooden hearts in this school, I can tell you. I hope people are nicer in 2065. It can't be much worse, at least not much worse than life in Hawksmead College for unwanted boys. I know I'm not really unwanted. My parents love me, and I love them more than anyone in the world. I do keep crying – in private. Nobody must see. Nobody must know. Not even Mini, who is now my best friend in the world.

My eye is getting better, but it's a good reminder to ignore McGrath. He's given up trying to be my friend and now just likes to make fun of me whenever he has an audience. "W…w..w.hat's the time, B.O.?" In class, he's particularly unkind, although the masters know better than to ask me a question. I don't understand why people are like this. Why does school have to be such an assault course? What have I done wrong? I'm good at English and love writing stories. The English master (Mr C) is the one teacher who doesn't make fun of me. He says nice things to me, especially when correcting prep. Prep is work we have to do outside of class in our own time. It's not exactly homework as we are very far from our homes.

I was happy today for the first time in a very long while. I got ten out of ten for an essay in English. Mr C asked me if I wanted to be a writer. I said yes, of course. My mouth was so dry with excitement that I decided to go to the drinking fountain. I turned the handle at the side and dipped my head down to the cold water. Somebody kicked me! I jumped back and looked around to see who it was, but nobody was there. A pinging sound caught my attention. I looked at the drinking fountain and saw a squashed airgun pellet in the bowl. I looked at my leg, and it was turning dark blue. The skin had split and was bleeding. Was someone trying to kill me? I looked all around me and then up at a window in a top dorm. A boy was pointing an airgun at me. I couldn't see his face. I raised my hands as I'd seen TV cowboys do when faced with a

Colt 45. I heard another crack, and some dust shot up near my feet – and then I could hear them laughing. I turned and ran back into the school building. The thought of reporting the incident never crossed my mind. They'd get me for sure if I did.

Fight! Fight! I was in the bogs, that's our name for the school lavatories, when the cry went up. I didn't want to see what was happening, so I stayed locked in my cubicle. It was Wilkins squaring up to Turnbull. I could hear the punches and the anguished cries. Both sounded hurt. Then I heard Matron who clapped her hands and told the boys to clean up and to report to her in fifteen minutes. She said that both would be deprived of hot cocoa and Wagon Wheels for a week – maybe longer if they didn't behave.

A lot of blood gets spilled in the bogs, mostly from people dropping shampoo bottles and not picking up all the broken glass. Shaving is also a hazard for some. A great "joke" is to nudge someone's shaving arm, hear them curse and then watch the blood flow. I have entered a mad world!!

Whoever you are, wherever you are, as you read my story, I hope your life is good. One day, I will be free of this place. One day.

CHAPTER NINE

'Hello Tina, it's Audrey.'

Tina was pleased but worried when she heard Audrey's voice on the estate agency's landline. 'Are you all right? You should have called me on my mobile.'

'My request is so mundane I didn't want to interrupt you negotiating a big sale.'

Tina laughed. 'Are you really inviting the whole town to your tea party?'

'Please tell me you'll come.'

Tina hesitated.

'I'm hoping this tea party will fill my new home with happiness and love. By the way, what can you tell me about a Mr Dryomov?'

Tina didn't know how to respond.

'Tina? Are you there?'

'I've not met him but, according to my boss, Trevor, he put in a ridiculously low offer. Fortunately, the estate's executors turned him down and then you came along offering a fair price, which is why we almost snapped off your hand.'

'Interesting. Now, re the tea. I've got the catering all sorted but I need a cleaning company. Is there one you can recommend? I've looked online, but as soon as I give my address they all lose interest.'

'Magdalena. She has an excellent team of Polish cleaners

who won't be in the least bit bothered by your, your – ' Tina couldn't say the word. 'I'll text you her number.'

~

Today, I herded cows for the first time. They are BIG!!! I didn't realise quite how big, and their udders are enormous. I have to admit that when I was under a cow attaching a pump to the four teats, I was scared. When the cow mooed, I leapt back and fell off my stool. And, when a cow moves, there is no stopping it. And if it kicks – watch out. She can break bones. I love the heat that comes from cows. I am always so cold that I like to be close to the animals as steam is actually rising from them. I did taste the warm milk but I prefer it chilled or hot – warm feels strange. Tomorrow, I'm back in the potato field, and I know that I will get bone cold but it's so much better than having my nose broken on the rugby field.

I didn't cry today. That's progress. Or maybe it's because of my friend, Mini. We go everywhere we can together. Some boys call us "queer", but I don't really know what they mean; we just like being close. I don't stutter when I'm with Mini. He's taught me that in the right circumstances, I can be normal. I'm not different. He's given me confidence and although I can still feel a juddering in my brain, and I still fear the letter 'W', I am more confident, but still not confident enough to raise my hand in class.

Mini has told me that the school play is *Cyrano de Bergerac* and boys rehearsing for the play will not have to go camping on the moor for three days. Mr C, my English master, is producing the play. I like him, and I know he likes me because I'm good at English. But he also knows I stutter when I'm nervous. I managed to get hold of a copy of the play and read about Roxane who charms handsome Christian and his sword-fighting friend, Cyrano. The only role I have a hope of getting is Roxane. At my prep school, I was always cast as the girl. Of course, in Shakespeare's day, boys similar to me would always play the girl. I have found a speech that I think will help get me the role. I know I can act if I can just not stutter. Of course, if there were a part for a stuttering actor I probably wouldn't get it! Mini has helped me learn the lines. I thought if I learned a speech, it would impress Mr C that bit more. Also, it's so easy to trip up over words when reading from a book. Mini thinks I have a good chance. He's a tremendous support. Without Mini, I would have run away a long time ago.

I've auditioned! I stood in line and was surprised that nobody made fun of me. Perhaps they were all too nervous. Eventually, it was my turn to walk on stage. I have read the whole play several times and rehearsed my lines with Mini so there was no risk that my mind would go blank. As I stood on the stage in the grand hall, I knew that this was my one opportunity to do something special, be someone special. When I looked out into the hall, I felt Roxane imbue my body, and I became her – and she was perfect. I spoke her words, flawlessly, without a hint of a stutter, and it was the greatest feeling I have ever enjoyed in my life. When I finished, Mr C stood and clapped.

"Well done, Oakes. The best audition of the day."

I felt so good when I heard those words.

"But, I can't give you the role because I cannot take

the chance on you not stuttering."

When I heard those words, I felt Roxane leave me.

"I won't stutter, sir. All the while I am Roxane I won't stutter. Please trust me, sir. I won't let you down."

Mr C asked me to read another speech which I hadn't learned. My whole body almost shook with fear as I looked at the lines. But then I felt Roxane's confidence flooding through my veins, and when I turned to speak, I knew that she was within every corner of my mind. And I got the role! I am so excited. Mini is also excited for me, although he is sad that I won't be going with him on the moor for three days. I'm sad about that too, but being Roxane fills me with happiness, with a joy I've not felt before.

CHAPTER TEN

Audrey couldn't help waking early each morning. Although the biting cold that blew through the old windows and corridors did not encourage her to get out of bed, the pressure on her bladder ensured she was downstairs making mint tea before 7 a.m. most days.

She hoped that by opening up her lath and plaster walls to the whole town, there was a chance that somebody would let slip information about what had gone on in the old house, even if it was second or third hand. Her husband was no longer with her; her grown-up sons had their own lives to lead, and she had nothing but old age to look forward to. If the nagging voice in her head was ever to be quelled, she had to act now. She owed it to her younger self. Occasionally, she had been a bit frightened of the dark shadows and accompanying creaks, but she would not be deterred.

Saturday arrived, and even for Audrey, who had been blessed with many special occasions during her adult life, it was a big day. She stirred the bag around in her mug and admitted to herself, as she sipped her herbal tea, that she was acting cool but did not feel it inside. She was nervous and wished her husband could share the responsibility. Too many people coming to her house scared her but too few scared her even more.

She took a shower, and whilst drying her hair she noted,

with pleasure, the high standard of cleaning. The lavatories would be available for both men and women, which certain guests may find awkward, especially if some men decided to use the "piss wall", an apt description Audrey had seen scrawled above the antiquated urinal. But, it had been a boys-only school and so there was only one set of lavatories.

The rest of her house was also spick and span, thanks to Magdalena and her team of Polish young women working all Thursday and Friday to lift the inevitable dust that had fallen since Audrey had moved in. While the girls were packing up their equipment, Magdalena had taken the opportunity to chat to Audrey. She was tall and, in Audrey's eyes, a complete knock-out with high energy and business savvy.

'Dirt,' Magdalena said, 'is never in short supply. Cleaning is boring but essential. Work is plentiful as dirt cannot be cleaned, cheap, from a call centre in Bangalore. If they want to steal my clients, they have to come here and scrub, and there are no better scrubbers than my girls.'

She kissed Audrey goodbye and wished her much happiness with her new home and life.

'Come to my party tomorrow,' Audrey said.

'I would love to, but we have two big jobs in Undermere for local council.' Magdalena opened the front door. The air was cold, but she didn't seem to notice. 'Bye-bye, see you soon. Have good party. You should charge entrance fee at door – make money.'

Audrey stood in her porch and watched Magdalena walk to her van but, before climbing in, she turned and called out to Audrey.

'Say goodbye to your grandson for me. He didn't say much, but he looks like you – typical English.' Magdalena laughed, waved, and climbed into the driver's seat.

~

I learned something today that has shocked me. Mr Gibbs asked all the new boys to go to the biology lab. I saw a projector sitting on a bench and was immediately excited. I love films, and looking at projection equipment is especially exciting. Mr Gibbs entered the lab, and we all immediately went quiet and stood by our stools. I cannot take my eyes off Mr Gibbs' hands. They are so horrible to look at and even worse to feel. He closed the door and, with his first sentence, he shocked and embarrassed us all. I cannot remember exactly what he said but here is the gist. I hope it's at least a hundred years before anyone reads this.

"Good morning, boys. Today, we are going to learn about the reproductive process – not of frogs, which I know you have been studying in biology – but humans – you and me – how we got here. Now, the temptation is to snigger and laugh, but this is a serious subject, and unless you enjoy five-mile runs followed by a five-minute cold shower, I suggest you button your lips until I ask for questions."

He ordered a couple of boys to pull down the blinds over the windows and asked me to turn off the lights. He went up to the projector and switched it on. A blurred image appeared on the white wall across the room which Mr Gibbs brought into focus. The picture was of a naked man. Mr Gibbs picked up a ruler and pointed at the man's penis and his scrotum. He told us that this was the man's equipment for making a baby. Every boy in the room felt inadequate. The next picture was of a naked woman, but we hardly had a chance to look at her before Mr Gibbs moved on to the next image. It was an outline drawing of a man with his penis all hard and at an angle. Mr Gibbs said that when the man is ready to make a baby, his penis gets hard because of the extra blood flow. The next picture was of an outline of a woman's insides, and it showed her vagina, her womb and her two ovaries, out of which she hatches an egg or two every month. The man and woman have to time it right in order for the man to fertilise the egg. At that point, I was completely lost and turned to look at Mini. Even though it was quite dark, we were able to see each other. Both of us were thinking – why would we ever do that? And then Kirby put his hand up and asked that very question.

"When a man loves a woman," stated Mr Gibbs, "he wants to help her make a baby, and in order to do that he has to inject her with his sperm. The sperm are like wriggly tadpoles that are carried in fluid into her womb, and the lucky sperm is the one that manages to stick his head into the egg first."

"What happens if other tadpoles stick their heads into the egg, too?" asked Kirby on behalf of all of us, as we were all wondering the same thing.

Mr Gibbs said that only one sperm was allowed in and that all the others would be rejected. It was at that moment I vowed never to get married. I don't know what convinces anyone to do what Mr Gibbs showed us. Another boy asked how long it would all take, and Mr Gibbs thought that forty-five minutes from beginning to end was normal. Kirby, who seemed particularly interested, held up his hand to ask another question.

"Sir, what makes the man's penis go hard, and once it's hard what makes it go soft again?"

Mr Gibbs rubbed his stubby fingers together and considered his reply.

"The man's wife makes the penis go hard, and once he has ejaculated into her, his penis quickly returns to its normal flaccid self."

There was one question I wanted to ask and, for the first time in many weeks, I put up my hand.

"Please sir, how does the man make himself ejaculate?"

Mr Gibbs rubbed his stubs even harder as he considered my question. I felt my cheeks going red, but luckily the room was fairly dark.

"The man moves back and forth within the vagina, and at the appropriate moment, his semen ejaculates from his penis and the sperm swim as fast as they can towards the egg. That is how we all come into this world. The key points you should retain are that it is only something that you need concern yourself with once you are married. Some boys and men like to practise the ejaculation experience on their own, but that is not why God gave you a penis. It is not a toy to be played with. It is a tube to facilitate urinating and when you are married, to help your wife make a baby."

"Sir, is it true that if a man pees into his wife's vagina, she will die?" Kirby seemed to have a lot of questions.

"No, that is not true because it can't be done."

"But if he did, would she die?"

"It is impossible for a man to urinate with a full erection, so the question is not relevant."

And with that, the blinds were lifted, and Mr Gibbs asked Campion, a chubby boy who is particularly clever, to carry the projector back to the headmaster's office.

I am amazed that any babies get born at all. The thought of my father doing that to my mother is impossible to imagine. It is so horrible, I vow in this diary never ever to do that.

CHAPTER ELEVEN

The first part of Saturday morning, Audrey utilised her limited calligraphy skills making signs:

Kitchen / Tea Room
Lavatories
Common Room
Dormitories

The local florist had placed vases of flowers in every dormitory room to cover any remaining musty smells.

Eleanor had closed her Olde Tea Shoppe following the Saturday lunch rush and had come to help Audrey serve tea.

'But, won't you lose business?'

'I've stuck a sign on the door informing my regulars that if they come up here they can partake in a free tea.' She cast an eye over the vast quantities of sandwiches, pastries and cakes in the kitchen. 'I have to admit, your caterers have done a good job. Logistics could be a problem, but not as long as people form an orderly queue.'

Tony Blake from *The Hawksmead Chronicle* appeared in the doorway with his camera. He was tall, wiry, almost gangly. Audrey hoped that she had been wrong about the meningitis. Any humiliation was a thousand times preferable to another baby undergoing the treatment her son had endured. She tried to read Tony's face, willing him to give her good news.

'Charlie's going to be all right,' he said with a big grin. 'It was touch and go for a while, but all is well now.'

Audrey was shocked by her reaction. Tears welled up, and she had to blink hard to prevent the excess rolling down her cheeks.

'Eden brought him home this morning,' Tony continued. 'You saved his life, Mrs Willatt. You saved his life.'

Audrey could not find the words to respond.

'Would you like a cup of tea? No charge.' Eleanor smiled. 'We need to celebrate.'

'Yes. Brilliant. I heard there's free cake, too.' Tony turned to Audrey. 'Would you mind if I took a shot of you in front of your house? Dad wants to do a big feature on the party. It could run for two issues.'

'Go on Audrey. Now is not the time for modesty,' Eleanor chivvied. 'Don't worry. If anyone comes, I'll pour the tea. After all, I am a professional.'

Audrey walked with Tony to the end of the drive and he positioned her in front of the tall, formidable boarding house, and beside a makeshift poster Audrey had taped to a piece of board.

Free Tea & Cake
All of Hawksmead, Welcome

The words were underscored by an arrow pointing to her front door.

Several passers-by stopped to watch the photography.

'Please come in,' Audrey beseeched, 'and help me warm my new home.' Glances and smiles were exchanged, and an intrepid few turned into a trickle and then a stream.

'If we have another child,' Tony said, as they walked back towards the house, 'we're calling her Audrey – if she's a girl, of course.'

'But it's not a royal name.' Audrey tried to disguise how deeply moved she was.

'Well it should be. And, if it's all right with you, we would very much like you to be Charlie's godmother. Neither Eden nor I are particularly religious but, after what's happened, we want to be – and we want to get Georgiana and Charlie christened. Please accept.'

Audrey wrapped her arms around the young man. Even if her plan didn't work out, coming to Hawksmead had already rewarded her in spades.

Young families, couples, individuals, Tony's father, Andy, and many others, crunched down the gravel drive. In the kitchen, people shuffled along the worktop counter, placing sandwiches on rigid card plates before receiving a cup of tea poured by Eleanor. At first, the chat had been a little forced but as the flow of people increased, the noise in the large, antiquated kitchen, with its hard, echoing, surfaces, became phenomenal.

Children gathered platefuls of fairy cakes and American-style muffins. And near to where Eleanor was pouring tea, there was a choice of soft drinks in cartons with straws stuck to the side.

'Few newcomers to the town,' Eleanor said to Tony, as she poured her umpteenth cup of tea, 'could have made a more positive impact than Audrey has done on our small community.'

The cacophony of chatter and laughter in the cavernous hallway pleased Audrey no end. It was exactly what the old house needed, but she was not sure how much she liked being the focus of such considerable attention. When she outlined her plans to develop the property, plans she had no intention of seeing through, she was surprised by the reactions, which were invariably supportive.

'You've set yourself a mighty challenge,' stated Colin Turner, a tall, gruff man with a florid face and a solid frame. 'But there's not one person in this room who doubts your determination to turn this miserable old building into a new and exciting asset for our town; one that will benefit all the people.' In his left hand, he was skilfully balancing a large muffin on top of an impressive pile of sandwiches. 'I missed lunch, owing to a poor round of golf, but was comforted by the thought that I would encounter a very good spread here. As you can see, disappointed I am not.'

They were approached by a stout woman with a distinctive rather than pretty face. 'I'm the mayor,' she said. 'I don't normally wear this much bling.' She gestured to the heavy gold-plated mayoral chain hanging around her neck. 'Except when I listen to rap, of course!'

Both Audrey and Colin Turner laughed.

'You're quite a celebrity, Mrs Willatt,' continued the mayor. 'And despite missing an afternoon of jam making, I couldn't not come and meet you. Most people give this house a very wide berth, even crossing the street, so I'm surprised you've got such a crowd. I've bumped into many people I know, and we all hope you'll do this every year. You've created a forum where neighbours who pass each other on the High Street with barely a smile are now firm friends.'

Audrey offered to give guided tours around the house, but party guests seemed reluctant to leave the comfort of the large groups, which disappointed her, although she didn't know what nuggets of information she expected to discover.

'The Falcon has landed,' Ted said as he eased his way up to Audrey, who was trapped in the corridor between a crowded hallway and an even more crowded kitchen.

'How lovely to see you, Christian!'

He laughed and did a cursory bow.

'I suppose your wife is minding your business?' Audrey had quite warmed to the publican.

'That's the reason she's so pale – she will not leave the inn. Of course, the invisible ball and chain around her ankle may have something to do with it!'

'And, you have your regular barflies to consider,' Audrey said.

'It was much better in the old days when the law made us close. This all-day opening is killing on the feet!'

'Would you like a guided tour, for old time's sake?'

'It's more than fifty years since I was last here. I was glad I was a local boy and not a boarder. I'm surprised anyone survived this place. Some didn't, of course, but that's a story for a very different day. Now, as the Americans say, I'll give the tour a rain check as I have just seen an old codger I've not spoken to for a while. So, thank you for making today happen. It's brought all sorts of unlikely people together.'

'I've not seen Cyrano de Bergerac, yet. Do you think he'll poke his nose in?'

Ted took a deep breath and looked intently at Audrey. 'The Michaelmas term when Vincent played Cyrano was brutal, and he suffered, particularly. It opened a fissure to his heart that alcohol has yet to heal.'

Ted eased his way through the throng to the hallway and Audrey made her way back to the kitchen, her thoughts far removed from polite chatter and tea cakes.

CHAPTER TWELVE

'Tina. How many times do I have to say it? You're a good driver with great motoring skills, but you drive too damn fast.'

Tina had made it clear when she first dated Sean that he was always going to be a passenger in her car. Now they were late for Audrey's tea, and he was complaining once again.

'Don't start. I'm not in the mood,' she snapped. 'I never drive too fast for the conditions or beyond my capability. Why can't you accept that?'

She waited for Sean to respond, but he seemed to be having difficulty choosing the right words.

'Sean, do you accept that I am a safe driver?'

She waited.

'Do you trust me,' she pressed on, 'to get you from A to B, safely?'

'Yes, of course I do.'

'Then why do you keep stamping your foot on a non-existent brake pedal? It's annoying *and* distracting.'

She turned into Hawksmead High Street and drove past the Falcon pub.

'Is it just going to be tea, or will there be booze, too?' Sean ventured to ask.

'What is your problem, Sean? Does Derby County mean so much to you, you can't even miss one match? They're playing again next week, for crying out loud.'

'I was just asking if there was going to be anything to drink? Did I mention football?'

'You didn't have to.'

They sat in silence, both pairs of eyes fixed on the road.

Look at that,' Tina said, indicating the number of cars parked near Audrey's house.

There were no parking restrictions on Saturdays in Hawksmead, which was good, but they would still have to park some way off and arrive on foot, as every parking space seemed to be taken. Although she exercised regularly in the gym, Tina hated walking. She had also spent quite a bit of time polishing her lovely VW Golf. Now, nobody would see the results of all her hard work; a shining trophy of success at such a young age.

She pulled the handbrake on, and Sean opened his door and leapt out. He hurried around the rear of the car and managed to open Tina's door before she pulled the interior handle. Sean's love for Derby County and his desire to rush around opening doors for her were beginning to be a bit of a turn-off.

'But he's drop-dead gorgeous, Tina,' said Suzanne, an old friend she had not seen since they'd had an embarrassingly drunken snog at the school leavers' party. 'And he's lovely. What's your problem?'

'He's twenty-eight and earns half what I do. He's got no ambition. He ducked uni and only trained to be an inventory clerk to earn enough beer money to go out with his mates. It's not a future.'

'But you ducked uni too,' Suzanne responded.

'I ducked uni as part of my strategic plan to get ahead, not through lack of ambition.'

'Fine. You make the dosh, and Sean's your handsome plus-one.'

'But what happens when we marry and have children?'

'Oh my God, Tina – you're pregnant!'

'No, no, but I'm thinking ahead.' She had met Sean on a job when he was carrying out an inventory for tenants who were leaving a property, and she was measuring it up for a speedy sale. She had fancied him on sight.

'You've always been good at thinking ahead,' Suzanne smiled. 'While the rest of us were trying to pick the next X Factor winner, you were planning your career path.'

'Exactly.'

'So, what's the typical career path for an inventory clerk?'

Tina took a deep breath. 'There is no career path, that's the problem. It's the kind of job middle-aged people do when all else has failed. I want Sean to reach for more; to set up his own inventory company and be the employer. There's almost no competition in Undermere, and nothing in Hawksmead. In London, checking-in and checking-out tenants is taken very seriously, and there are loads of inventory companies; but here, it's much more relaxed, with landlords often doing the work themselves. Sean has a chance to corner the inventory market; but despite my less than subtle hints, as long as he has a bit of cash in his wallet, he's happy.'

'He's happy because he's got you,' Suzanne said. 'Tell him, he can't keep eating your gorgeous cake and having it too.'

The two young women looked at each other and both burst into fits of giggles.

'That came out all wrong!' Suzanne hiccuped, and it brought on another bout of giggles. When she had just about recovered, she fought to speak through tear-filled eyes. 'You know what the answer is?'

'What? Restrict the cake?' They both doubled-up with uncontrolled laughter.

Suzanne searched her pockets as mascara tears streamed down her cheeks. Finally, she found a small pack of tissues and was able to wipe her face and give her nose a massive blow. 'Right. No more talk of cake. The answer is, *you* focus on earning the big bucks and, when a sprog arrives, Sean stays home to do the childcare. Problem solved.'

They hiccupped in unison but were too exhausted to laugh.

Tina clicked her VW fob, and the indicator lights flashed confirming that her shining beauty was locked. She took Sean's hand, and they walked at a brisk pace along the pavement towards the boarding house. Tina was not dressed for the cold – she never was; style was always her driver. As they approached Audrey's new home, she sneaked a peek at the top window and was relieved to see only clouds reflected in the pane.

'We should go up there,' Sean commented, much to her surprise.

The two crabbed their way between a Range Rover and Honda and, as they approached the open front door, were confronted by a cacophony of voices coming from the house.

'Oh my God, the whole town is here,' Tina declared.

The hallway was jam-packed and it took quite a lot of excuse-mes and close encounters for Tina to lead Sean through the chattering mass to the rear corridor and into the kitchen, where they entered the queue for sandwiches and cake. At the far end, Audrey and Eleanor were pouring cups of tea. They seemed surprisingly calm, Tina thought, bearing in mind the amazing number of guests.

'Tina!'

Tina pulled her eyes away from the array of fairy cakes and cream puffs and beamed across at Audrey, giving her a manicured-and-varnished thumbs-up. After much sideways shuffling, the young couple arrived at the tea station, and Tina introduced Sean. In return, Audrey introduced Eleanor.

'I thought you'd know each other,' Audrey said.

'Tina does not yet fit the profile of the average customer at the Olde Tea Shoppe,' Eleanor responded. 'Which is either the retired or young mums meeting other young mums with their children.'

'Mrs Willatt,' Sean said. 'I've passed this house a thousand times and always wondered what it was like inside. Is it okay if we explore?'

'Finally, somebody wants to look around. Please go into every room. Nowhere is out of bounds. Have fun. Fill the house with your youth and love.'

With a beaming smile, Sean took Tina's hand.

'Why don't we explore after we've had tea and cake?' she said, pulling back on his arm.

'There's loads of food. It'll still be here when we get back.'

Tina felt dragged by Sean as they weaved through the party guests towards the stairs in the hallway. For a moment, they were blinded by a flashbulb.

'Audrey's a really cool lady,' Sean said, keeping a firm grip on Tina's hand.

'I know this house backwards. I measured it up for sale. I don't need to explore it.'

'I bet she was really hot when she was young.' Sean almost hauled Tina up the stairs to the half-landing. He looked at the faded sign pointing to the lavatories.

'Maybe later,' he said.

'Well, maybe now for me. I'll follow you up.' Tina extracted her hand from Sean's and headed for the lavatories. She didn't really need to go, but she had to get away from him.

CHAPTER THIRTEEN

Sean climbed the few steps to the first floor corridor. It was surprisingly dark, despite the glowing bulb hanging on its plaited flex. He looked at a beautifully inscribed sign on one of the doors: *Common Room.*

'Common Room – for common people?' He laughed at his own joke, turned the knob and pushed open the door.

He wandered into the drawing room and took a few moments to admire the original plaster cornicing and marble fireplace.

'Impressive.' The door swung to behind him.

Ensuring he was alone, he went down on one knee. 'Tina, me darlin', would you do me the great honour – ' He shook his head and laughed and got back up onto his feet. 'No, she'll think that way too uncool.'

He wandered over to the Victorian sash window and looked through the grimy panes to the walled garden below.

'Would you like a wagon wheel?'

Sean spun round. He felt the hairs rise on the back of his neck as he searched the room for the source of the young voice.

~

Hello dear reader in 2065, I hope wherever you are, whatever you are, that the world is treating you kindly. If it is, it's made a lot of improvements. Poor Mini, it's time for him to leave for three days' camping on the moor. It's been raining hard for the last few days. I told him that he had to keep warm and laugh at every discomfort. Daddy says that laughing at a problem diminishes it. Mini is stoic; he may be small – he is Small! – but, he is strong and popular. I'm going to miss him – and I'm going to be alone in the boarding house, which I'm not looking forward to because it's quite spooky at night. Matron will be here, so I should be okay.

Today, we started rehearsing. A boy called Hart is playing Cyrano and he is very good. He doesn't like me, as a person, but when I become Roxane, he changes towards me. I'm a good actor. As Robert, I stutter, but when I am Roxane, it's like she's taken over my mind and body. I am her. I love her. She is beautiful and clever and sweet.

I have made a new friend. Paolo Ynsfran is from Paraguay in South America, and he is playing Roxane's duenna – a sort of older chaperone for Roxane. He is very nice, and I like him a lot. I have about eleven hundred lines to learn, but Hart has about eighteen hundred. The play has five acts, and Roxane is in four of them. I love her so much. I want to be her forever. I am so excited about the play.

Mr C fired a starting pistol during rehearsal for a battle scene, and it gave me such a shock that my knees buckled under me. He was cross that I'd over reacted, but I could tell that he regretted his words. At lunchtime, he said that he was giving us the afternoon off to learn lines and to rest. I didn't know what to do. Roxane knows all her lines. She is confident in a way that I will never be. As I was walking back to the bike shed, Mr C called out to me from his car and invited me to go home with him for tea. He drives an MG 1100, the same as my mother does, so it's nice to get into a familiar car. I like Mr C because he says kind things.

We drove to a house on the outskirts of Hawksmead. It's a nice place, smaller than my home but very cosy. It's nice to be in a homely environment after being so cold but, in a way, it made me yearn for home even more. He made a pot of tea and also put out biscuits and a jam sponge cake. He's not married and looks young. We had a good conversation about the play and how it was coming along. I am impressed by his plans for the set and am so excited to be part of something so big and so special. I sat on the sofa, and Mr C put the tray with the tea things down on the coffee table. I didn't stutter once. Not once. He made me feel so comfortable and he really does like my Roxane. He kept talking about her. It may be hard for you to believe, but people see me differently now. When they look at me, I think they see Roxane – I don't mind why people are nice. I just want them to be nice. I don't want to be punched or shot with an airgun ever again.

We talked about films and TV programmes, and although Mr C sat a bit close to me on the sofa, I enjoyed the sponge cake. After tea, he looked up film times in the local newspaper, and he took me to the cinema in Undermere. We went to see *Lawrence of Arabia*, but I didn't like it. It's full of cruelty. Towards the end, I asked Mr C if I could go into the foyer to make a phone call. He was reluctant to let me go, but I promised to wait for him by the box office. I rang home. I had enough pennies to make a call, and my mother called me straight back. She was so pleased to hear my news about the play and was absolutely thrilled when I told her about Mr C taking me to his home for tea. She promised that she and Daddy would drive up to see the play on the Saturday night. I am so excited. This is my dream. I am going to be an actor. I am not going to stutter ever again.

When my mother said goodbye and I put down the receiver, the film had ended, and Mr C was waiting for me. He said he was going to take me out for a meal before driving me back to the boarding house. We went to a smart restaurant in Hawksmead and I had Chicken Kiev. Mr C used his fork and knife to carefully pierce the chicken as he was worried that I would press too hard and squirt juice all over my shirt and jumper. He had a glass of wine, and I had apple juice. For pudding, I chose apple pie and custard and almost scraped away the bowl, it tasted so good.

Mr C drove me back to the boarding house and said hello to Matron. He reminded me that rehearsals were to start at 9 a.m. As all the boys are away, there is no chapel service. I shook Mr C's hand and thanked him for the most amazing afternoon. Matron was really nice to me too. She made me hot cocoa and gave me a Wagon Wheel which I said I would save as I was still full of apple pie. We watched some TV, but I fell asleep. She woke me up and walked with me up the creaky old stairs to my dormitory room. I like her. I don't know her name. We just call her Matron. I don't think Mr C even knows her name as he calls her Matron, too.

After three intense days of rehearsal, *Cyrano de Bergerac* is really taking shape. On Sunday night, the boys returned from the moor – cold, ill, bedraggled and much the worse for their experiences. I looked for Mini who thinks he has flu – or pneumonia, as he can't stop shivering. The showers are full of boys trying to get warm and clean off all the grime from the moor. In the Common Room, the talk is of two older boys who are missing. Part of the training was canoeing on the River Hawk, but the heavy autumnal rain has swollen the river, and they can't be found. Mini said that the river swept the boys down to the humpback bridge where a man saw them trying to grip the slippery stones.

CHAPTER FOURTEEN

Tina pulled the chain and watched the force of water swilling around the decorative toilet bowl. She opened the door and crossed to the washbasins, conscious of a tall, blond man washing his hands a few basins to her left.

'This is a first for me,' he said.

Was he talking to her? She was not a hundred per cent sure.

'I'm not used to sharing with woman.' He looked at her.

Tina smiled. 'It's a first for me, too. Some of the graffiti is quite fruity.'

'My name is Spartak.' He approached her with his hand extended. 'It is clean. I give you my word.'

Tina laughed and hastily dried hers on a paper towel. 'Tina Small.' They shook hands and she almost jolted from the electrical charge as her fine bones were encased by his palm.

'Yes, I know who you are. I wanted to buy this house.'

She froze for a moment, her mouth slightly open. 'The Russian brothers.'

'Please do not judge me too harshly. My brother is like bull in tea shop.'

'I had heard.'

'Well, it is very pleasant to meet you. We are looking to develop more land, more old houses. Point me in right direction, and I will make you rich.'

'It was very nice to meet you, too.' She turned away from him and headed for the door.

'Nothing illegal or immoral, I assure you. All I want is advance warning, so I can get my chicks in row.'

'Ducks,' she corrected him.

'I apologise. I am not being entirely honest. I would like to take you out for drink because you are the most beautiful woman I have seen since I come to UK.'

Tina looked at the man who was almost twice her age and felt an overwhelming wave of desire, which shocked her. She couldn't help but compare her boyfriend, Sean, and his lack of ambition with this sexy man whose sculpted looks were complemented by his drive to enrich himself, a quality Tina profoundly understood.

'I bet you say that to all the estate agents!' The door opened behind her, and she jumped out of the way.

'I hope I'm not interrupting anything,' said a young man with a smirk. He headed straight for the urinal, unzipping his fly en route.

'Time for me to go, I think,' Tina said, and she slipped through the door which swung to behind her. She eased her way through the throng to the top of the stairs and looked down into the hallway, which was buzzing with chatter.

'I'd like us to live in a grand house like this,' whispered Sean into Tina's ear as he wrapped his arms around her waist from behind.

'Then you'd better start earning more money.'

'Don't worry – I've got plans. Follow me.'

He almost dragged Tina up the short flight of stairs and down the long corridor to the stairway at the end.

'Where are we going?'

'To meet your little ghost boy.'

Tina pulled back on his hand. 'It was just the clouds

reflected in the glass. An optical illusion.'

'Really?' He led Tina up the next flight of stairs to the second floor. Boards creaked with every step they took. 'It's a bit chillier up here.'

'Can we go down?' Tina almost begged.

Keeping a firm grip on her hand, Sean climbed the final flight of stairs to the top landing. He let go of her and walked across to the window. 'Wow. Great view from here. You can even see the old school on the moor. Glad I didn't go there. It looks like a bloody prison or a lunatic asylum. Hey, I've got an idea. Why don't you go back down and take a photo of me at the window with your phone? See if I look like a ghost.' He laughed.

Tina didn't bother to respond. Instead, she entered the top dormitory room. Audrey's clothes were neatly folded on the narrow beds. On the windowsill was a glass vase with a generous bunch of lilies. Outside stood the oak tree, its leaves turning red and gold.

Sean came up behind her.

'Why is she sleeping in here? There's a much bigger room downstairs.'

'Sean, we've gone as far as we can. '

'You're right. Let's get out of here.'

'You go on ahead.'

'What about tea? Do you think she'll mind if we leave?'

She dug in her bag and pulled out two twenty-pound notes. 'Here. Take a taxi.'

He looked at the money then at Tina. 'What's going on?'

'Go home. We'll talk later.'

'Are you dumping me?'

'I'm sorry.'

'This is bollocks. I'm not leaving without you.'

'Please, Sean.'

'What if I can't get a taxi? They're always busy on Saturdays.'

'I'm sure you can cadge a lift off someone.'

'It's this house. You've lost your mind.' He snatched the cash out of her hand. 'Call me tomorrow when you're thinking straight again.' He swung the dormitory door back on its hinges so that it bounced against the old plaster wall.

Tina sat on Audrey's bed and put her face in her hands. She sneezed. She looked up – her eyes were swimming. On the windowsill the petals of the Spirited Grace lilies had opened and were emitting their intoxicating fragrance.

She delved into her handbag and set about repairing the damage her tears had inflicted on her cheeks. Less than happy with her work, she put her powder compact away, got up and opened the door.

Her heart skipped a beat.

Across the landing was a lone figure standing by the window. 'We meet again,' Spartak said.

He came over to her and she instinctively slid her arms around his neck. All thoughts of Sean evaporated from her mind as she tilted her head back and their lips touched.

CHAPTER FIFTEEN

'Bugger that,' said Colin Turner, the local councillor and buildings' surveyor Audrey had met earlier. 'He's full of hot air. Don't let him bully you. If you have any trouble, Mrs Willatt, let me know, and I'll rally the Hawksmead cricket team. He wants to put up a bunch of boxes on this site, but not while *I'm* on the planning committee.'

'We hope you'll be very happy in Hawksmead. This party was a brilliant idea,' said the councillor's wife. 'If you fancy a game of tennis, my local club has indoor courts.'

Before Audrey could respond, Colin cut in. 'And, if you need any advice re building works, give me a call.' He handed her his card. 'No charge.'

'Hi, I'm Jason.' Audrey turned to look into a lean, tanned, wrinkled face, offset by blue twinkling eyes. 'Thank you for the great tea. It's been a wonderful get-together for the town.'

'My pleasure. I am so pleased you could come.' She shook Jason's outstretched hand.

'Do you play tennis?' he asked.

Audrey was slightly taken aback by the question. 'Yes, a bit. It seems to be a popular sport in Hawksmead.'

'I bet you're good. I belong to a great club with air conditioning.'

Audrey put her hand up to her nose to contain a sneeze. 'Excuse me. It's the lilies. My nose is buzzing.'

'We should have a game.'

'That would be lovely.'

As soon as Jason was out of earshot, a woman – stick thin with hooded eyes, an ever-present smile and exquisite taste in clothes – kissed Audrey on each cheek and half-whispered in her ear. 'He's married. We widows must watch each other's backs.'

Audrey laughed. 'I knew he was married. A pity. He reminds me of a boy I went out with when I was fifteen. Very handsome.'

'What happened to him?'

'After a couple of weeks, I gave him a frank talk.'

'Why? What had he done?'

'Oh, absolutely nothing, except being liked by my dear mother. As soon as she said, "Oh, he's nice," I knew it was time to kiss him goodbye.'

'By the way, my name's Maureen.' She held out her bony right hand which Audrey shook. 'If you're not otherwise engaged on Monday evenings, perhaps you'd like to join our bridge set? We alternate between each other's homes; make sandwiches, coffee, et cetera. You do play, don't you?'

'Of course. That would be lovely. But perhaps when I'm a bit more sorted. Although I do already have the sandwiches,' Audrey laughed.

As if a plug had been pulled out in an old enamelled bath, tea party guests and new friends came to say goodbye and offer return invitations. Audrey was greatly admired for taking on the big old house, especially given its grim reputation.

It was the dome of his bald head that attracted Audrey's attention, then his white dog collar. Head thrust forward creating a slight stoop, what could have been quite a stern appearance was mitigated by smiling blue-grey eyes and a confident and friendly shake of Audrey's hand.

'Mrs Willatt – Longden, Reverend William.'

'Are you from the church next door?'

'Yes. To answer your unspoken question – why is a man of eighty-five still in the pulpit? I derive my income from my pension. I do not need to draw a stipend, which helps the Methodist Church. You should come and join us for tea and biscuits when you have a moment. We are raising money to sort out the rising damp that is so affecting our walls.'

'I would love to,' Audrey said. 'Churches fascinate me and, sometimes, I am almost tempted to believe.'

'Since the departure of my wife, Lily, I rattle around in the church manse. Come and visit, no prior appointment necessary – or you can find me at the church, ten a.m. every Sunday. Non-believers are most welcome.'

'I think I may have heard your bells.'

'That'll be Saint Michael's down the road – Church of England. We only have one bell, and it's cracked.'

Tina uncoupled her hand from Spartak's at the top of the stairs that led down into the hallway. There were still a few party guests, holding glasses of Prosecco.

'Tina!'

She looked down at Audrey and a tsunami of blood flooded her cheeks. She gave a little wave and hurried down the stairs followed by Spartak.

'Thank you, Mrs Willatt, it's been a wonderful event.' She kissed Audrey on each cheek.

'Please call by anytime.' Audrey turned to Spartak. 'Thank you for coming, Mr Dryomov. Are you here to make me an offer?'

'Not to buy but to renovate. I have very good team of hardworking men. Here is my card.' As if he were a conjuror, his business card appeared between his fingers.

'Thank you.' Audrey took the card. 'I'll be in touch should I need a quote.'

'And also,' Spartak said, 'if you change your mind and would like to sell, I know we can come to price that will keep smile on your face for a very long time.'

Audrey looked at Tina. 'I saw Sean storm out a little while ago. I hope everything's all right.'

Spartak put his arm around Tina's shoulder. 'Everything's just fine, Mrs Willatt. We must go. I thank you for tea. It exceeded my most optimistic expectation. I believe, when a good thing is presented to me on a plate, it is rude not to accept.' He steered Tina through the hall and out of the front door.

By the time the final tea party guests said their goodbyes and stepped into the chilly air, it was dark. Audrey made a special point of remembering names and faces but her attention was continually drawn to a tall man, wearing a herringbone jacket and silk tie, whom she had seen earlier chatting to Ted, the publican. She was sure he'd been watching her almost as keenly. She smiled to herself – it wasn't only Tina whose endorphins were on the march that Saturday afternoon.

The penultimate guests left and the gallant stranger from the train extended his hand. 'Malcolm Cadwallader, widower. A bit of a mouthful.'

She slipped her hand in his and a frisson of excitement ran through her. 'Audrey Willatt, widow. How nice to see you again.' She felt his warm, dry skin as she looked up into his eyes. 'You disappeared before I could thank you properly.'

He smiled and released her hand. 'I'd left my car at Undermere station, so had to get back on the train. This excellent tea is more than recompense for my small service.'

Why was a widower much more attractive than a divorcee? Audrey pondered. Perhaps it was the finality of death as opposed to the baggage of divorce that made Malcolm so appealing to her. She liked the way he had dressed for the occasion, and she liked his posture. As a former ballerina, Audrey always admired good posture. She also particularly admired the shape of his head with its balanced cheekbones and jaw, and how his blond hair gave him a hint of boyish youth.

'Willatt – a truly distinguished old English name,' Malcolm stated.

'It was my husband's.'

'Of course.'

'Cadwallader?'

'The last and greatest King of Wales. Seventh century, so the DNA is a bit thin!'

Audrey laughed. She settled her blue eyes on his and felt sixteen again.

'Has anyone told you that you're the spit of Audrey Hepburn?' he asked.

'You're too kind. I do have a bit of Dutch – like her.'

'Really?'

'Van Staaten.' Audrey inwardly smiled as she considered the slender link that connected her family's genes with the Netherlands. 'My great-grandfather was the painter Louis van Staaten.'

'I'm astounded!' Malcolm paused. She watched him gather his thoughts. 'I was selling a few items that belonged to my late wife at Fielding's, the auctioneers, when I saw this amazing watercolour of medieval buildings lining a canal in Flanders. The reflections of the barges in the water are second to none. I stayed for the auction and paid about seven hundred and fifty pounds; more than I've ever paid for a painting, but it gives me enormous pleasure.'

'If he'd painted in oils, it would have cost ten times as much.'

'You must come and see it.'

'Do you have etchings, too?' Audrey's marriage to Duncan had been successful from every angle and had produced two wonderful sons and two grandchildren. Why was she even toying with the possibility of a new romance?

Malcolm smiled. 'I paint a bit. I like to go up on the moor. Some of my best ideas have come to me in that wonderful wilderness.'

'What kind of ideas?'

'I was in marketing. I'm good with words; creating concepts for advertising campaigns – that sort of thing. Sadly, I do not possess your great-grandfather's artistic gift.'

They talked, in the dimly lit hall, oblivious to the debris around them and to Eleanor, who was hovering in the corridor that led to the kitchen.

'Do you like walking?' Malcolm asked.

'I do.'

'Have you walked the Ridgeway, yet?'

'I can see it from my bedroom window.'

'If you like, we could walk it together. You should definitely climb it before winter sets in.'

He entered her number into his phone and they said goodbye with another charged handshake. Audrey closed the front door as Eleanor emerged from the corridor. For a moment, the two women looked at each other.

'It's this house,' Audrey said. 'It seems to turn people on – or maybe it's the lilies.'

'I've lived in Hawksmead a long time, but he's the first man I've seen who comes close to getting my cake to rise,' Eleanor said, laughing. 'If you don't want him, send him down to the Olde Tea Shoppe. Tell him there's a cream meringue waiting for him.'

Both women guffawed.

'Why is he so attractive?' Audrey asked herself as much as Eleanor.

Eleanor pondered for a moment. 'It's our time of life. We've got our homes, we've had our families – we're no longer looking for a go-getter, a high achiever. What matters to us now are shared interests, shared pleasures, a kind character – and if there's a decent body thrown in, then that's a bonus.'

'He's very slim.'

'And has a young voice. Definitely not a smoker,' Eleanor added. 'Right, let's get on with sorting out this mess.'

'I absolutely won't hear of it.'

Rather than clearing up, they shared the remains of a bottle of Prosecco, then gave each other a sisterly hug before Eleanor said goodbye and stepped into the night.

Audrey let the door close and heard the latch click into its keep. She slid home the heavy bolts at the top and bottom, and sighed. She was alone – and didn't much like it.

There was a creak behind her.

A shiver rippled through her body.

She turned. 'Hello? Anyone there?'

Upstairs, along the corridor, she heard a door hinge squeak. Then a floorboard creaked and creaked again. She waited. She wanted to run. She was in an unfamiliar house, in an unfamiliar town, and every nerve was telling her to get out. How she yearned for the cacophony of recent chatter.

The footsteps were definitely male and getting nearer. She took a deep breath, determined to remove all tremor from her voice. 'Who's there? The party's over. It's time to go home.'

'Mrs Willatt?'

The source of the voice appeared on the half-landing.

Audrey let out a sigh of relief. 'Sean. What are you still doing here?'

'Sorry. I fell asleep.' He walked down the creaking stairs into the hallway. 'Has everyone gone?'

'Yes. I thought you had, too.'

'I came back. I wanted to speak to Tina. Did you see her?'

'I did.'

'Did she say anything about me?'

'No. We only had a brief conversation.'

'I tried her phone, but it went straight to voicemail.'

'I'm sure all will be fine in the morning.' She pulled back the heavy door bolts.

'I heard a voice, earlier. But no one was there.'

She reached for the door latch.

Sean stood very close to her and almost whispered in her ear. 'He sounded very young.'

'It must've been one of the children having fun. The chimneys act as echo chambers.'

'He asked me if I wanted a wagon wheel. A wagon wheel? Why would I want a wagon wheel?'

'A Wagon Wheel is a chocolate coated biscuit sandwich,' she said, drily, and swung the door open. 'The wind's picking up. Do you have a car?' She held the door as cold air refreshed the hall.

'No. I'll walk down the High Street and pick up a taxi at the railway station.'

'I hope you get things sorted out with Tina. She's a lovely girl. Really smart and go-ahead.'

'That she is. Goodnight, Mrs Willatt.'

She closed the door and bolted it, again.

For a moment she allowed the pervading silence to envelop her. 'Being a widow sucks, Duncan.' She wiped away an escaping tear.

The kitchen looked pretty good, thanks to Eleanor's sterling work. Cling film covered plates of uneaten sandwiches and cakes. Although there was still plenty of cleaning up to be done, Audrey had all the time in the world to sort it out in the morning.

She flicked on various feeble lights as she walked through the house, no longer needing the bunch of keys as she had unlocked every internal door. She had loved seeing so many people talking and laughing and sharing in the excitement of being together within a building that they had often crossed the road to avoid. In fact, she had almost forgotten why she had hosted the tea party in the first place.

Audrey noticed that the lights were on in the old drawing room and went to switch them off. Hot water pipes clanged together as if hit by a hammer.

She held her breath, her ears pricked for further sounds. Could there be someone else still in the house? The pipes clanged again – and she breathed out.

She went back downstairs and entered the laundry room. Despite its age, the boiler still pulled its weight, and with the help of a separate pump sent hot water through the old lead pipes. Audrey turned a knob and, protected by the thick glass window, saw the flames die back to a single pilot light.

She made a mug of cocoa, ate a couple of leftover sandwich triangles, and climbed the stairs to the half-landing. She focused her mind on Malcolm and tried to ignore the creaking floorboards that were accompanied by the wind's pitiful moan.

'Can I really fall in love again at the age of sixty-five?' She spoke the words out loud. 'Is it really possible?'

She walked along the corridor to the washroom and wondered whether she could ever again feel the same kind of love she had felt for the father of her boys. Or could it only ever be affectionate companionship? No, what she felt within her slim frame was not affectionate companionship but a sensation that took her back to when she had happily given up her virginity, to the accompaniment of Procol Harum's *A Whiter Shade of Pale*.

She laughed and pushed open the washroom door. 'Girl, there's still life in the old bones yet.'

Following her usual swift ablutions, Audrey carried her cocoa up to the top dormitory room, flicking on and off lights as she went. She smiled when she saw her single bed with its old school blankets. A lily, taken from the bouquet, had been placed on her pillow. She guessed it was Tina. What had she got up to with the Russian? She shivered as a cold draught rattled the ill-fitting window.

CHAPTER SIXTEEN

The clock in St Michael's Church struck the midnight hour as Kirill Dryomov pulled his white van to a halt. His big brother was going soft, becoming English, more of a doe-eyed spaniel than a Russian bear. Not Kirill. His face, as opposed to Spartak's handsome features, looked like it had been flattened by a shovel, the result of too many fights. If people crossed him, he punched them. Man or woman – it didn't matter. His brother may not have the stomach to deal with the old stick, but Kirill most certainly did. It was a simple matter of honour, or deep-down resentment grown from a lifetime of playing second balalaika to an older brother who was popular with women and their mother's clear favourite.

Across the street, the old school boarding house almost glowed in the street lights. He could break in now and throttle the scraggy English woman's neck. He'd enjoy that. So far, he'd killed two people in Moscow and hurt quite a few since he'd followed his brother through passport control into Britain's open arms. Of course, as his brother reminded him, the British police were not quite so easily bribed as the police and public officials in their home town of Kaluskovye.

He opened the rear doors to his van and removed an old axe.

Tina had spent the evening with Spartak following Audrey's tea party but had decided not to stay the night in Undermere's four-star White Hart Hotel. Her parents were cool about her sleeping with Sean but would definitely kick up a fuss if they knew she'd chucked Sean and had sex twice with Spartak all in the same day. Perhaps it was time to look for her own place.

The Old Military Road from Undermere back to Hawksmead seemed especially dark as the headlights on Tina's Golf strained to probe the blackness. She had no desire to live in a city or a large town but there was no doubt that the countryside at night could be really spooky. The wind was picking up off the moor, and the stark branches against the midnight sky looked like something out of a horror film. When she had broken up with her first boyfriend, Gavin, her brother had taken her to a special screening of *The Scars of Dracula* to try and take her mind off the heartache. Images of Christopher Lee as the blood-sucking count flashed through her mind.

The moon came out from behind a dark cloud, and the angular trees lining the road ahead looked especially eerie in the silvery light. Tina wished she'd stayed with Spartak in the hotel bed; the thought of snuggling up with him seemed a very good idea, but it was too late now to turn back.

A dark shadow scampered across the road and Tina slammed on her brakes.

Damn!

It was a fox, she was sure, but her nerves were playing tricks with her mind. Ahead, the road turned to the right, a typical blind bend. Tina straddled the middle of the road to take the optimum line and then she saw something up ahead.

Almost beyond the range of her headlights was a small

figure, the moon casting whoever it was in its strange, cold light. She stamped on her brake and came to a stuttering walking pace.

She checked that all her doors were locked. Through her windscreen, she saw the figure standing in the road, staring at her. He was wearing a coat, which was flapping back and forth in the gathering wind.

Fear stirred her guts, then a blinding light killed her night vision. A large vehicle blasted its horn behind her. Terrified of an impact damaging her pride and joy, Tina floored the accelerator.

The wind was turning into a gale as spots of rain splattered onto her windscreen. She knew the vehicle behind could crush her little car, but she was driving straight at a helpless child. Adrenaline coursed through her body as she debated which ditch to swerve into. And then the road veered sharply to the left by the turning to the former school. The boy miraculously became a fence post and the long flapping coat was a gate swinging back and forth in the increasing wind. Tina swept past, spurred on by the headlights tailgating her Golf. Was the boy just a trick of the moonlight? She swiftly arrived at the humpback bridge and knew she was going too fast, but if she braked hard, the vehicle behind could propel her into the river.

She screamed as her car almost took off at the apex and thumped down on the far side, a real test for her German-made suspension. She pulled the wheel and managed to prevent the Golf from crashing into the stone wall that lined the side of the bridge.

The vehicle was still following close behind, so Tina pressed her accelerator and headed for Hawksmead High Street. She was going way over the speed limit as she left the Old Military Road, and almost didn't notice the flash of a speed camera competing with the full-beam headlights in her rear-view mirror.

Audrey's house came up on Tina's left and she skidded to a halt by the entrance to the drive. The vehicle following swerved around her, slowed, blasted its horn, and sped away. It was a Range Rover similar to Spartak's. Why would he be following her to Hawksmead? He said his home was in Undermere.

Tina didn't know what to think. Her whole body was shaking. Loads of impatient people drove Range Rovers. As for the boy standing in the Old Military Road with the flapping coat – it had just been her imagination, and no more real than the big man standing in Audrey's driveway, with oak leaves swirling around him, and holding what looked like – in the glow from the streetlights – an axe.

Was she going mad? Was this a dream? A nightmare? A Hammer horror? A few hours earlier, she had been consumed with desire in the top dormitory room, and now she was consumed with fear. What was the house doing to her? Nothing had gone right since she'd first entered that hateful building.

She ground her beloved gears and fought to find first. Her clutch plates connected, her front tyres squealed, and she roared off with her mind in turmoil.

~

Audrey awoke with a start; she knew she'd been dreaming but couldn't remember what it had been about. The room was pitch black and very cold. Outside, it was clearly blowing a gale. She pulled the sheet and blankets more closely around her shoulders, wishing that she'd bought a duvet. More annoyingly, the half-drunk mug of cocoa was causing unwelcome pressure on her bladder – or, perhaps it was the Prosecco. She did not relish the cold, dark walk to the lavatories and wondered whether she was too young to have a Victorian potty tucked under her bed, as she'd seen her grandparents do when she was a little girl.

She closed her eyes and tried to slip back into sleep but, after a few seconds, she knew she had no choice but to get up. She flung back the covers and felt with her toes for her slippers. She debated putting on her dressing gown but decided that would slow her down. She stood and reached for the doorknob, which she turned. Out on the landing, a little of the sodium lighting from the High Street gave her enough illumination to find the light switch. The house was quiet; eerily quiet, Tina would say, whereas for Audrey, she felt that her new home was at peace. She was still getting to know its many little ways but, as she walked down the shadowy stairs, she was excited about the man she had met for a second time and the possibilities that lay ahead. Finding the truth about what happened in the boarding house fifty years ago suddenly seemed of secondary importance.

She came to the half-landing and felt along the wood-panelled wall for the switch. She turned on the light and smiled. Debris from her tea party littered the floor and surfaces, reminding her of the delicious touch of Malcolm's hand.

The washroom, with its hard floor and walls, was particularly cold as Audrey sat down in one of the cubicles. Her mind relaxed with her body and sleep overcame her. Her head flopped forward, waking her with a start, but even in those few seconds of sleep, she'd had a dream about a little boy, that felt stark and very real. She shivered in the cold cubicle, her thin nightdress providing little protection.

Audrey washed her hands and looked at her reflection in the mirror. She gave herself a wry smile; she knew she looked good for sixty-five, but she was no longer a pin-up, a top Lucie Clayton fashion model; a dolly bird who earned lots of cash wearing clothes designed by Mary Quant.

At the age of seventeen, she had been selected, together with four other models, to fly to Australia and attend sporting events wearing Mary Quant's latest collection. It had been a big story at the time as one of the models was the girlfriend of a member of the sixties' pop group The Monkees. Audrey had loved all the attention. Her parents had seen her on the evening news, flying off with the other girls to Australia where they were treated like film stars. The trip launched her modelling career and put a lovely sum of money in her bank account. The only downside was leaving her new boyfriend, Duncan, whom she'd met at a party in Sevenoaks. She and Duncan had clicked immediately. He was witty and cheeky, a cool dresser, physically fit and very classy. When she had kissed him goodbye at Heathrow Airport, she had secretly been thrilled to see his tears.

Audrey still felt tired but yearned for the comfort of dawn so left the lights on as she made her way up the stairs. She opened the door to her bedroom and switched on the light. All was as she had left it before heading for the lavatories.

She slipped between the sheets of her bed and was comforted by the cold cotton encasing her. She looked up at the bare bulb illuminating the room and thought about her life and the reason why she had moved to Hawksmead. She knew she mustn't lose sight of that but other plans, other desires, were now jostling for her attention.

She closed her eyes and could see the light bulb's feeble beam through her eyelids as sleep took her back to her ballet school in the heart of the Sussex countryside. She was on stage, holding hands with Curly McLain, singing *People Will Say We're in Love*. And she really had been in love with Curly, or rather Lauren, who had been Audrey's "pash" since she'd first arrived at the boarding school, aged eleven. Audrey had fought to get the role of Laurey Williams in *Oklahoma!* the musical, just so that she could spend as much time as possible with Lauren. She'd even written home to her brother and begged him to lend her his favourite six gun and holster so that Lauren as Curly would look like a real cowboy.

It was a sad day for Audrey when she left the ballet school aged fourteen. Her parents had been advised that short tendons in her legs prevented her from progressing as a ballerina. She was in the front passenger seat of her father's large Mercedes car, driving back at the end of the summer term, not relishing the prospect of attending a local school where she would be the new girl.

'Fourteen is an exciting time in your life,' announced her father, out of the blue.

'Is it?'

'Yes, very exciting, especially as you will now be at a day school,' continued her father as they drove through the beautiful Sussex countryside. 'Do you like The Beatles?'

'Of course. Everyone does.'

'Who's your favourite?'

'You know who,' Audrey said, wondering why her father had raised the subject. He liked Doris Day, The Seekers and German beer-drinking songs – why was he asking about The Beatles? But Audrey was happy to think about them, although she didn't have enough money to buy their LP.

'It's Paul, isn't it?' asked her father.

'Of course, who else could it be?'

'Mummy says a lot of her friends like John.'

'All the girls in my school love Paul.' Audrey did not tell her father she had written to Paul, declaring her love. She didn't know his address but felt sure that *Paul McCartney, The Beatles, Liverpool*, written on the envelope would definitely get her letter to him. Her old pash, Lauren, would always hold a special place in her heart, but there was no doubt that Paul was now her new and forever pash.

'Boys like girls, and it's important that you understand the whole process.'

'What process?' She was relieved he could not read her mind.

Her father had to scrape a hedgerow to prevent a head-on collision with a mini being driven at sixty miles an hour in the opposite direction.

'Blithering fool!' he shouted. Audrey hoped the scare would change the subject.

'Shall I put the radio on?' she asked.

'In a minute. I just want to clarify a few things. Boys and girls, as you may have noticed, are different in many, many ways. Girls are pure, and boys are — '

Audrey waited for him to finish the sentence. 'Boys are not pure?' she offered.

'They may be pure, but they do not have pure thoughts.'

'How do you mean?'

'Boys have a – a penis, and it can have a mind of its own.'

'A penis has a brain?'

'Not exactly, but it does control the brain.'

'Does yours control your brain?' Audrey asked, warming to the conversation.

'Good God no!' said her father, his cheeks flushing under his fourteen-year-old daughter's gaze. 'Not at all. But, you are now of an age when boys see that you are budding, and that can be awkward.'

'Budding?' Audrey asked, genuinely perplexed.

'You know… bras and things.'

Audrey looked down at her budding breasts. 'You mean my bosom?'

'Well, it's not quite a bosom yet, but they *are* budding.'

Audrey was pleased that her father had noticed the rapid change that had happened to her during the summer term of 1964. 'You think boys will notice?'

'Most definitely, and they may want to see them… without a bra.'

Audrey felt a frisson of excitement at the thought of showing off her bosom. 'I don't mind.'

Her father took his eyes off the road in alarm. 'You jolly well should!'

'I don't mind at all,' Audrey said, really beginning to enjoy the conversation. 'What harm can it do?'

'It's what it leads to.'

'Leads to?'

'Boys will not stop there.'

'Where?'

'At your… your breasts.'

'They won't stop at my breasts?' Audrey asked. 'Where will they go?'

'They'll want to go where they should not, and that is how we get unwanted babies. Do you understand?'

Audrey understood. She'd had full instructions from girls at her school on exactly what boys wanted and what she should let them do and what she should not. But she was really enjoying giving her father the run around, so feigned ignorance.

'Daddy, where will boys want to go?'

'If you let them, they'll want to go south.'

'South? I don't understand.'

Her father took a deep breath. 'South. Where your knickers are.'

'My knickers? I don't think you've got this right, Daddy. Boys like to kiss and, sometimes, touch tongues. Why would they want to go to my knickers?'

'I can assure you they do.'

'But why?' Audrey asked. 'What's there to interest them?'

'Best discuss it with your mother. I want to listen to the news.' He turned on the radio.

'...that is the end of the news. And now the shipping forecast, issued by the Met Office on behalf of the Maritime and Coastguard Agency...'

Audrey looked out of the car's side window as the BBC's Home Service shipping forecast warned of gales in Rockall, Malin, Hebrides, Bailey and Fair Isle. She knew exactly why boys wanted to go south.

'It's going to be a lovely day,' her father said. 'You should go swimming.'

'Will you buy me a bikini? One-piece swimsuits are so boring.'

She looked at the road ahead as the bright sun sent shafts of light through the canopy of trees.

Audrey opened her eyes and was surprised to see that the sun was up. At this time of year, it must mean she'd overslept. She thought about her dream and smiled to herself, before throwing back the blankets and swinging her feet to find her slippers.

Her phone beeped; she picked it up and checked the screen. It was a text. She read it; she read it again and tapped in a short reply. She hurried out of the dorm but, at the first turn on the staircase, she slipped and stumbled. She removed both slippers and carried on, her bare feet at the end of long, slim legs slapping the stairs as she rushed to the washroom.

She stepped into the cavernous shower area and turned her head up to the large rose. Shafts of freezing water cascaded over her face and naked body. She wanted to wake up; she wanted to be sharp; she wanted to be at her best.

CHAPTER SEVENTEEN

It's a few days since I last wrote my thoughts down, so I have quite a bit to tell you – and it's not happy news. On the Monday morning after the weekend break on the moors, the whole school was brought together for morning chapel. Every member of staff looked very solemn, and for the first time, the headmaster seemed unsure of himself. We didn't sing a hymn, but he went straight into an announcement.

"Christopher Wilkins and David Turnbull were canoeing as part of their Duke of Edinburgh Award. Both lost control of their canoes and were tipped into the water. Their bodies were found by the police, and their parents have been informed. It was a tragic accident, and although it may be considered ill-advised to have ventured onto the river, the ethos of our school is that risk is a part of living."

I whispered a prayer of thanks to Roxane for sparing my life. Mini said that neither boy was wearing a life jacket as it was too difficult to use the paddles with one on. Mr Gibbs then informed us of future events and that Monday was to be a normal school day.

Disturbingly quickly, we all got back into our usual routines as winter truly set in, despite it being early November. Snow covered the moor and farming duties involved cleaning out the barn and helping with the cows. No more potato picking – hooray! I have got used to the regime, and thanks to Roxane and playing a major role in the school play, I have earned the respect of even the nastiest of boys. The older boys in the boarding house still call Mini and me the queer twins but it seems to be done with some affection, as long as we take their turns to clean out the bogs. I don't mind. It's all about surviving to Christmas, and I'm happier than I thought possible in this place. And I like myself a bit more – Mr C says that I have genuine talent and that if I keep practising I will rid myself of my stutter. I hope so. Mini says it's all in my mind, and we laugh.

~

Malcolm, sitting in the driver's seat of his Honda Civic, looked at his phone and checked the local weather forecast for the day ahead. It was going to be sunny in the morning, but an icy blast was heading in from the east bringing rain from mid-afternoon. He thought about his wife, Mary, who had been the belle of Hawksmead. He remembered the first moment he'd seen her when he was aged sixteen. David Winstanley was having a gathering at his house. There were quite a few girls aged fourteen and Malcolm was entranced by their female forms. Mary was five foot four inches tall, slim and sweet, and Malcolm promised himself that one day he would marry her. But it took two more years at boarding school, three years reading English at Oxford, and two years of working and living back with his parents before he met her again, by chance, in Hawksmead High Street. In fact, she saw him coming before he saw her and she called out his name. He was immensely flattered that she remembered

BRIDGE TO ETERNITY

him at all, let alone his name. She'd been up at Edinburgh University studying for a Philosophy PhD and was home for the summer holidays. They chatted about mutual friends until Malcolm plucked up the courage to ask for her phone number.

Nearly fifty years on, driving his Honda Civic to Audrey's house, he felt the same intense excitement. He'd fancied Mary in every way a man desires a woman and was pleasantly surprised by the same surge he felt coursing through his veins when he first saw Audrey. Of course, life was more complicated these days, but at least he could text an invitation rather than having to summon up the nerve to invite her out on the phone.

She was the first Audrey he'd ever met – it was an unusual name for the post war generation. He admitted to himself that he was nervous and had taken great care with his appearance, but getting the balance right between looking smart and being comfortable was not always easy. Today, he'd had to dress for warmth but, at the same time, he wanted to wow Audrey. He could be considered too old for her at the age of seventy-five but his fitness, coupled with his excellent mind, wiped a good twenty years off his slate – at least, that's what he told himself.

The doorbell rang, and Audrey almost skipped down the stairs. She reached the half-landing and looked into the cavernous hallway, taking care not to catch her shoe on the offending floorboard.

'Just coming!' She hurried down the final flight and did a quick self-check of her clothes as she crossed the hallway, kicking aside used paper plates and plastic champagne flutes. She grabbed her coat, hat and gloves off a coat stand she had bought from a local bric-a-brac shop, and pulled back the bolts.

She opened the door to a tall man, silhouetted by the autumnal, early morning sun, and to the head of an axe embedded in the thick oak panelling.

'I see the axe man cometh,' Malcolm said indicating the axe cleaved into her door.

Audrey stared at the axe open-mouthed.

'Any idea who did it?' he asked.

It was the first axe she could recall seeing, outside of a film or on TV, and it scared her. She licked her lips and tried to control her breathing. 'I think it may have something to do with a certain Russian property developer.'

'You must let the police know.'

Audrey tried to free the axe.

'May I?' Malcolm placed his hand gently on her shoulder.

She smiled up at him and stepped aside. He used the length of the handle to lever the axe head free from the aged oak. 'At the very least, it's criminal damage,' he said.

She took the axe and placed it in her hallway. Letting Malcolm help her with the axe was a perfect ice-breaker. She must make sure to thank the Russian, she thought, smiling inwardly at her forced levity.

'Usually, I don't worry about double-locking, but I think I will now,' Audrey said, rummaging in her handbag for her keys.

She made sure that the door was fully locked and slipped her hand through Malcolm's arm. They headed off down the short drive, past Malcolm's Honda, to the main road.

Turning right, they walked in happy silence along the footpath towards the River Hawk.

'I've not been this far out of town,' commented Audrey as they turned a corner in the tree-lined road and she caught sight of the narrow, humpback bridge.

'There's no path over the bridge,' Malcolm said. 'We'd better walk in single file. I'll go first.'

'Why should you go first?' enquired Audrey, enjoying Malcolm's company more with every step.

'I'm older than you and taller. The oncoming cars will see me more easily.'

Audrey smiled and let go of his arm as they walked to the apex of the stone bridge. Malcolm continued to the far side. She paused and looked down at the fast flowing water. Malcolm hurried back to join her.

'We're living dangerously, standing like this.'

Audrey squeezed his arm. 'It's beautiful.'

'You should see it when it's in flood – it's savage.'

Audrey looked through the trees lining the riverbank to the faint outline of a distant building rising from the steaming peat bog.

'Hawksmead College – now closed, of course. It's where the boys who boarded in your house used to go every day for lessons.'

'Let's go up there.' Audrey gave him her brightest smile.

A car crested the bridge and braked hard to avoid them.

'Anything to get you off here!' Malcolm took Audrey's hand and led her down to the north side of the river.

~

There's been a terrible accident. I'm almost too sad to write it down, but you've helped me a lot, you person reading this in 2065 – your understanding has given me courage when I needed it most.

This morning, it was particularly cold on the moor. Condensation on the window panes had frozen on the inside. I dressed up as warmly as I could then Mini and I went down to the shed to collect our bikes. My teeth chattered as we pedalled. The cold went through my gloves, and my bare knees have never been so blue. There was a dense mist across the moor, and the school formed only a faint outline. As we approached the humpback bridge, the road looked like a black satin ribbon. Mini came alongside me, pedalling hard. As we cycled together onto the bridge, without warning, our wheels slid out from under us, and we landed hard on what I learned to be black ice.

We were both in shock, our knees bruised and bleeding. What had happened? It took a moment or two for us to be aware of a car coming towards us, sliding uncontrollably on the ice. I rolled as close as I could to the side of the bridge but Mini was not so quick. The car scooped him up, and I heard his bones crack as he was crushed between the bumper and the stone wall. The MG 1100 was badly damaged, and I'd never seen a schoolmaster cry until that terrible moment.

The police asked me what happened, but no one at the school wants to talk about Mini. I will write to his parents, but I don't know what to say. Do I say that I have lost a friend? Do I tell them that I loved him? What will they think of me? Will they think I'm queer? At night, I look at Mini's bed, and I can't stop crying. His mattress has been rolled up, and all his personal knick-knacks removed. McGrath calls me a baby, but I don't care. Mini is dead. He's dead and I loved him so much.

~

The Old Military Road was fairly straight. A high hedgerow

to the left blocked their view, but to the right were ploughed fields giving way to peat moorland.

'It's been a while since I walked along this road,' Malcolm said. 'Usually, I'm in my car and I forget how beautiful it is out here.'

'Crataegus monogyna,' responded Audrey, indicating the hedgerow.

Malcolm laughed. 'Common hawthorn. Did you study Latin?'

'I know the Latin name for a few plants, but at my ballet school French was more important. It's the language of dance.'

Twenty minutes later, they passed a rusting triangular sign warning motorists that a school was up ahead. A few minutes' further walking and a side road opened up to the right with a sign on the far corner announcing in weathered letters: *Hawksmead College.*

They turned right and walked along the narrow road, bounded by hawthorn hedges that required trimming after bounteous summer growth.

'Did your parents send you to Hawksmead College?' Audrey asked, happy to have her hand warmed by Malcolm's crooked arm.

'No, it was a boarding school for troubled boys, designed to build character through a variety of physical challenges. At least, that's what it said in the prospectus. Anyway, it was way too alternative for my parents. They sent me to more of a classic British boarding school in Kent. A sort of poor man's Eton with a uniform less grand but still with detachable stiff collars. It now has girls, but in my day, it was cold, sadistic, and I hated every moment.'

'But your schooldays were still the happiest days of your life. No?'

Malcolm burst out laughing. 'I hope the happiest days of my life are still to come.'

Audrey squeezed his arm as they continued walking towards the old school, breathing in the damp moorland air and relishing its mix of odours.

'I was a fag,' Malcolm stated, 'and earned ten shillings for the privilege.'

Audrey laughed. 'In other words, you were a personal servant to an older boy?'

'Yes, to the head of house. A good-looking boy called Stuart Feltwell. It was a poisoned chalice because I was accused by my peers of passing on information to him. I didn't reveal anything, but other boys thought I did. Feltwell was kind to me, but he liked his privileged position too much and made sure that no junior mistook his friendly demeanour for weakness. His beatings were a regular occurrence and inflicted for the tiniest transgression. It was an alternative form of bullying.'

'Sadly, bullies do quite well in our world,' Audrey said.

'Like your Russian friend.'

'He's the first Russian I've ever met, and he reminds me of Rudolf Nureyev. I loved him when I was a little girl. He was beautiful and courageous.'

'As are you! My apologies. That was a bit forward.'

Audrey couldn't contain her smile as a warm glow engulfed her body.

Malcolm stopped walking and turned to her. 'You must inform the police.'

'I may be wrong blaming the Russian. He looked much more interested in bedding my estate agent than embedding his axe in my door.'

'Interesting.'

They stood close together as they shared the view of

rolling hills with their scattered clumps of trees.

'It is beautiful,' she said. 'But it must have been a frightening, lonely view for a young boy arriving for the first time at the big school. Is that the ridge you promised to take me up on?' She pointed to a high ridge in the distance.

'Yes. We must go up there before it gets too cold.'

As one, they started walking again. Their easy, relaxed chatting carried them along the country lane towards the remote edifice of the former boarding school. On their right, they came to a couple of houses built in classic 1980s architectural design.

'There was much argument about the construction of those two properties,' Malcolm said. 'People felt that it was the thin end of a nasty property development wedge. But they needn't have feared. Once Hawksmead finally lost its textile mill, there really was no pressure on housing – until recently, of course. Now, the council can't wait to show its credentials by giving planning permission to anyone with a trowel… or, indeed, an axe.'

'Well, the axe is mine, now.' Audrey laughed, expressing far more confidence than she actually felt. She slowed, took a deep breath of damp moorland air, and cast her eyes over mile upon mile of open countryside, criss-crossed with ancient stone walls and peppered with tiny, remote cottages. 'My mother taught me many things, but perhaps the most valuable was the ability to relish the moment.'

'I am most definitely relishing this moment,' Malcolm responded. 'People talk about companionship in old age, but this walk with you has wiped fifty years off my clock.'

'And fifty years off mine too – and some to spare,' Audrey laughed, giving Malcolm's arm another squeeze.

The sun had already reached its high point of the day and

was now slipping behind a chimney stack rising above the imperious, empty school building. The immediate grounds were unkempt, with weeds carpeting the gravelled drive and apron. The mighty walls had, for the most part, succumbed to ivy and other climbers, encasing the old school in a green straitjacket. The windows, a mix of architectural styles, revealed no life within; copper pennies on the eyes of a dead body.

'I can only imagine the horrors that once lurked within,' Audrey said, more to herself than Malcolm.

'It was the era. Children were clay to be moulded, especially young boys, far from home. Discipline was the byword. There was no warmth. No affection. No love. Just hardship.'

Audrey looked at Malcolm and was surprised to see tears sparkling his eyes.

'Anyway,' he continued, 'it's closed now. No more suffering.'

They stood, side-by-side, in the shadow of the empty building.

Audrey broke the silence. 'What's to become of it?'

'There's talk of turning it into a hotel and conference centre, but the cost of conversion seems to be prohibitive.'

'They should tear it down and give the land back to nature.'

'Little chance of that. Parts of it are fourteenth century.'

'Perhaps we should head back. It's getting a bit chilly.' She shivered. 'I could make us soup for lunch.'

'Why don't we go to the Old Forge? They do a very tasty set meal.'

'Sounds lovely.'

They walked at a steady pace along the country lane that led back to the Old Military Road. With every passing year,

Audrey believed it became harder to turn good acquaintances into real friends, but she hoped that Malcolm would prove to be an exception. She'd lost the only man she'd ever loved and had felt like ending her own life to free her of the pain. If she hadn't had family who loved her, Audrey was sure she would have taken the easy way out. Now, little more than a year after the funeral, she wanted to live every minute of every day she had left.

It was early afternoon by the time they reached the Old Forge Restaurant with its low beams, inglenook fireplace and scattered diners at the coffee stage. In the rear yard, Audrey had spotted a man in spattered chef's clothing enjoying a post-lunch cigarette.

The manager put on a good show of being pleased to see them, but Audrey knew the chef would be annoyed at having to cook for latecomers.

'Are you going to buy Hawksmead College too? You clearly like big houses,' Malcolm asked, offering Audrey the bread basket.

She smiled and took a hunk of wholemeal. 'Is it for sale?'

Malcolm poured red wine into their glasses. 'It's so relaxing being retired. Not having a deadline is one of the best things about growing old.'

'Having children aged me. I was young when my first boy was born and then when my youngest went to university, I looked in the mirror and saw my mother's face.'

'Well, she must've been a beauty.'

Audrey smiled and lifted her glass in a salute to Malcolm.

'Why did you move here?' he asked. 'Why Hawksmead of all places?'

'I heard it was home to a handsome widower.'

'Touché.' Malcolm lifted his glass.

'I was lonely in Sevenoaks. My lovely husband had moved on and left me rattling around in the family home. I needed a reason to get up in the morning. I had a bit of spare cash and thought that I would turn an unloved building into one that was full of warmth and laughter.' She took a sip of wine to hide her lie.

'Your tea party was an inspiration and a wonderful success, but warmth and laughter are quite a challenge to achieve in a building as austere as the old school boarding house.' He reached for his glass of wine but took a sip of water instead.

'Actually, I think it's going to be quite easy,' Audrey said. 'Many people come to walk the Ridgeway and to enjoy the wonderful moorland scenery. I intend to convert it into a hostel and offer cheap, simple, accommodation. Perhaps, if you're not too busy, you'd like to help me.'

Audrey's mind was in turmoil. Was that a lie or the truth? Was that a marriage proposal or a business offer? They looked at each other; and for a moment, neither had a word to say.

After simple but tasty rural fare, Malcolm got up from the table and appeared a little unsteady. 'Please excuse me; I need to see a man about a dog. Red wine during the day has twice the effect.'

Audrey watched him straighten his back and walk with purposeful strides to the men's lavatory. She looked across at the manager and squiggled the air with her hand. He nodded and brought the lunch bill over. Audrey offered her debit card and the manager slotted it into the wireless card reader. After tapping in her pin, the card and receipt were handed back to her. She slipped both away in her handbag.

She spotted Malcolm emerging from the men's lavatory and pretended to read messages on her phone. Out of the corner of her eye, she saw him approach the manager.

'I'd like to settle our bill, please,' she heard him say.

'You're too late. Madam has already paid.'

'Could you let me know how much it was?'

'Madam gave me explicit instructions not to.'

Audrey put her phone away in her bag as Malcolm approached the table. He was followed by the manager carrying their coats.

'Audrey,' Malcolm said, his tone reproachful. 'What have you done?'

She gave him her full megawatt smile. 'It's a small thank you for a wonderful day.'

The late afternoon was still fine as they walked along the quiet streets of Hawksmead, each lost in their own thoughts but relishing the other's company. A chill breeze had picked up, giving them both the excuse they needed to wrap an arm around the other. At the far end of the High Street, they waited for a white VW Golf to speed by, driven by a pretty young woman Audrey realised was Tina, before crossing to Malcolm's Honda, parked in her drive.

'Come to my place for tea.' Malcolm said.

'Are you suggesting that I accept a ride with a strange man and drive off to some mystery location?'

'I have homemade damson jam, and an original van Staaten eager to make your acquaintance.'

CHAPTER EIGHTEEN

Malcolm parked outside a classic early Victorian terrace of three cottages as Audrey's phone beeped in her handbag. She took it out and looked at the screen.

'It's Tina, the estate agent who sold me my house. She wants me to text her when I'm home, safely.'

'Well, well, well,' Malcolm said. 'To think at the age of seventy-five, I cannot be trusted to preserve the honour of a young woman.'

Audrey laughed and they both got out of the car. She closed the door and looked at Malcolm's pretty garden with its wooden pergola spanning a path of Yorkshire paving stones leading to the front door. To the left was a small rose garden with neatly tended beds, all ready for the harsh winter to come.

'It's exquisite, Malcolm,' she said, genuinely moved by the beauty of the cottage and setting.

'It's a bit small for me, height-wise,' he said, joining her. 'But Mary set her heart on the place and, since her passing, I've not found a good enough reason to sell, apart from the occasional bumped head.'

He swung open the white-painted wooden gate and indicated for Audrey to walk up the path to the front door, painted light blue with mottled glass panels. He followed her, fishing in his pocket for his keys. He unlocked the door, immediately causing a loud beeping noise. He eased his way past her to an understairs cupboard and tapped in a code on an alarm pad. After a couple more beeps, the annoying sound ended.

'Come in, come in,' he said and closed the front door behind her.

She looked at one of several framed photos lining the narrow hallway.

'Did you take them?'

'Yes, in the days when film ruled the photographic world.' He switched on the hall light. 'I've not taken to digital.'

'Is that Mary?' Audrey gestured to a portrait of a honey-blonde young woman.

'Yes. I wish I'd used black and white film stock. After fifty years, the colours are not what they should be.'

'She's beautiful. I can see why you fell for her. What happened?'

He looked away. Audrey waited. There was a heavy silence which Malcolm eventually broke. 'Breast cancer. It's not a subject I care to give oxygen. Tea?'

Audrey smiled. 'You read my mind.' She looked again at Mary's portrait then slipped off her walking shoes before following Malcolm into a small but perfectly furnished sitting room. The rear wall was now an archway to a dining area, and beyond, Audrey could see through French windows to a beautifully tended little garden with a centre patch of lawn, a wooden pergola, and assorted shrubs and bushes in neatly weeded beds.

'I'm impressed. You have an exquisite home, so different from my boarding house.'

Malcolm turned on more lights. 'And here is your great-grandfather's painting.' He gestured to a landscape watercolour of a windmill, artisan cottages, boats with rust-coloured sails, and coal-carrying barges moored to the bank of a wide river. 'He was an absolute master. Look at his reflections in the water. Not sure which river it is, but the region is definitely Dordrecht. Would that be right?'

'I think so.'

'It's what I look at when I eat my breakfast.' He entered the kitchen, and Audrey heard him filling a kettle. A few minutes later, he placed a plate of buttered crumpets on a mat depicting a comedy fox hunt, which was one of six protecting the dark, rosewood dining table. He took two fine porcelain plates out of a sideboard and a couple of silver butter knives from a drawer. From another drawer, he removed two white, lace-trimmed napkins.

'I'll get the tea.' Malcolm disappeared into the kitchen.

Audrey stood by the French windows, staring into the garden. She imagined Malcolm and Mary as a young couple, sharing the excitement of their new home, all those years ago. She thought about Duncan and their first flat in Beckenham, bought for five thousand pounds. They'd been so happy.

'Tea,' announced Malcolm. He placed a porcelain teapot on a stand.

'Your garden is a perfect tonic for all the ills in our world.'

'That depends. Now it looks good as I've put it to bed for the winter but come spring and summer, it's a constant battle between man and nature.'

Audrey laughed.

'I intend to plant vegetables next spring so that I get some return for all the hours.' He pulled out a rosewood dining chair with a tapestry padded seat and Audrey took her cue to sit down. He sat on her right at the end of the table and offered her the plate of crumpets.

'Jam?' Malcolm indicated a porcelain pot, with matching lid and cut out section for the teaspoon.

'Mmm, truly scrumptious. I'll need another long walk.'

'Your stairs,' Malcolm said, reaching for the teapot, 'will ensure you keep the weight off. Where are you sleeping?'

'I'm in a room at the very top of the house. Did you not go up there at my housewarming?'

'Er, no, I didn't venture far. Isn't it a bit out of the way?'

'I like it. Something about the room appeals to me.'

Tea turned into high tea and then an early light supper. It was gone ten p.m. by the time they got into Malcolm's car and drove back to Audrey's new home. He swung into her driveway and as soon as he'd brought the Honda to a halt, he leapt out and opened the passenger door. She looked up at him and couldn't help admiring his tall, slim frame and surprising athleticism. She climbed out of the car into the distinctly chilly night and allowed him to escort her to her front porch. They reached the door and she turned to face him, residual light from the High Street giving his contours an ethereal glow. She slipped her arms around his neck and their lips met. Within moments a gentle kiss turned into one that was full of passion under a three-quarter moon floating in an almost clear sky.

Audrey was surprised by her awakened desire and wondered if there could be a happy future with this handsome man, an eventuality that had definitely not been in her game plan.

'Come in for a nightcap,' she whispered.

'I'm driving.'

'No need to hurry up in the morning. I make good mint tea.'

Malcolm eased his body away. 'Let's go back to my

cottage. It's warm and cosy.'

She kissed him, gently.

Audrey heard Malcolm firing up his Honda as she closed the heavy oak door and flicked on the dim hall light. The house was quiet and seemed content but stark compared to Malcolm's lovely cottage. The floor was still littered with debris from her tea party. She smiled – but her face froze when she saw the axe leaning against the wall, and she quickly looked away.

CHAPTER NINETEEN

Tina had an early viewing of a property in the morning, so had decided not to stay the night with her new lover. She always drove too fast, but despite campaigns by various parent groups, Hawksmead did not have speed humps or cameras apart from the one near the humpback bridge, for which Tina would, in all probability, receive a penalty ticket. She was still shaken from her experience after the tea party and was convinced that she was now seeing ghosts, thanks entirely to her involvement with Audrey's house. Grade II it may be, but she wished Spartak had bought it and razed it to the ground. Their relationship had survived the first twenty-four hours – he had sworn on his mother's grave that it wasn't him who had chased her in a Range Rover – but her parents were unhappy that she had missed their family Sunday lunch to spend the day with him.

She had decided not to take the Old Military Road back to her parents' home in Hawksmead but the much longer and less lonely arterial route. She entered Hawksmead at the southern end of the small town and rejoiced in seeing the street lighting. Her spirits lifted, she pressed the accelerator and roared up the empty High Street. As she cut across the white line in the centre of the road to make a perfect entry into Woodland Rise, her retinas were blanched by full-beam headlights coming from a vehicle speeding in the opposite direction.

Malcolm felt good as his size ten shoe pressed down on the accelerator. He hated wearing spectacles, but even he succumbed when driving at night, and now his lenses were magnifying the glare of approaching headlights. Instinctively, he swerved hard to his left but his side mirror slapped the approaching car's side mirror with a combined speed of ninety miles per hour, smashing them both.

Tina leapt out of the car she loved and had just damaged for the very first time. How could she have been so stupid, and who was the idiot driving in the middle of the road? She looked across the street and recognised Malcolm as he got out of his car. Why was he driving so fast? Had something happened? Weren't old people meant to just pootle along?

'Are you all right?' Malcolm called.

'Yes. Are you?'

They gave each other a thumbs-up.

Tina pulled off a loose section of mirror and got back into her car. Instead of turning left into Woodland Rise and heading to her family home, she continued up the High Street, at a leisurely pace, and brought her car to a gentle halt. She stepped out and shivered, not from the chilly night air but from gut-wrenching fear that enveloped her as she looked up at the old school boarding house, eerily silent in the sodium-coloured street lighting.

She felt a painful twinge of guilt for selling the great unloved pile to Audrey, and wanted to be sure that she was all right. The man with the axe may have been no more real than the boy with the flapping coat, but Malcolm speeding away was definitely not a figment of her imagination.

The moon came out from behind a cloud and added to the spectral ambience of the house, as droplets of water crystallised in the midnight air. And then she saw him – his young, pale face clearly lit by the moon, looking down from the top landing window.

Tina stood motionless, caught in the boy's stare, her eyes locked on his until a cloud passed in front of the moon and released her from the boy's grip. She had Audrey's mobile phone number. Should she call and warn her? But what would that achieve? She jumped back into her car and spun the front wheels on the damp tarmac.

~

Something has happened which you may not believe. I'm not sure I actually believe it myself. Two nights before the opening of *Cyrano de Bergerac* and my parents coming to see me in the play, I woke up in the night, bursting for a pee. As you know, my dormitory is at the top of the boarding house and, to get to the bogs, I have to walk down two flights of narrow, wooden, creaking stairs that make a terrible din no matter how hard I try to be quiet. The way is lit by dim, yellow, night lights that create a strange glow in the freezing air. Shivering with cold, I stopped at the half-landing. To my left were the wide stairs that went down to the main hallway. From nowhere, a boy approached me. He was smaller than me and, in the gloomy light, I was convinced he was my friend Mini. I said hello to him, forgetting he was dead. The boy did not respond. He came up to me and stared into my face. It wasn't Mini. I mumbled an apology, but the boy just continued to look at me. Then he turned, and I watched as he went down the main stairs into the hallway and disappeared from view.

Bursting, I rushed to the bogs. It was only when the

pressure was off, I realised that when the boy walked down the stairs, there was absolute silence – not one floorboard squeaked.

I left the bogs and walked slowly back to where I had seen the boy. I looked down into the hallway and then rushed upstairs to my dorm, caring not a jot about the noise I was making. When I was safely in my narrow bed and had the sheet and blanket over me, I finally took a breath.

CHAPTER TWENTY

Audrey emerged from the kitchen and walked along the corridor, back into her entrance hallway, steaming mug of cocoa in hand. She deliberately avoided looking at the axe and took her time climbing the creaking stairs, turning on and off lights as she went. Her mind was completely consumed with thoughts of Malcolm. She hardly knew the man but would have slept with him on their first date, as she did after just one date with her husband. Of course, that was in the Swinging Sixties when miniskirts and marijuana, peace and love filled her world.

In the top dormitory room she took off her clothes and pulled on cotton pyjamas. Lying between the sheets under thin boarding-house blankets, she felt way too excited to sleep and wished she'd accepted Malcolm's offer to return to his sweet cottage. If she rang him now, she knew he would drive over and collect her. She looked at her phone, which she had plugged into its charger, and debated calling him. What a day she'd had. How life changes on a sixpence. Her reason for coming to Hawksmead suddenly seemed almost inconsequential to the desire she felt for a man that three days ago she'd known only as a Good Samaritan who'd helped her with her bags.

She eyed the row of tired old books, sitting on the top shelf within the bookcase. They looked untouched for many a decade, apart from a large encyclopaedia that had a small thumbprint in the thick dust.

Decision made, she flung back the bed covers and swung her bare feet onto the scarred floorboards. For a moment, her hand hovered over the phone. She took a deep breath and sighed and turned her attention to the faded spine titles above long-dead authors' names.

Dust made her sneeze as she flicked through the various tomes and then she looked at the child-sized thumbprint.

She pulled on a thick lambswool sweater and had to use two hands to lift the heavy encyclopaedia off the shelf. The worn cover was locked with a small brass clasp. She blew as much dust off the book as she could and sat across her bed leaning against the cold, yellowed wall. She opened the tome and flicked a few pages and then her heart raced with excitement, for in a large, jagged, cut-out section was another book. On its dark blue leather cover was written *1965* in faded gold. She eased the little book out of its hiding place and looked at the flyleaf:

This is the secret diary of Robert Oakes
DO NOT READ UNTIL 2065

Audrey's heart missed a beat as she turned to the first entry, written in pencil in a neat, carefully rounded, schoolboy's hand. She read the first sentence, and all thoughts of Malcolm and her new life evaporated from her mind.

I am thirteen years old and frightened. I am not very bright. When stressed I cannot get the words out. My parents took me to a doctor. He recommended vigorous physical exercise in an outward-bound school. He said it would cure me of my stutter and help me with my school work.

Audrey read the diary straight through but paused to wipe her eyes on her bed sheet before reading the final two entries.

Roxane has saved me again. When I am her, I do not think about Mini. I think about Christian, speaking beautiful, poetic lines to me that were written by Cyrano. I think about misplaced love and how we are all too frightened to reveal our thoughts. But I don't know what my thoughts are. They are very confusing to me. I like being Roxane, I like dressing up as her, and I like people thinking I'm pretty. When I look in the mirror and see Roxane, I feel the best I've ever felt. No wonder they call me queer!

My performance of Roxane received a standing ovation. Not once did I stutter when I spoke my lines. My parents are staying in a hotel in Undermere and seem really proud of me. Last night, I went to bed happy for the first time in a very long while. But something woke me in the early hours of this morning. For a moment, I thought I heard Mini calling me. I tried to go back to sleep but, scared of wetting my bed, I decided to go down to the bogs. When I reached the half-landing, the way looked clear in the dim lighting – and then I saw him, Mini, standing in the hallway looking up at me. I felt a great pull inside me to be with him.

Silently, the boy climbed the stairs and came towards me. It wasn't Mini. I could see tears in his eyes and rope burns around his neck as he reached out his hand. Icy tendrils stroked my cheek before I found the courage to escape to the bogs and lock a cubicle door. Who is he? What does he want? I wept for my friend Mini as I shivered and waited for the sound of boys getting up for the new day.

Once the washroom had emptied, I cleaned my teeth and rushed up to the dorm to get dressed. Down below, I heard the distant chatter of boys leaving for chapel, and Matron starting her Morris 1000. Then the boarding house fell quiet. On my pillow was a letter from my mother; inside, I found a crisp one-pound note. My parents had come to say goodbye, but Matron couldn't find me and told them I'd left for breakfast.

I am writing this through my tears. Mini has gone, Roxane has deserted me, and I am back to the stuttering, blubbing boy I truly am. I know my parents love me, but I wish they'd taken me home.

Someone is coming up. I can hear the stairs creaking. Time to hide you, my friend.

Audrey hugged the diary as if it were the boy himself. The dormitory room was freezing cold, and condensation on the old window panes had turned to ice. She pushed back the bed's sparse covers and slid her feet into her slippers.

This is the secret diary of Robert Oakes
DO NOT READ UNTIL 2065

Tears poured from her eyes as she wept for the boy who had written his private thoughts in the very room in which she slept.

Exhausted with emotion, she saw the encyclopaedia, with

its cut-out section, and decided to put the diary back in its secret home where it had lain hidden for fifty years. She touched her fingers to her lips, passed the kiss on to the diary's leather cover and returned the encyclopaedia to its place on the shelf. She turned off the light and went to the window, and was about to close the fraying drapes when the moon emerged. Through the frosting pane and cold air, she could just make out the humpback bridge and the meandering black serpent of the River Hawk.

CHAPTER TWENTY-ONE

'Fifth position,' ordered Elizabeth. Audrey tried to move her feet without the book sliding off her head.

'If the book falls off your head again, you will be punished much more severely,' Diana said with glee.

Audrey felt the book sliding down the back of her head and woke up before it hit the floor.

Through the window she could see the first signs of dawn. Her sheets were sodden. She had no choice but to get out of bed and roll them up. She peeled off her clinging pyjamas and put on her dressing gown.

Lost in thought, she went down the wooden stairs barefoot, no longer noticing the accompanying chorus of creaks and squeaks. She stopped at the half-landing and looked down the stairs that led to the hallway. This was where Robert Oakes had met the ghost boy. Who was it he'd heard climbing the stairs to the top dormitory room?

Audrey entered the washroom and dropped the rolled bed sheets on the floor together with her pyjamas. She hung her dressing gown on one of many old iron hooks and used her usual cubicle. Her breath billowed out in the cold morning air. She pulled the long chain with its porcelain handle, walked into the communal shower, and checked there was a towel hanging on a hook. She turned on the water and jumped clear before the icy spray could soak her. It took about three minutes for the water to get warm and by then, Audrey's thin body was shivering with cold. She turned her face up to the spray and thought about Robert Oakes standing in her shower, scared, cold, lonely. How bereft of love he must have felt that first day of school. From her own experience, she knew that most parents want to do the very best for their children, little realising that they may be handing them over to people with hidden vices.

Warmed through, she stepped out of the shower and quickly wrapped herself in her towel and dressing gown. She walked into the washroom and cleaned her teeth; the mirror above her was misted with condensation.

In the kitchen, while the kettle was coming to the boil, Audrey popped the damp sheets and pyjamas in one of the old washing machines, poured soap in the dispenser and switched it on. She wished she'd worn her slippers as the tiled floor was numbing her feet. Looking around for salvation, she spied two old rugby socks she'd found in the washing machine when she first arrived, and put them on.

The oil-fired boiler had been on low all night to ensure she had hot water for her shower. Now, it had to pull its weight and heat the freezing house. She turned a knob and was pleased to see the roar of flames through the thick viewing glass.

'Not that it will do much good,' Audrey said out loud to herself as she re-entered the kitchen and made a cup of mint tea.

Warmed from her drink but still scantily attired, she climbed the stairs up to her dormitory room, completely lost in a world that had existed in her house fifty years ago.

She opened her bedroom door and stopped dead. Her breath came in short snatches, and her body shook as blood drained from her face.

On the floor lay the encyclopaedia together with all the books that had rested on the shelf for fifty years. How had they fallen on the floor? Audrey had never watched any films about ghosts or poltergeists, not out of fear, but because she could not suspend her disbelief. And yet, on the floor lay the heavy encyclopaedia and all the other books. Perhaps there was more to the supernatural than she'd given credence.

She knelt down and opened the encyclopaedia, and was relieved to see the diary was still in its hiding place. She picked it up and placed it on her pillow. She looked at the high shelf and saw it was broken in two. Examining it closer, she saw the ends were riddled with tiny holes.

'Woodworm – not a poltergeist.'

There was a creak behind her.

She didn't look. Her heart pounded. How she wished Malcolm was with her. Screwing up all her courage, she turned to face she knew not what.

Caught in a draught between her bedroom window and the window across the landing, the dormitory door was swinging gently back and forth on its old hinges. Audrey laughed with relief. She looked at the boy's diary sitting on her pillow and slipped it out of sight, underneath.

BANG!

Audrey jumped. The door had slammed shut. She closed her bedroom window and took a deep breath.

'Get a grip, girl.'

She grabbed a few, trusty, practical items of clothing and quickly got dressed. Handbag in hand, she was about to leave when she had another thought. She removed the diary from under her pillow and contemplated returning it to the cut-out section within the encyclopaedia, but decided to pop it into her bag.

She looked around the room, now messy as a teenager's. 'I'm here, Bobby. You're going to be all right.'

CHAPTER TWENTY-TWO

The travel kettle came to the boil. Audrey popped a Yorkshire teabag in a mug and poured on the boiling water. She was fired up. She had a plan. Her hand went to turn on her Philips radio to listen to Radio 2, but she did not press the button, preferring the sound of her own mind rather than the distraction of lively chat.

She blew her tea and thought about Robert and his friend Mini, who had been killed on the humpback bridge; and the two older boys who had tried to claw their way out of the swirling torrent. She thought about the boys' parents, especially Robert's, and could not contain the tears that rolled, unchecked, down her cheeks. She also thought about the ghost that Robert had seen. Who was he? Was he really a ghost? Do they actually exist? She sipped her tea.

Audrey slipped on her coat and her wool-lined hat and gloves. She looked at the axe leaning against the wall by the front door in the hallway, turned the latch and pulled the door open. A great hulk of a man was standing on her doorstep – and her mouth dropped open.

'Good morning Mrs Willatt,' Spartak said. 'Thank you for excellent tea party. It was kind of you to invite us all.'

'How can I help you?' She tried to sound calm.

'I believe you have something of mine.' His voice was gruff and deep and – Audrey thought, much to her annoyance – incredibly sexy.

'I've told you, my house is not for sale.'

'I hear you. I have come for axe.'

'Axe? Explain yourself.'

'My little brother got over excited, and – '

'Left an axe embedded in my door.' She indicated the deep cut in the old oak.

'I sincerely apologise for distress caused.'

'There was no distress on my behalf. Your little brother is the one with whom you should be concerned. I suggest you keep him on a tighter leash.'

'I give you my word he will not trouble you again.'

'Good.' Audrey stepped through the doorway forcing Spartak to step back. She turned her back on him and closed the door.

'What about axe?'

'Apology accepted.' She used her key to double-lock the door and turned to face the handsome Russian. 'Now, you'll have to excuse me as I have a busy day.'

'It's my axe. You cannot keep it.'

'And my door will not heal.'

'It has sentimental value. I ask you to return it to me.'

Audrey removed her phone from her bag.

'Who you call?' he asked, looking less sure.

She ignored his question as she swiped the screen.

'Please. All I want is axe.'

She scrolled through her contacts and selected one. She put the phone to her ear.

'I will return when you are less busy.' He spat out the words as he stormed off down her short drive towards his van, where another man was sitting at the wheel.

'Hello.'

'Malcolm, it's Audrey.' She listened to his happy

response. 'I have an errand to run this morning. Could we meet for a late lunch? I'll give you a call.'

Tina, seated in her car across the street, watched the van pull away, forcing a taxi, about to overtake, to brake hard. She was in a state of shock. She had wanted to check that Audrey was okay, following the clash of mirrors with Malcolm, and to take up her invitation to drop by for coffee. She had not expected to see her new boyfriend, or the man in the driver's seat of the van.

Realisation dawned. She had broken up with Sean and slept with a Russian whose brother, she now realised, was probably an axe murderer.

She started her engine and inadvertently attracted Audrey's attention. Damn! What was she going to say? She lowered the driver's window as Audrey peered in.

'Hello, Tina. I hope you're well. Did you want to see me?'

'No,' Tina said. 'Well, yes, in a way. I just wanted to check that you were all right.'

Audrey looked at the remains of the side mirror hanging by its wires. 'I'm fine, but I see that your car has had a bit of a mishap.'

'Your gentleman friend and I had a coming together last night. We slapped mirrors. Nobody's fault.'

'Well, it's very good of you to call by,' Audrey said. 'I'm off to the library to do a little research.'

'On your house? On the ghost boy?' She looked up at Audrey but could not maintain eye contact and stared at her hands in shame. 'I shouldn't have sold you the house.'

'You had no choice. I was determined to buy it.'

'Would you like a lift to the library? The pavement's a bit slippery.'

'Thank you. I think I'll walk. I need to blow away the

cobwebs.'

'Let me put the house back on the market. Something bad lurks in there. I've seen him. It should be torn down. Destroyed. Please, don't go back in there. Not alone.'

'Thank you for your concern, Tina, but the only bad thing I've seen lurking around here is the company you keep.' She strode off, leaving Tina feeling even more wretched.

CHAPTER TWENTY-THREE

Since arriving in Hawksmead, Audrey had visited the town's Victorian library building several times, not for anything in particular but because she loved the smell of old books. She could also use the library's computers if she needed to do anything that was too fiddly for her phone; and there was the convenience of an ATM for withdrawing cash in warmth and safety.

Audrey went up to the front desk and was greeted by Shirley, a woman of similar age to her.

'I would like to look at newspapers from fifty years ago. Do you have old copies filed away in a vault by any slim chance?'

'In those days, newspapers were photographed on film,' Shirley said, clearly delighted to see Audrey again. 'We've an old viewer, somewhere.'

Audrey moistened her lips, doing her best to rein in her excitement. 'What level of bribery would it take for me to have access to the films and the viewer?'

'A cup of tea in the Olde Tea Shoppe would be nice,' Shirley said, smiling.

'You're on, and I'll throw in an Eccles cake.'

'Black Forest gateau is my cake of choice. But, before we get too excited, let's check that the bulb hasn't blown in the viewer.'

Audrey followed hot on Shirley's heels to a storeroom at

the back of the library. The viewer was bolted to its own table which, conveniently, was on castors. Together, the two women wheeled it out and, despite its awkward, supermarket-trolley-like movement, they managed to push it to a spot where there was both an electrical plug socket and a table for the rolls of film.

Shirley plugged in the viewer, and Audrey turned on the switch. The light bulb came on.

'Leave it on. I'll go and get the rolls of film for…?'

'September to Christmas 1965,' Audrey answered.

A few minutes later, Shirley returned with a heavy cardboard box with *David Greig the Grocer* stamped in fading black ink on the side.

'I hope you've got plenty of time. Is there anything in particular you're wanting to read?'

'Some boys died who attended the old school. One of them was killed in my house.'

'I see. Well, I must get on with some work. Don't shout if you need anything.' Shirley smiled and walked away.

Audrey searched through the rolls that had been marked in blue ink; red copper showing through the faded script. She decided to start with the town's local newspaper, *The Hawksmead Chronicle*, and quickly figured out how to thread the film into the viewer. She picked up a roll marked September 1965.

Audrey was impressed with the old technology. If a story caught her eye she could zoom in and read the text in large type. Strangely, the roll of film started in August rather than September, so she scrolled, as fast as the machine would allow, through stories that made the headlines in what the press call the silly season.

That Magnificent Young Man in His Flying Machine was a headline she could not resist and very quickly she was reading about Ashley Ward, an eleven-year-old schoolboy, who flew his father's Cessna at Biggin Hill and was called the youngest trainee pilot in England. To see over the controls, he had to sit on two cushions.

Audrey scrolled on with a smile and thought back to when she first took to the road and had no licence and no brakes worthy of the name. Her father had brought home plans for a soapbox cart, drawn up by one of his designers in his construction company. A carpenter had cut pieces of wood to length so that she could nail them together and build a cart big enough to take both her and her young brother. She received five shillings out of her mother's housekeeping to buy pram wheels.

She and her brother loved their soapbox. They lived at the southern end of Sevenoaks on a residential hill called Brattle Wood, where the family had moved when Audrey was seven. The first time she and her brother rode the cart together, they had crashed into the kerb, flipped into the air and landed on the loose gravel road with both suffering badly scraped knees, hands and elbows. It didn't put Audrey off. She persuaded her father to bring home more wood, and for two shillings she managed to buy another set of pram wheels. Now, she and her brother could race. Very few families owned a car, so the road was mostly clear for the young drivers. Her brother was fearless, but Audrey was heavier, so her cart went faster, sometimes too fast, and she had to take quick action to avoid serious injury.

Audrey continued scrolling on through the film roll until a headline jumped out at her together with a picture of Robert Oakes in his school uniform. She read the article as quickly as possible but took her time when it came to the coroner's summation:

The schoolboy was the last to leave the boarding house and so no one saw what happened. It is assumed that in his haste not to be late for chapel, he tripped on the stairs and, in the resultant fall, broke his neck. His body was discovered in the hallway by his English master, who had called in at the boarding house to congratulate the boy on his performance in the school play.

The deaths of four boys, in one school, in one term, is highly regrettable and the school is urged to reconsider its duty of care to the pupils in its charge.

Audrey pushed her chair away from the viewer, ignoring the tears filling her eyes and pouring down her cheeks. What had happened? The last entry in the hidden diary had been: *Someone is coming up. I can hear the stairs creaking. Time to hide you, my friend.*

Who was that person, and did he or she have anything to do with the boy's death? Audrey mopped her face dry and dug deeper into the article.

Crown Courts in England and Wales, are giving parents the choice of paying for their miscreant sons to undergo rigorous correctional training at Hawksmead College, an independent outward-bound institution, in order to spare their little darlings from attending a government reform school such as Borstal. The physically rigorous regime that is part of the curriculum at Hawksmead College is considered by the courts to be sufficiently tough and preferable to the curriculum of crime that is the norm in approved Borstal detention centres.

However, the secret agreement between Prime Minister Wilson's Labour administration and Hawksmead College was exposed, not just through the unfortunate deaths of four innocent pupils, but by the savage injuries inflicted on fellow pupils by young thugs who should be wearing suits with arrows rather than open-necked shirts and corduroy shorts. Once the cosy arrangement between the courts and a school struggling to make up its numbers came to light, many parents removed their children and the school governors were forced, in certain instances, to refund the parents' deposits.

Audrey scrolled on to see if there were any further articles about the school and found a short piece recording that Neville Gibbs, the headmaster of Hawksmead College, was to take early retirement. He planned to return to Nepal where he had lost his fingers and toes attempting to be the first to climb Mount Everest.

Audrey pushed her chair away from the viewer and sighed. So that was it. The deaths of four boys, in one school term, were simply a footnote in history – if that.

A cup of coffee with a digestive biscuit nestling in its saucer was placed on the battered viewing trolley in front of Audrey.

'You look like you need it,' Shirley said.

Audrey smiled. 'Thank you. May I ask how long you have lived in Hawksmead?'

Shirley looked around the library. An elderly man, seated at a long table littered with newspapers, appeared to be asleep. On the far side, in the young people's reading area, a primary school teacher was holding the attention of a group of children.

She turned back to Audrey. 'I was born here. Quite a few years before you were even a glint in your father's eye.'

'Not so many years. What can you tell me about the big school?'

'It was bad news for the town when the last pupils left the college. Many businesses closed down. The shop that sold the school uniform and games kits closed immediately.'

'How long ago was that?'

'It happened right in the middle of the banking crisis and it's been empty ever since.'

'What about the deaths of four boys in one school term? Do you remember anything about that?'

Shirley looked uncomfortable. 'No one in their right mind in that cold autumn will ever forget what happened. The weather was freezing, but those poor boys in their corduroy shorts still had to camp out on the moor. Two boys drowned in the river. Why they were in the river, canoeing, was never explained. But it was in full flood and dangerous. Another boy died on the bridge on his way to the school. That seems to have been a tragic accident, although it turns out that the driver of the car was a master at the school.'

'What was his name?'

'It was never released. I don't know why,' Shirley said with a shrug. 'Anyway, he'll be dead by now.'

There was a pause. Neither spoke.

'Well, I'd better get back to work,' Shirley said. 'We volunteers cannot stand around chatting all day!' She turned to go.

'The fourth boy,' Audrey stated. 'What do you know about the fourth boy who died? The one who fell down the stairs.'

Shirley looked even more uncomfortable. 'You're happy in your new home, aren't you?'

'Very.'

'Best leave it at that.'

'I know a boy died in my house.'

'If only it had been just one boy.'

Audrey thought about the ghost of a boy that Robert wrote about in his diary. 'Was there another boy who died?'

Shirley nodded. Tears welled up in her eyes and she slumped down in a chair sobbing quietly. She searched her sleeves for a handkerchief or tissue. Audrey came to the rescue, offering a perfectly ironed lace-trimmed hanky.

'I'm sorry,' Audrey said.

Shirley shook her head and took the hanky. 'You weren't to know. His name was Edward Holden. One morning, during his first term, we met on our bikes. I was twelve at the time, and he was thirteen. It was frosty cold, but it was a Sunday, so we were both just filling time. It sounds silly now, but we fell in love and promised each other that we would marry as soon as we were aged twenty-one – the age of consent back then. We met every Sunday, and Eddie told me about the school, the harsh physical regime, the bullying and… and…' Shirley trailed off.

'What happened?' Audrey took Shirley's hand.

'Eddie told me that he was having trouble with an older boy. He'd tried to kiss Eddie. One day, while Eddie was taking a shower, the older boy interfered with him. I didn't really understand what Eddie was telling me, but I could see his distress. The following Sunday, I rode on my bike to our meeting place by the bridge, but Eddie didn't show up. I was nervous about cycling to the boarding house as our meetings were secret. I thought that maybe he'd been punished for meeting me. The next day, at my school, a girl I didn't like came up to me and told me that my boyfriend was dead. When the boys woke up on the Sunday morning to go to chapel, Eddie was found hanging by his bed sheet in the hallway.' She sank her face in her hands. 'I loved him.'

Audrey watched as memories from fifty-five years ago

came back with full intensity.

It took Shirley a couple of minutes to find herself again and, after wiping her face with Audrey's sodden handkerchief, she managed to rally a smile. 'That's not what I expected when I awoke this morning. You're the first person I've told. Not even my dear husband, God rest his soul, knew about Eddie and me. They say it's haunted, the boarding house, your new home. That Eddie still walks the stairs. If you see him – tell him, Shirley sends her love.'

She got up from the chair and looked at Audrey's handkerchief. 'I'll wash this.'

'I don't remember seeing you at my housewarming party.'

'I thought about leaving Hawksmead and did for a while. But I always wanted to be close to Eddie's spirit. I didn't want to leave him alone in that house – but I could never go in – never.'

CHAPTER TWENTY-FOUR

It was late morning when Audrey left the heat of the library and stepped out into the cold air. She embraced the icy prickles, keen to shake off the deep sadness that had enveloped her. Not just the death of Robert Oakes, but the suicide of Edward Holden. Thankfully, Malcolm was available to meet for lunch, and the thought was already lifting her spirits.

Every now and then, as she walked through the small town, a guest from her tea party would say hello, and Audrey rejoiced in the friendly conversations. She approached her home from the far side of the street and took a few moments to look at it. Her eyes drifted up to the top window where Tina believed she had seen the face of a schoolboy.

Come on. Show yourself. Don't leave me out. Audrey shook her head and crossed the road. She walked up her short drive, unlocked the heavy front door, and curled down her mouth when she spotted the deep gouge caused by the axe blade. She entered the hall and closed the door securely behind her. She wanted to freshen up, to make sure she looked her best for Malcolm.

Facing the closed door, with her back to the hall she felt a cold chill of fear, like bony fingers crawling up her spine. Behind her, she heard a creak. What would she see? Would it be the ghost of a boy Shirley still loved, fifty-five years after his death? Heart pounding, she turned and looked into her hallway. It was as it should be, just a hallway, large and gloomy; the weak autumnal sunlight filtering through the rippled Victorian window panes.

She breathed out and walked to the base of the stairs.

'Eddie. I met Shirley this morning, and she asked me to send you her love. She thinks about you every day and misses you very much.'

She cocked her head as if waiting for a reply. 'Look at me. I'm talking to myself, now.'

She placed her hand on the wooden handrail and a foot on the bottom step. She looked up to the half-landing and climbed the stairs, accompanied by their usual creaks and squeaks. At the top of the first flight, she turned and looked down into the hallway. She now understood why people in the town were so reluctant to enter her house. Too much had happened within its solid walls.

She felt the vibrations before she heard the faint ring of her mobile phone. She opened her bag and dug deep to retrieve it. The screen displayed the name *Malcolm,* and her heart skipped a beat.

'Hello handsome,' Audrey said, with a teenage smile.

'Well, that's the best answer to a phone call I've received in a very long while,' Malcolm laughed. 'In fact, according to my excellent long-term memory – ever! I should be with you in about twenty minutes. I've booked us a table at the… well, I'll leave it as a surprise. Suffice it to say, I have my own tankard hanging on a hook over the bar.'

Audrey slipped her phone away and, warmed by thoughts of lunch with Malcolm, walked up the stairs to change into something just a little more inviting than her thick trousers. They kept out the cold chill that would emanate off the dark waters of the River Hawk, but as Malcolm was picking her up in his car, she thought a dress was more appropriate. She got to the top floor landing and crossed over to the window. She looked down into the High Street and spotted Malcolm's Honda. What a gentleman; so considerate of him to give her a bit of time to smarten up.

She turned away from the window and entered the top dormitory room. Relief flooded through her – it was as messy as when she had left it. She quickly peeled off her clothes and selected a favourite daytime dress she'd picked up in the local Oxfam charity shop. She put it on, felt for the zip, smoothed the skirt, grabbed her bag, had a quick look around, and headed out of the room.

Thank you are two words that can mean a lot in the right context, but written in the dust that lay on the window pane across the top landing, they scared Audrey more than she thought possible. It was nearly lunchtime, not midnight, and yet she was petrified; almost too fearful to walk down the stairs.

'Get a grip, girl,' she murmured. She took a deep breath and could feel her heart pounding. She licked her dry lips and tried to swallow her fear.

'You're welcome, Eddie. You're very welcome.'

She hurried to the top of the stairs and ran down faster than she knew was safe. She reached the half-landing and looked down the wide stairs leading into the hallway. Malcolm was outside waiting for her. She was tempted to run into his arms, but she knew she had to keep a lid on it or she, too, would be too frightened to live in the old school boarding house.

She took another deep, calming breath and headed for the washroom. She switched on the lights and popped into her favourite cubicle. She didn't much like the long chain with its old porcelain handle, but the rush of water was certainly powerful and the natural action calmed her nerves. She came out of the cubicle and washed her hands.

Audrey knew she had not written *thank you* on the window pane and there was nobody, to her knowledge, in the house. So how had it got there? What rational explanation could there be?

She brushed her teeth – her hair, still thick and enhanced by colour, she gave a light flick with a hairbrush.

'I think that's as good as it gets,' she said to her reflection and hurried across the washroom. She opened the door, switched off the lights, and entered the dark corridor. Spurred by fear, she ran to the half-landing and almost skipped down the stairs. In the hallway, she lifted her coat from the wooden stand and was about to turn the door latch when she heard a loud creak coming from the staircase behind her.

She froze. 'Eddie… Shirley told me what happened. You can rest, now.'

There was another loud creak. She had to hold her nerve. She took a deep breath and turned to face the hallway.

Standing on the half-landing was a powerfully built man. In his hand was the axe. Audrey glanced down at the spot where she had placed it after Malcolm had removed it from her door.

'I Kirill Dryomov – Spartak's brother. I come for axe and take look round.'

Audrey could feel her heart rate increasing, but she was determined to stay calm. 'You're becoming a nuisance.'

'No!' His response was loud and echoed in the almost unfurnished hall. 'You are the nuisance. We want you out of here. Gone. Do you understand, lady?'

'I understand that you have damaged my front door, broken into my house and are now threatening me. I suggest you get out before I call the police.'

Kirill laughed and walked down the stairs. 'Sell the house, lady.' He sauntered up to her, the axe loosely held in his left hand.

'Why do you want it so much?' She looked into his rough face and searched for some of the good looks that imbued his older brother. 'Is there buried treasure, is that it?'

'You steal it from us – like you steal axe.'

'Nonsense. Your Russian pride is hurt. No more than that. Move on to another project.'

'Are you not frightened? Just a little bit?'

She saw the corners of his mouth quivering.

The doorbell reverberated around the hall.

Audrey twisted the latch and pulled open the front door. Malcolm was standing on the step. His smile froze on seeing Kirill, who eased his way past Audrey. 'Thank you for axe. It was stolen from van.'

Audrey did not respond. Kirill looked at Malcolm. He gave him a brief nod, turned, and walked down the drive, the axe swinging at the end of his sinewed arm.

'You must call the police,' Malcolm urged as he helped Audrey put on her coat.

'It's good to see you.' She held his face in her hands, partly to stop them shaking, and kissed him on the lips. 'I have big plans for you and me.' She locked her front door and took his arm. 'I'll tell you over lunch. Where are we going?'

'I've booked a table at the Rorty Crankle Inn.' They walked to his car, which was still parked across the High Street. 'It offers the most amazing views of the moor, and the food is home cooking at its very best.'

Audrey looked at the smashed side mirror, held together with copious strips of sticky tape.

A massive beam spread across Malcolm's face. 'A slight misjudgement on my part.'

Audrey laughed, relieved to be out of her house and in the company of such a charming man.

The Honda, with its two happy occupants, headed towards the River Hawk. Malcolm slowed as they approached the bridge; fifty years on, it was still only wide enough for one vehicle.

'My heart races every time I drive over this bridge,' he said, accelerating to climb up the sharp incline.

Audrey thought about Robert's friend, Mini, falling off his bike and being crushed by a car.

'In the morning, it can be very icy,' Malcolm continued. 'I think it's the refrigerating effect of the water below. I try to avoid it as much as possible.'

Audrey breathed a quiet sigh of relief when they came down the north side.

The Honda roared along the Old Military Road, past the turning to Hawksmead College and up a gentle gradient towards the high ridge. Malcolm pulled over by a sign with an image of a camera. They got out, and the air whipped around Audrey's thin dress.

'A little of this can go a long way,' she laughed, hugging her coat to her.

'This beautiful expanse has been like this all my life. I hope it never changes. Of course it will. But for now, for the time I have left, I hope that we can come to this spot and share its wondrous beauty.'

Holding her coat closed with one hand, she slipped the other into Malcolm's. He gave it a gentle squeeze and looked down at her. She was fifteen again, and he was twenty-five. She hadn't wanted to wait when she was fifteen and in love with Paul McCartney, and she most certainly was not interested in wasting any time now.

'Warm hands, warm heart.' Malcolm smiled. 'If your husband was half as happy as you make me, he was a very lucky man.'

CHAPTER TWENTY-FIVE

There were quite a few vehicles in the seventeenth-century coaching inn car park but still plenty of spaces for Malcolm's Honda.

'Wait there.' He opened his door and the wind almost snatched it out of his hand. Bent against the razor-sharp air, he went around to the passenger door and used both hands to hold it open.

The wind was so strong, Audrey and Malcolm were almost propelled through the inn's battered door. Harry, the landlord, gave Malcolm a cheery welcome. His handsome ruddy face was topped off with a head of dark curls.

'Could you point me in the right direction?' Audrey asked, as she tried to recover her hair.

While she headed for the ladies, Harry gave Malcolm a double thumbs-up. 'You've landed on your feet there, mate. She's an absolute corker.' He escorted Malcolm to the dining section of the pub.

'I'm not sure I'm even awake.' Malcolm slapped his own cheek. 'This could be an amazing dream. If it is, don't wake me up.'

'You'd better hope she doesn't fall for *my* charms. I'll do my best to keep my natural charisma in check.'

'I am here!' called out Cathy, holding open the swing door to the kitchen.

Malcolm smiled at the comfortably plump, blue-eyed

beauty, armed with a spatula and wearing a food-spattered striped apron. 'Hello, Cathy. I'm like a teenager on a first date. I want to demonstrate my feelings, but I'm scared of blowing out the flame.'

'Have you bought her anything special?' Cathy asked. 'A brooch? A necklace? A bracelet?'

'Er, no, not yet.'

'What about flowers?'

'I meant to. It slipped my mind.'

'Any romantic gesture at all?'

'I saved her from a madman with an axe. Does that count as romantic?'

Harry laughed. 'Halloween has a lot to answer for!'

'Apart from a "brief encounter" on the train,' Malcolm continued, 'I've only known her since her housewarming party last Saturday. I'm trying to keep real but it's no good!'

'I don't blame you, mate,' Harry said. 'She's gorgeous.'

'Harry, you're on very dangerous ground.' Cathy waved her spatula, threateningly, as Audrey emerged from the ladies.

'I know it's crazy, but it feels so wonderful,' Malcolm said. 'Why would she be interested in me? You should have seen the men at her tea party – their tongues were hanging out, even though most were at least twenty years younger than her. She simply emanates perfection. Or am I completely deluded?'

'I hope so,' Audrey said, poking Malcolm gently in the ribs.

'Audrey,' Harry said. 'This is my wife, Cathy. She's your chef for the day.'

'I hear you've moved into the old school boarding house,' Cathy said, shaking Audrey's hand. 'Was there nothing smaller for sale?'

Audrey laughed. 'I have plans.'

'Well, so do I, and it's to cook you and your handsome friend the best meal you'll ever eat this side of the moor!' They all laughed as Cathy retreated to the kitchen.

Harry showed them to their table. 'We're open all the way through until eleven tonight, so take your time.'

Audrey and Malcolm declined Harry's menu and said they wanted Cathy to surprise them.

'Ooh, she'll love that.' A few moments later, Harry returned with two crystal-glass flutes sparkling with champagne. 'On the house,' he said.

Malcolm and Audrey toasted Harry and Cathy and then they were left alone. For a moment, quite a long moment, they looked at each other.

Audrey broke the silence. 'The Rorty Crankle. Odd name. What does it mean?'

'I don't have the least idea. I think it's joke words, made up to mean something long forgotten. Probably very rude.' He smiled. 'How was your morning before that thug arrived?'

'I was in the library with a lovely person called Shirley. Do you know her?'

'What sort of age?'

'My sort of age. Well, a few years older. She's lived in Hawksmead almost all her life.'

'Although Hawksmead is my home town, for many years, I lived in Manchester.'

'Was that where you met your wife?'

'No, my wife was from Hawksmead too, but we had to move because of my work.'

'You were in marketing?'

'Yes. I've always had the gift of the pen. Coming up with marketing concepts and pithy copy was my stock in trade.

I'm lucky. I got out before the internet took over. Words are cheap these days. Everyone's a blogger or writing acerbic comments on Facebook or Twitter – I'm sure they're having fun, but it's hard to monetise. In the 1970s, 80s and 90s, it was possible to make a very good living looking out of the window, opening my mind and allowing a brilliant idea to take root. Of course, not every seed that flew in was a rose; occasionally, what seemed promising would turn out to be Japanese knotweed!'

Audrey laughed as Harry arrived with their starter – beetroot and gin-cured salmon with freshly baked soda bread. For a few moments, they ate in silence.

'Why did you not have children?'

Malcolm paused his chewing and thought about the best way to answer Audrey's direct question.

'Of course, you can tell me to mind my own business.' She popped a piece of toast in her mouth.

'We tried. We tried everything. Unfortunately, IVF came too late for us. I think it wrecked our marriage. We didn't divorce, but we were divorced in every other way. They couldn't put their finger on it. She had the eggs, and I had plenty of little guys, but the chemistry wasn't there. We thought about adopting but we were getting on and the adoption agency put us near the bottom of the list. I expect we could have adopted a troublesome child, but neither of us wanted that. It was a baby we wanted. We had money, not to burn, but I was making a good living; we had lovely friends who all had children; but what she and I didn't have was love. Neither of us said it out loud but, deep down, she blamed me and I blamed her. We muddled through until she died. You and your husband were a bit luckier.' He took a sip of champagne.

Audrey steepled her fingers. 'I have been very lucky. Two

boys, two lovely daughters-in-law, two grandchildren; it doesn't get any better, save for the fact that my keep-fit fanatic of a husband had repeated heart attacks until, finally, the one that killed him. He quit smoking when he was young; didn't drink much; was careful about what he ate…' Malcolm watched her blink back her sudden tears. 'Sixty-five – ' Her voice caught in her throat. 'Not even three score and ten.' She took a deep breath. 'Fortunately, touching wood, a weak heart is a gene my sons appear to have ducked.'

Malcolm caught the smell of beef wafting through from the kitchen and abandoned the remainder of his salmon. 'I'm sorry you've had to suffer such grief. How have your sons coped with the loss?'

'They miss him, but not quite as much as I'm sure he would like. Growing up, they had to live with a father for whom winning was in his DNA.' She smiled. 'Beating fellow highfliers, whether it was at squash, tennis or sailing that boat of his, gave him way too much pleasure. Of course, it's why he earned the big bucks. But, ultimately, the boys suffered issues with confidence, self-esteem. It's tough being the son of a successful go-getter. Still, his death has enabled me to help them buy bigger homes and to invest in the old school boarding house.'

'Invest?' Malcolm queried, raising his eyebrows.

'That's what I want to talk to you about, but something scrumptious is about to arrive.'

Two plates of steaming beef Wellington replaced the salmon starters. 'That looks magnificent, Harry,' Malcolm said, admiring the puff pastry wrapped fillet. 'Be sure to compliment the chef.'

'Nothing gives my misses greater pleasure than sweating over a hot stove for you, Malcolm. It annoys the hell out of me watching her cook for you with so much enthusiasm! By the way, when are we going cycling, again?' Harry looked at Audrey. 'Malcolm was quite the athlete in his youth. I've seen more of his padded cycling shorts than is healthy for any man.'

Harry walked off without waiting for a response.

'He's a good mate,' Malcolm said. 'He's seen me through a few rocky times.'

Audrey picked up her knife and fork. 'I am so pleased I changed into a dress. I don't think my slacks could have withstood the pressure. Bon appétit.'

'And here is the perfect accompaniment,' Harry said, proffering a wine bottle to Malcolm. 'A Cabernet Sauvignon with a rich oak flavour.'

'Pour away, but just give me a drop,' Malcolm said. 'I'm the one at the wheel, although my car is insured for anyone to drive should we both be incapacitated!'

Harry poured one and a quarter glasses. He placed the bottle on the table and, with a bow, he dramatically backed away.

'I like it here,' Audrey said, as she reached across the table to squeeze Malcolm's hand. 'If I had my own tankard, I would hang it above the bar, too.'

Malcolm laughed. 'Even Harry doesn't really know why he chose to buy the Rorty Crankle when he could have bought a pub in Hawksmead or Undermere. He said it was the moorland air and the total peace that did it for him, rather than any business sense.'

For a few moments they ate in silence. Malcolm was more than happy to accept Audrey at face value, but there was one question he knew he had to ask. He put down his knife and fork and looked across the table. 'What brought you to Hawksmead, Audrey? Why did you really buy the boarding house?'

Audrey put down her knife and fork and took a sip of wine. She picked up her napkin and dabbed her lips. 'I'm on the run – I robbed a bank and used the cash to buy the first building I could afford.' She said it with such gravitas that for a moment Malcolm was almost taken in.

'That was a line from a play I was in for an amateur theatre group,' Audrey continued. 'I got rave reviews.'

Malcolm laughed with relief. 'I'm not surprised.'

'By my being a bank robber or by my acting?'

'Hawksmead has an amateur group. You should join.' He took a forkful of food as Audrey took another sip of wine.

'The truth is,' she said, 'I've experienced life in Broadstairs, by the grey sea with its high cliffs; and I've experienced life in Sevenoaks with its money and commuting bankers. My generation, retired stockbrokers and their partners, are living smug, contented lives on the golf course, until someone like me becomes a widow. At first, my friends gathered round; I was invited everywhere, but then I began to notice that their husbands were absent. Frankly, it became clear that I was only on the guest list when the wives were grass widows, but not for the important events. Even though I was in my sixties, I was seen as competition, which I most certainly was not. So, I had a choice – be a lonely widow in Sevenoaks and wait for my friends to become widows too, or start a new, exciting life in a place far away from everything familiar. I looked at a map of England, stuck a pin in Hawksmead and searched online for properties for sale. I saw the old school boarding house and simply made a derisory offer, sight unseen. Nobody was more surprised than me when the offer was accepted. I think the charitable trust that owned it was fed up with paying council tax and other maintenance costs.'

'Where does the man with the axe fit in?'

'It was a petty tantrum, although I am going to change the back-door lock.' Audrey lifted her wine glass. 'It's so good not being the driver!' She took a deep glug.

'What about your children, your sons? They must be disappointed that you're not on hand for free babysitting?'

'Probably. But, as happy as I am to be a grandmother, I want to be me too. And, though my sons and their wives may protest, I know that weeks would go by without my seeing any of them. That's normal. Anyway, I shall still see them and, when I do, I'll have something to talk about.'

Harry approached the table and looked at the clean plates. 'Cathy will be very pleased.'

Audrey looked up at Harry. 'It was absolutely delicious.'

Malcolm added his high praise and caught Harry's eye and winked.

'Don't think I didn't see that!' Audrey laughed, stretching across the table to squeeze Malcolm's hand.

'I'll bring the dessert menu,' Harry said, taking away the plates. Audrey picked up her wine glass and looked at Malcolm.

'To you… the handsome marketeer.'

Malcolm picked up his glass, barely touched. 'To you, beautiful in every way.' They both took a sip.

'Are you up for a challenge?' Audrey asked.

'Of course. Always.'

'Help me turn the old school boarding house into a sanctuary full of warmth, laughter and great food for visitors to the moor.'

Malcolm withdrew his hand from Audrey's and used his napkin to dab his brow.

'It's a house that needs love,' she continued. 'It has seen tragedy and loneliness and fear, and I want to imbue it with joy.'

Malcolm replaced the napkin on his lap and looked into Audrey's sparkling eyes. 'I am honoured that you should ask me to share such an important venture, although I'm not sure how many useful years I've got in the tank.'

Before Audrey could respond, Harry came up to their table. 'And what would you two lovebirds like for dessert?'

'Just the bill, please Harry,' Audrey said.

They fought over the bill and then agreed to split it fifty-fifty. They said their goodbyes, put on their coats, and stepped out into the chilly late-afternoon air as the soft autumnal sun began to slip down towards the horizon.

'This is just the beginning,' Audrey said.

It was fully dark and bitingly cold when Malcolm turned into Audrey's short drive and came to a halt. For a moment, they sat in silence and then Audrey reached out for his face and turned it to her, looking into his eyes.

Malcolm slid his arm under Audrey's and their mouths met. Old instincts took over, and soon they were kissing like teenagers at the end of a first date.

'Let's go in,' she whispered.

'I have a nice, big, comfy bed in my cottage.'

'We can push two beds together. Anyway, we only need one.'

They broke apart and got out of the car. She took Malcolm's arm and led him to her front door.

'My cottage is very cosy and warm,' shivered Malcolm.

Audrey laughed. 'The heating is on. We can always go to your cottage later.'

'Is there a reason why you have not moved in your furniture?'

'I'm renting out my home in Sevenoaks, furnished –

anyway, I'm here to start again. Together we can turn this old house into the Hostel on the Moor.'

'Hostel on the Moor; I think I saw the film. It didn't end well.'

Audrey laughed as she turned the key in the lock and pushed open the heavy oak door. She switched on the light and the flickering strip lit the gloomy hall. 'Lighting is the first thing we need to get right.'

Malcolm stood on the threshold while Audrey slipped off her coat and hung it on the old clothes stand. 'I'm going upstairs to the top dormitory. You can go home and watch *Countdown* on TV and fantasise about Rachel Riley, or you can come upstairs with me.'

Malcolm stepped into the hallway. He turned to close the door, but the draught caught it and the slam echoed loudly through the building. Audrey helped him out of his coat and hung it next to hers. She reached for his hand and led him across the hall and up the first flight of stairs. Malcolm looked at the old school sign pointing to the lavatories.

'I may just have to take a detour,' he said.

'I'll be waiting.'

'Would you come with me? This house is distinctly creepy.'

Audrey took Malcolm's hand again and led him along the dark corridor to the washroom. She opened the door and switched on the lights, revealing the rows of washbasins and lavatory cubicles.

'All mod cons,' she said. 'But I think future walkers on the moor will draw the line at sharing a shower with a stranger.' She pointed at the cubicles. 'Take your pick. The one closest is my personal preference.'

'Thank you,' Malcolm said.

'I'll wait outside.' She turned and left him alone in the

washroom.

Malcolm entered a cubicle and looked at the various messages scrawled on the wall. Being tall, he could see one that was high up by the cistern. As he leaned across the toilet bowl to read it, the door opened and closed in the cubicle next to his.

'Interesting writing on the wall,' Malcolm said. *'Matron's watching but it's Gibbs who's feeling.'* He smiled. 'Three apostrophes and all used correctly.'

There was no response from the neighbouring cubicle.

'Audrey? Are you there?'

Silence.

Malcolm carefully aimed for the bowl and was pleased to see that there was soft tissue and not old school Bronco non-absorbent lavatory paper. He pulled the chain, and water rushed down from the old metal cistern into the porcelain bowl. He opened his door and saw that the door to the neighbouring cubicle was closed. He pushed it, but it appeared bolted.

He crossed to the washbasin and looked at his ageing, handsome face as he soaped his hands. The main door to the washroom opened and Audrey put her head around. 'This girl's getting impatient,' she said with a big smile.

Malcolm looked at Audrey then at the cubicle next to the one he'd just used.

'Everything all right?'

'Yes,' he said. 'I was... I was just admiring some of the writing on your lavatory wall. Excellent grammar.'

Audrey took Malcolm's hand and led him along the corridor to the half-landing where he stopped and looked down into the hallway. Draped across the handrail were some fresh sheets which she put over her arm. He followed her up the short flight of stairs to the long corridor, and up the next two flights. Every step they took was accompanied by creaks and groans from the aged oak floorboards.

When they reached the top landing, Audrey flicked the light switch and glanced across to the window. 'Thank you' could just be discerned, written in the dust.

'Your ghost?' panted Malcolm.

'My Russian, I think. Done with his fat forefinger.'

'Perhaps I'm not quite as fit as I thought I was,' Malcolm said, as he sucked in a lungful of air.

'You will be after a few weeks.' She opened her bedroom door and turned on the feeble light.

Malcolm shivered. 'There's a definite chill.'

'I'll soon warm you up.' Audrey took his hand and gave it a squeeze. 'Wait there. I'll just be a jiffy.' He watched her throw the clean sheets onto a spare bed and swap around the thin and stained mattresses.

'Do you need any help?'

'Room service is not what it used to be.'

Malcolm laughed. 'Of course, back at my lovely, warm cottage, I have a very comfy mattress on my *double* bed, and one of those modern duvet thingies.'

Audrey chuckled as she tucked in the sheets and blankets. She crossed to the window and pulled the worn scrap of curtain material. 'Only the owls can see us up here, but…'

She looked across the dingy dormitory to Malcolm, and opened her arms. 'Welcome to my boudoir.' She came up to him and tilted her head back. For a moment, they stood facing each other – then the light bulb on the landing blew.

Audrey laughed. 'Good idea.' She turned off the dormitory light.

Later, lying wrapped in each other's arms, Audrey

whispered: 'I knew I didn't need contraception but I thought you might need Viagra – how wrong was I?'

'It's been a long time.' He kissed her gently.

'I wasted too many years planning for a future that was snatched from me. Now, I don't want to think beyond tonight.'

CHAPTER TWENTY-SIX

Malcolm stirred, and he felt Audrey wake in his arms.

'Are you okay?' she whispered.

'I have to go.' He kissed her.

'Don't leave. I want to see the sunrise with you.'

'I have to go to the bogs.'

'Bogs?'

'The little boys' room.'

'Bogs. I've not heard you call it that before.'

'Ah, well, there's a reason for that – it's this house.'

'I don't understand.'

'After I graduated from Oxford, I taught English and drama for a short while up at the old school. It was an interim job before I got into marketing.' He leant in to kiss her again but couldn't locate her lips. 'I won't be long. Don't go anywhere!'

Malcolm eased his way off the narrow bed and slipped on his boxer shorts and T-shirt. He felt his way along the wall to the door and turned the knob. Pale light spilled across the landing from the window. He reached for the handrail, and although he had no desire to go down two flights of stairs to the bogs all on his own, his call of nature was getting more urgent.

Barefoot, he walked carefully down the stairs to the usual accompanying creaks. He arrived at the half-landing and looked down the long flight into the dark hallway. For a fleeting moment, he thought he saw a boy lying on the tiled floor but it was only a shadow caused by a balustrade. He shivered and was enveloped by overwhelming sadness. In the top dormitory room, he had just experienced the happiest moments of his seventy-five years, but now, standing on the half-landing, looking down into the gloom of the large hallway, he knew there was no escape from the past. He was held in the grip of a misery that had cursed his marriage to Mary and clouded every waking moment of his life since.

'Malcolm?'

He swung round and stared at Audrey, the contours of her slim frame encased within a sheer nightdress.

'What happened to Robert Oakes?'

It was fifty years since he'd last heard that name. His head throbbed as adrenaline powered his pumping heart.

'It was an accident.' His voice cracked, and he closed his eyes as the memory of a beautiful young woman flooded his mind. 'He was Roxane in my production of *Cyrano de Bergerac*. Exquisite. Fragile. Vulnerable. She touched something deep inside me. I wanted to protect her. I wanted to protect him.'

He felt a tongue of freezing air wrap around him.

'What happened?' Her voice came from the far end of a long tunnel.

'It was a Sunday morning. I found him alone, in the top dormitory room.'

'What did you do?'

'Nothing! I did nothing. But, he misunderstood me.' Malcolm turned his back on Audrey and gripped the handrail. 'I told him Roxane would live in my heart, forever.'

Silence.

Not a breath.

Not a creak.

He had to explain. 'I reached out for him. I wanted to protect him, but he ran away.'

'And you caught him here, on the landing?' Her voice sounded as cold as metal.

He nodded, roughly wiping away an escaping tear. 'I needed him to understand. I grabbed his arm, but he pulled free and tripped on a raised floorboard.' He felt Audrey's eyes boring into him. 'Why are you asking me about Robert Oakes?'

'He was my little brother.'

Despair filled his veins.

'I came here to find the truth,' he heard her say. 'But the truth has found me.'

Head bowed, Malcolm listened as her bare feet padded down the stairs into the hallway.

Icy tendrils of air made him turn. In the gloom was a boy. A boy he'd not seen for many years.

CHAPTER TWENTY-SEVEN

Audrey's hand shook as she poured boiling water into a teapot. She put the kettle down and sobbed for a little brother she hardly knew. She had come to Hawksmead to try and discover the truth but had betrayed her family by making love to the man responsible for her brother's death.

How she despised herself.

From the hallway, she heard Malcolm cry and then the sound of his body, thudding down the wooden staircase.

'Malcolm!' She hurried out of the kitchen, along the corridor and into the hallway. Near the base of the stairs lay Malcolm, broken and twisted. She whimpered, and her knees buckled under her.

He groaned. Her hand flew to her mouth. His eyes opened, and he looked up at her. She slid her hand under his head, so it was no longer resting on the cold, tiled floor, and strained to hear his words.

'I saw him. I saw Bobby. He spoke to me. He said… he said…' His eyes flickered and shut.

Audrey gently laid his head back on the hard floor. She hurried upstairs, her bare feet taking two steps at a time. She had to get her phone.

'Emergency. Which service do you require?'

'Ambulance. As fast as possible.' Audrey gasped as she tried to control her breathing.

'What is the nature of the emergency?'

Phone in hand, Audrey almost flew down the stairs. She reached the half-landing and looked down at Malcolm, lying on the floor in the hallway. 'My friend has fallen down the stairs,' she panted. 'He's seventy-five and is badly injured.'

'Is he breathing? Is he conscious?'

'He's breathing but not conscious.' She rattled off her name and address. 'Please send an ambulance.'

'An ambulance has been dispatched and will take approximately ten minutes. Please check the airway and confirm to me that he's breathing normally.'

Audrey ran downstairs and put her phone on loudspeaker. She rested her hand on Malcolm's chest. 'Yes, he's breathing but it's not good. He's badly hurt.'

'Is he in any immediate danger?'

'No.'

'Can the paramedics gain access to the location?'

'I'll open the front door. We're just in the hall.' Audrey got up and ran across to the front door which she pulled open. A cold draught flicked her flimsy nightdress. She hurried back to Malcolm and carefully slid her hand under his head.

'Can you tell me what happened?' asked the operator through the phone.

Before Audrey could respond, Malcolm stirred. 'He wants us to be happy.'

'Could you please state exactly what happened?' asked the operator, her voice strident on the phone's loudspeaker.

'I was so pleased to see him,' Malcolm continued. 'I rushed to tell you and stupidly tripped on the stairs, the way Robert tripped all those years ago. What an old fool.'

'The ambulance is outside,' said the operator. 'Good luck.'

Audrey heard the ambulance arrive in her drive.

'He was a gifted actor,' Malcolm rasped. 'Something magical happened when he walked on stage. There's not a day gone by when I have not thought about his Roxane.' Malcolm's eyes closed as a paramedic entered the hallway, carrying a heavy medical bag followed by an emergency ambulance driver wheeling a bright yellow stretcher.

'Malcolm!' Audrey said trying to shake him awake.

The paramedic eased Audrey out of her way and set about examining Malcolm.

'What's his name?' she asked Audrey.

'Malcolm. Malcolm Cadwallader.' And quietly, to herself, 'Mr C'.

'Malcolm, my name's Sandra and I'm going to examine you. Are you having any trouble breathing?'

'My ribs hurt, but I can manage all right.'

She placed her fingers over his right wrist and looked at her watch. After what seemed an eternity, she looked up at her colleague then spoke to Malcolm. 'I'm going to give you a little examination. Let me know where it hurts.'

She started with his head and slowly moved her hands down his arms. Malcolm emitted a dry, piercing cry.

'He has a dislocated left shoulder and fractured radius.' She continued down. 'Fractured ribs.' She reached his hips and Malcolm cried out again. 'Fractured pelvis.' She felt down both his legs.

'Malcolm,' Sandra said to him, 'we're going to get you off the floor and onto the stretcher, but before we do that, my friend, Toby, is going to give you something to ease the pain.'

Audrey watched as, with surprising speed, the paramedics set up a drip which they inserted into Malcolm's right arm.

'Ma'am,' began Toby.

'My name's Audrey. Audrey Willatt.'

'Mrs Willatt, could you tell us what led to Malcolm's fall?'

'Mr Cadwallader, Malcolm, was standing at the top of the stairs when I left him to go to the kitchen and make a pot of tea.'

'Did you see what happened?'

'No, but I heard his cry from the kitchen and ran back here.'

'Did he tell you how he fell?'

'He said he tripped on a raised board at the top of the stairs. I've only just bought the house and not had time to fix it.'

'And there's nobody else in the house?' Toby helped Sandra fit a neck brace.

'No. There's nobody else here. Just Malcolm and me.'

'No family members?'

'No.'

'No children?'

'No. There's no one else here.'

'No dogs?'

'No.'

Toby turned to Malcolm. His eyes were closed, and he was breathing more easily. 'Malcolm, Mr Cadwallader. Can you hear me?'

Malcolm opened his eyes.

'Were you pushed? Did somebody push you?'

Malcolm tried to shake his head. 'It was a silly accident.' He whimpered as he was eased onto the low-lying stretcher and strapped into place. Audrey slipped her bare feet into a pair of walking shoes and grabbed her coat off the stand. She followed the crew out of the house, into the freezing rain, leaving the front door open. She hurried past Malcolm's car to the ambulance parked at the end of her drive.

'Aren't you going to lock your house?' Sandra asked as she and Toby raised the trolley and slid Malcolm into the ambulance.

Audrey looked back at her open front door, as rain turned to luminescent hailstones in the weak light from the hallway. 'I won't come with you,' she said. 'I'll follow on shortly. Where are you taking him?'

'Undermere General Hospital. Are you sure you don't want to come with us?'

'We'll wait for you to lock up,' Toby said.

'No, I'll get dressed and make my own way to the hospital. Thank you for taking care of him.'

Shivering uncontrollably, Audrey re-entered the hall and pushed the door shut. She ran upstairs, dressed quickly and then picked up Malcolm's jacket. She searched his pockets and found his house and car keys, his wallet and phone, and shoved them in her handbag. She hurried back down to the hallway. On the floor was her own phone, which she retrieved.

Slamming the front door, she ran to Malcolm's car, slipped into the driver's seat, slid it forward and fired up the engine. She took a few seconds to find the switch for the lights and the stalk for the wipers. She had no idea where the hospital was but decided she would follow the road signs to Undermere and then use her phone to direct her to the exact location.

The car was an automatic so finding reverse was easy. She backed out of her drive and stopped in the road. What was she doing? Why was she rushing to the hospital? For a moment, she considered what had just happened, then turned back into her drive and switched off the engine.

She closed the car door and entered her hallway. The old

school boarding house was quiet. There were no squeaks or creaks, just still, cold air. She stood in the dimly lit hall and a conversation that had changed her life when she was aged twenty came back as though it were yesterday. She was in the drawing room of a large Victorian house, watching her Aunt Margot pour tea into fine porcelain cups.

'I don't know what to do, Auntie. I'm completely torn,' said the young Audrey. Her aunt handed her a cup of tea and picked up a sharp knife to cut a slice of homemade Dundee cake.

'Well,' said her aunt. 'Let me see if I can help you. On the one hand you have Joey, who is rich, successful and has bought you a car; and on the other hand you have Duncan, who is young, penniless but full of potential.'

'That's about it. They both have their qualities.'

'However, I can assure you that you do not love them both equally.' Her aunt skilfully placed a slice of cake on a porcelain plate and handed it to Audrey. 'I'm going to ask you two questions and I want you to give me your first response to each. Question one: imagine that you will never ever see Joey again – how does that make you feel?'

Young Audrey shrugged. 'Not good. I love him.'

Her aunt pressed on. 'Second question: think about Duncan. Imagine never, ever, seeing him again. You have seen him for the last time. He is out of your life. How does that make you feel?'

Audrey snapped back to the present and looked about the hallway. She was alone. Her wonderful aunt who had helped to change the course of her life was gone. She was totally bereft. Totally alone. Her life had lost all meaning. Was she simply a loose end counting down to her own demise? She felt for the wedding ring on her left hand and that, too, was gone.

'Duncan! I miss you. I bloody miss you!' She fell to her knees as tears flooded her eyes.

It did not take long for the cold floor to bite and for her whole body to be convulsed with shivers.

'I love you, Ordy.'

What was that? Who had spoken? She used the heel of her hands to push the tears from her eyes. All she could see were blurred objects and dark shadows. Was that a shape on the half-landing?

Her coat sleeve was a poor sponge as she attempted to clear her eyes. She looked up again and tried to focus.

CHAPTER TWENTY-EIGHT

It was still night when Audrey was permitted to enter the intensive care unit at Undermere General Hospital. She stared at Malcolm lying in the mechanised hospital bed, his face covered by an oxygen mask. A bag on a hook was attached to an intravenous line that disappeared into his arm. A cardiac monitor relayed the peaks and troughs of his beating heart, and a drainage bag attached to the bed was collecting his urine. On a trolley was a defibrillator.

Gavin, a nurse, placed an upright chair near the bed. 'He's sedated. He has a broken hip, a fractured left arm, and a dislocated shoulder, which we will relocate under general anaesthetic. He will be in hospital for some while. I'll be back, shortly.'

Audrey nodded and Gavin left.

Joshua, Audrey's miracle son, shouted from the living room. 'Mum, it's dad. I think we should call an ambulance.'

Duncan was slumped in his usual chair. His right hand was clamped to his left arm and his shirt collar, soaked with sweat, was tight around his swollen throat. He looked up at Audrey, his face contorted with pain as his tongue – grotesquely long – lolled out of his mouth.

The door to the ICU opened and two orderlies entered together with Nurse Jablonski and Dr Ryder, a registrar in her thirties who looked as though she had been working all night.

Nurse Jablonski gave Audrey's shoulder a gentle shake and Audrey's dilated eyes looked up at the pretty blonde nurse. 'Is he still alive?' She gripped the nurse's arm as she got to her feet. 'Tell me the truth.'

Dr Ryder turned to Audrey. 'We're taking him for a scan. We believe he may have a subdural haematoma caused by the bang to his head. If he has, he will be operated on immediately to remove the blood and stop the bleed.'

'What about his heart?' Audrey asked.

'For a man of his age and with his injuries from the fall, his heart is holding up pretty well. We've just got to put the broken bits back together.'

Audrey watched as the bed was wheeled out.

What fall?

Duncan had had a heart attack – he didn't fall. Perplexed, she looked out of the window and saw the sun rising over the hospital car park.

She heard a familiar ring tone and, instinctively, picked up her handbag from the floor and opened it. She took out her phone. Green *Answer* pulsed and she swiped the screen.

'Mrs Willatt, Audrey. It's Tony, Tony Blake.'

'Tony Blake?'

'I'm the photographer from *The Chronicle*.'

'The Chronicle?'

'You saved our baby.'

'Your baby?'

'You recognised the symptoms of meningitis.'

'Sorry, I'm a bit muddled.'

'I took your photograph and wrote the story about your haunted house. I came to your tea party.'

'I don't understand.'

Following Duncan's first heart attack more than twenty years ago, Audrey had suffered repeated nightmares. After his death, lack of sleep brought on by grief and stress had turned her nightmares, from which she could shake herself awake, into sleep terrors from which opening her eyes, walking around, even talking, did not free her from the images projected in her mind.

'Mrs Willatt? Is everything all right? My dad had a call this morning from a friend who saw an ambulance outside your house last night.'

Audrey looked at the empty space where the bed had been. 'I think something terrible has happened.' She furrowed her brow. 'Malcolm. Yes! Malcolm Cadwallader. I remember. He fell down the stairs. He's badly hurt.'

'Where are you now?'

'I'm at the hospital.' The hand holding her phone dropped to her side. She had to think. She had to clear her mind.

She picked up her bag and opened it to replace her phone and saw Malcolm's wallet, phone, and house and car keys. He had told her he had seen her brother – but that was impossible. What other lies had he told her?

'Excuse me,' Audrey said to the receptionist at the front desk in the intensive care unit. 'I have Malcolm Cadwallader's wallet and phone. Could you keep them safe for him?' She placed them on the counter.

'We prefer valuable items to be kept by family members,' replied the receptionist.

'I'm not family.'

'But you're his wife?'

'No.'

The receptionist frowned. 'His partner?'

'No.'
'But you're his friend?'
'No. I'm not his friend. I will not see him again.'

CHAPTER TWENTY-NINE

Tony Blake was excited. He couldn't help it. The newshound within him smelled a story. He scrolled down the names in his phone.

'Dad, hold the front page. I think I have something.' He gave his father an account of his brief conversation with Audrey.

He kissed his baby son goodbye, gave his wife a quick peck and almost leapt into his family-sized Skoda Octavia with its two child seats in the rear. The roads were particularly icy, and rush hour was building, so it took at least half an hour to get to Undermere General Hospital.

Tony hated paying for parking, but he knew that the hospital's out-sourced contractor operated a ruthless system of fines. He also knew the layout of the hospital well, having spent quite a bit of time wandering around when his son had been ill. He found his way to the intensive care unit and was about to try and blag his way past the receptionist when he saw Malcolm Cadwallader being wheeled back into his room.

'Granddad!'

He followed the orderlies into the side ward, ignoring repeated requests for him to return to reception. Malcolm was awake and looked at Tony, his mouth covered by an oxygen mask.

'Audrey rang me, Granddad. She told me what happened.'

The orderlies secured the wheels on the bed while Gavin, the nurse, checked that all the readings were in order. Once he was happy, he looked at Tony.

'Your grandfather has had a lucky escape. There's bruising but no bleed to the brain. We've just got to sort out the various broken bones and nasty dislocation of the shoulder and he'll be fit as a fiddle again.' He turned to Malcolm. 'I'll be back shortly with some more painkillers.' He smiled at Tony and followed the orderlies out of the room.

Tony looked at the monitor with its multi-coloured numbers and lines and at the bag supported on the side of the bed, about a third full of urine. He leaned in towards Malcolm. 'Would you like a drink?'

Malcolm removed his oxygen mask with his good arm and placed it below his chin. 'Thank you. My mouth is very dry.'

Tony picked up a plastic jug with a lid from the bedside trolley and poured a small quantity of water into a plastic cup. He held it whilst Malcolm took a few sips. He returned the cup to the trolley.

'I'm a friend of Audrey's. She told me what happened last night. I came over to see her.'

'She was here? At the hospital?'

'Yes,' Tony said.

'Please give her a message. It's very important.'

'You can tell me. I'll make sure she gets it.'

'I... I...' The words caught in his throat, confirming to Tony that there was definitely more to this story than simply falling down the stairs.

CHAPTER THIRTY

Audrey followed the road signs back to Hawksmead and parked Malcolm's car in her driveway. The morning air was bitingly cold and, as she entered her cavernous hall, her house did not feel much warmer.

She closed the front door and its bang echoed briefly. On the floor, near the base of the stairs, were remnants of medical packaging left by the paramedics last night. She looked up the stairs to the half-landing. What happened? Did Malcolm really see Bobby? Or was that the lie of a guilty man?

'Bobby! It's Audrey. I'm here. I've come to say goodbye.'

She stood and waited.

'I will always love you. You were never forgotten – not by Mummy, not by Daddy, not by me.'

The house replied with a heavy silence.

Audrey, her whole body weary, trudged up the stairs to the half-landing. She was desperate for a shower. She walked along the narrow corridor to the washroom and used her usual cubicle. She pulled the chain and peeled off her clothes, dropping them on the old terracotta tiled floor. In the large communal shower area, she turned on her usual tap. Icy water cascaded over her face and down her drawn, thin body. She didn't care. She soaped herself as best she could, but the cold water prevented her from making much lather.

Shivering almost uncontrollably, she towelled her skin dry, rubbing herself fiercely as she walked back to the main washroom area. She looked at her naked form in the mirror. She had achieved what she set out to do when she first decided to buy the old school boarding house, but she hadn't factored in the possibility of falling in love with the man responsible for her little brother's tragic death.

'I've failed, you, Mummy. I've failed you.'

Leaving her clothes and wet towel on the floor, she picked up her handbag and opened the washroom door. She would leave Hawksmead today. She looked back at the long row of toilet cubicles, complemented by the long row of washbasins. For a moment, she thought she heard Bobby's voice, but she knew it was in her head.

She let the washroom door close and, barefoot and naked, she trudged along the corridor to the half-landing. She looked down the stairs into the hallway.

'The Russians can have it.'

Her skin almost tinged with blue, she climbed up to the top landing and entered the dormitory. She looked at the dishevelled bedding from the night before and expected to be consumed with shame, but all she felt was overwhelming sadness. She shivered, and hastily dressed in the warmest clothes she had.

Still shivering, she pulled the two suitcases out from under her bed and placed them on top. She opened the lids and wasted no time folding clothes as she stuffed in as many as she could, leaving a rejected jumble of trousers and sweaters amongst the bedding.

Across the room, Audrey saw the encyclopaedia lying on the floor. She lifted it up and placed it on a bed. In the cut-out section she expected to see Robert's diary.

Where was it?

For a moment she felt sickening panic, but then she remembered it was in her handbag. She took it out, sat on her bed, and looked at the diary's fly leaf with its handwritten inscription:

This is the secret diary of Robert Oakes.
DO NOT READ UNTIL 2065

She turned to the first page; her brother's record of that autumn term sparking so many childhood memories for her. She read the short diary through to the last line, now knowing that the footsteps Bobby heard coming up the stairs were Malcolm's. She kissed the leather cover and placed the diary in her handbag.

It took some effort to close the two suitcases and carried the heaviest down into the hall. She went back upstairs into the washroom and packed as many toiletries as she could into her wash and make-up bags. Leaving them on the half-landing, she trudged up to her bedroom to collect the second suitcase. She hauled it off the bed and looked around the room. She thought about her little brother and his love for Mini, and she thought about her misplaced love for Malcolm.

She picked up her handbag and lugged the second suitcase down the two flights to the half-landing.

Something was wrong. She was sure she had left her wash and make-up bags at the top of the stairs – they were gone. She carried her suitcase down into the hallway and was shocked to see her toiletries and numerous items of make-up scattered across the tiled floor. It looked like an angry statement by somebody – or some*thing*.

She picked her way to the front entrance, put down her suitcase and opened the door. A great gust of wind snatched the latch from between her fingers and the heavy oak door slammed shut. She tried to open it again, but it wouldn't budge. An icy chill caused her to give an involuntary shiver.

Was some spectral presence in the hallway with her? She focused on the hardened woodgrain in the old timber door, too scared to turn around and take a look. She had loved her brother, but the thought of seeing him in ghostly form terrified her.

'I'm leaving, Bobby, and it is time for you to leave too.' She spoke without turning to look.

A sharp crack sent a jolt through her and Audrey felt her knees buckle. She screwed her eyes shut and blocked her ears against the creaking sound. She shook almost uncontrollably. Taking deep breaths, she turned around and opened her eyes.

Hanging at the end of bed sheets, twisted around his neck and tied to a newel post on the half-landing, was a young boy, his head at an impossible angle. She did not recognise his face, which was distorted and livid, with eyes bulging from their sockets; but she knew it was Eddie Holden, the boy Shirley had talked about with such deep sorrow when Audrey had visited the library.

She tried the front door again and it opened. She reached for her suitcase, but the door slammed shut. She turned the latch and pulled, but it wouldn't budge. Screwing up her courage a second time, Audrey turned around and looked back into the hall. Standing at the top of the stairs, wearing corduroy shorts, was her little brother.

'Bobby!'

The name came out in little more than a whispered croak as she dropped her handbag and ran to the base of the stairs.

Something pulled the boy from behind and his arms

flailed at an unseen foe.

'*NO!*' Audrey screamed.

The boy stopped and looked down at her.

'Please don't!' She looked up into his sweet, sad face, big sister and little brother staring at each other for the first time in more than fifty years. 'I can't bear to see you fall.'

He smiled, touched his fingertips to his lips and blew her a kiss. Audrey felt embraced by a great warmth as he walked silently down the stairs and came towards her.

The front door blew open.

Bobby smiled, and she watched him walk across the hallway and out of the house to a place Audrey could not imagine.

She sank to her knees and wept, as fifty years of grief poured out. She thought about her dear mother breaking the devastating news to her. How her mother had fought to keep calm as she relayed to Audrey what had happened to Bobby.

The Oakes family had been solid and strong, but within ten years of Bobby's death, she saw her family disintegrate. Her father felt the loss of his only son every bit as keenly as her mother and dealt with the pain by distraction: distraction work; distraction sailing; distraction dating; anything that would occupy his mind. But her mother could not find any solace, despite throwing herself into her local amateur dramatic plays, meeting smart friends for bridge, entertaining frequently, and swimming at the local country club. It didn't work. Ten years on, Audrey saw the pain of loss in all its rawness when her mother told her she had breast cancer. Of course, everything was done to cure her of the disease, but in the mid-1970s, the technology was crude and the results more miss than hit. The cancer spread, and Audrey saw it was a blessed release. She knew that her mother loved her every bit as much as she had loved Robert, but now that Audrey was settled in her own home with her lovely Duncan, it was time for her mother to slip away into painless oblivion.

But how would her mother respond if she knew that Audrey had slept with the man who was responsible for Robert's death? How would her father react at the age of eighty-nine? He was happily married to his favourite sailing companion and still in very good health. If she told him what had really happened, if she showed him Bobby's diary, it could tip him over the edge and into his grave.

Roughly wiping away her tears, she knew she had to get out of the house. There would be no Hostel on the Moor. Despite its Grade II status, she hoped the old building would be destroyed.

Audrey picked up her handbag and opened it. She removed the front door keys and threw them onto the floor, amongst all her discarded make-up and toiletries, and hurried out of the house, leaving the door wide open.

Seeing Malcolm's Honda in her driveway sent ripples through her body.

What now? Had all hope of a future together been shattered by the truth?

Audrey walked past the Honda to the end of her driveway. Across the road, she saw a parked transit van and spotted Kirill Dryomov sitting at the wheel with the engine running. She may as well tell him now that the house was up for sale.

Checking for traffic, she stepped into the road and walked across to the van. Kirill looked in her direction and pulled away before she could speak to him.

She watched him go. No matter. The estate agency could arrange the sale.

She crossed back to her drive and looked at Malcolm's car. She would drop the keys off at *The Chronicle* and send a message to Tina, in case the car had to be moved before Malcolm was well enough to drive it – if he survived.

She was about to walk down the High Street when she changed her mind and headed towards the Old Military Road. She pulled the strap of her handbag over her shoulder and dug her bare hands deep into her pockets as moisture from her breath crystallised in the biting chill.

She could not remember ever feeling this wretched. Her head was a jumble of conflicting emotions laced with overwhelming guilt. Had she really seen Bobby? Had he really smiled or had it all been in her troubled mind? Shoulders hunched against the freezing air blowing off the moor, she paid no attention to the white transit van, following her some way behind.

Lost in so many thoughts, Audrey approached the humpback bridge over the River Hawk. The narrow strip of road glistened like a black silk ribbon. Her shoes were for walking and had good rubber grips, but she was not prepared for the slipperiness of the ice that coated the road, and she had to grab the stone wall at the side of the bridge to stop falling over.

She took a few calming breaths and steadied herself. She would be gone from Hawksmead soon, but she'd had to make this final pilgrimage to such a significant place in her brother's short life. The sun was up and the trees were almost entirely shorn of leaves, so Audrey could see across the moor to the Ridgeway and the forbidding sight of the former outward-bound boarding school. She thought about Bobby with his terrible stutter, trying to survive in such an austere environment; and his friend, Mini, being crushed on the bridge fifty years ago, exactly where she was standing now. She looked down at the river, awash with churning water, and thought about the two boys Bobby had written about, who had drowned trying to claw their way out of the swirling torrent.

Who remembered them now?

Who remembered Bobby?

CHAPTER THIRTY-ONE

Kirill didn't know what to do. He had driven to his brother's house that morning, as usual, and in no uncertain terms had been told to piss off. Spartak's skank of a girlfriend had recognised Kirill as the man with the axe and had decided to end the brief affair. Girls like that were dirt cheap in Russia, but his brother appeared to have fallen for her and blamed Kirill for the break-up. Why was it his fault? If the widow had not been so objectionable, he would not have been standing in her drive with an axe when Tina saw him.

The whole town knew that the Dryomov brothers had wanted the boarding house but when Audrey stole it from under their noses, people had lost their fear and openly laughed. The humiliation he felt was driving all reason from his mind. But it wasn't just losing the house that annoyed him, it was Audrey herself – her lack of fear, her scrawny frame, her very existence.

And now there she was, standing all alone on the bridge. To his surprise and horror he felt a surge in his pants. What was he thinking? She was twice his age. The blast of cannons from his phone blew apart his fantasies and his brother's name on the screen deflated his lust. He lifted his right hand and his grubby fat thumb hovered over the green *'Answer'* before swiping it.

'Zdravstvuj,' he said, reluctantly.

~

The torrent of water rushing between the bridge's three stone arches frightened Audrey. Her mother had loved swimming and would go in the grey-green sea even when it was freezing. But it wasn't the cold that bothered Audrey; it was water's merciless power to kill.

She was six and in charge of looking after her four-year-old brother as they ran down the road with buckets and spades gripped in their little hands.

'You can play on the beach but you're not to swim.' Audrey had begged her mother to let them go on their own. 'If you want water for a sandcastle, you can fill your buckets from one of the rock pools.'

In the 1950s, there were few cars and crossing the road to the broad steps that led down to the beach was easy and safe. Audrey was mature for her six years and always took great care of her little brother.

The tide was out and there were plenty of rock pools for Bobby to explore. It was a sunny afternoon and lots of little children were on the beach having fun including a coach load of boys being minded by Roman Catholic nuns, looking hot in their flowing black habits. Audrey remembered seeing her brother playing with some boys by a shallow rock pool. They had a little boat and were building a harbour.

Her mother had given Audrey a shilling – easily enough to buy two ice creams. There was quite a queue leading up to the white-painted beach hut, and she waited patiently to be served, completely unaware that her little brother was in the process of being rounded up by one of the nuns. She did not see him being told by a pinched face to hold hands with another little boy. She did not see him being marched up the beach towards the waiting coach. She did not hear his protests or the nun ordering him to be quiet. She could only imagine the fear her little brother must have felt as every step took him further away from his big sister. Ice filled her veins as she thought about the nuns pushing her little brother up the coach's steps and with a hand on his back guiding him down the bus to one of the rear seats. She could almost hear, sixty years on, his scream when a nun slammed the door shut and the coach's engine rattled into life.

~

Kirill terminated the connection to Spartak. He would go and pick his brother up in his own good time. He licked his cracked lips as he contemplated the thin female form leaning against the side of the stone bridge. It wouldn't take much to grab her, tie her up in the back of his van and later, much later, dump her body out on the moor. What was it about this old woman that was driving him so crazy?

He opened the van door and felt the icy blast coming from the east. He liked the cold. He liked the bleakness of winter, the stark branches on the trees, the hard ground and the biting air. He smiled. He was downwind. She wouldn't hear him coming.

CHAPTER THIRTY-TWO

Tony had been moved by Malcolm's story and was keen to meet up with Audrey to get the complete picture. He contemplated phoning but decided to go straight to her house instead. The morning rush hour clogged the main roads, so he had taken the longer but less busy route across the moor along the Old Military Road. As he drove, he could feel his Skoda being buffeted by the easterly wind; snow was starting to fall, and soon his wipers were battling blizzard conditions. Although confident that his car was sufficiently reliable, he did feel vulnerable and began to regret his choice of route.

~

Kirill's phone buzzed in his pocket and the cannons boomed. He hurried back to the warmth of his van before he answered his brother's call.

'Do her no harm.' Spartak's voice through the phone's speaker bounced off the van's metal interior. 'You hear me? If anything happens to that woman – *anything* – I will go straight to the police and report this conversation.'

Kirill was shocked by Spartak's intuition. How had he known what Kirill was contemplating?

~

Snow blew into Audrey's face and prickled her skin but she could not lift her mind out of the despair into which she was sinking. She should be thinking of her sons and those that loved her today, not suffering the misery of her family's past. But the past had come around full circle and she could see no future for herself. She looked up from the fast-flowing river and through the sparse trees to the moor now carpeted in white. She could just make out the soulless edifice of the old school. Her parents had wanted nothing but the best for her and her brother; her sweet brother who stuttered but dreamed of being an actor. Audrey's childhood had been very happy – ballet lessons, piano lessons, bike rides and roller skating. No knee pads or wrist guards in those days – just pure fun and the occasional scrape.

~

Was it Bobby's scream that made Audrey look towards the beach or a cry from a seagull? She saw that the tide was coming in and the waves were building, crashing fiercely onto the sandy shore. Although she couldn't see her brother, she didn't want to lose her place in the ice cream queue. Normally, she wore glasses, so the children building sandcastles on the beach were all a bit of a blur. Bobby was a good boy and knew not to go in the sea without his big sister. But Audrey's sense of responsibility got the better of her, and she broke away from the queue. She ran towards the rock pool where she had last seen her little brother as the rising tide hurled massive rollers onto the beach. With water swirling and sucking at her ankles, she saw that a section of beach was now cut off by the sea. Was Bobby playing behind the rocks?

She waded into the foamy water to get a better view of the dwindling beach, her focus entirely taken with scanning the shoreline and not the mighty rollers building behind her.

~

Kirill started the transit van and turned on the wipers to clear the snow from the screen. The woman was still standing on the bridge. Why? Was she insane? Even Kirill, who liked the cold and snow, would not stand exposed to the elements without a hat and gloves. An idea sparked in his mind.

~

Tony had his lights dipped and his wipers working hard as he tore along the Old Military Road. He passed the turning to Hawksmead College and continued on, slowing as he approached the bridge. As a precaution, he hooted his horn.

~

Kirill's van was almost at the bridge when he saw Audrey turn her head. She must have heard something. Perhaps a car was coming in the opposite direction? He touched his brakes, but it was as though he didn't have any. His wheels locked, but the van continued in a straight line, heading directly towards Audrey who was standing with her back to him. She was about to be the cushion between his van's large bumper and the bridge's stone wall. In desperation, he blasted his horn and pumped his brakes. His brother would never believe that he had not intended to kill the woman, but that was exactly what he was about to do.

~

Tony crested the bridge and saw the white van, and then, to his perplexed horror, Audrey's lone figure standing in peril. He overreacted and slammed on his brakes, but his car's anti-locking system had no effect on his speed as he slid on ice towards the van and the woman who was now trapped in a pincer with nowhere to go.

~

Above the roar of water flowing under the bridge, Audrey had picked up a sound and turned her head. The message conveyed by her eyes that two vehicles were about to crash into her, triggered neurons in her brain to send an urgent message to her ballet-trained legs. Her muscles contracted, propelling her body up and back over the top of the low stone wall.

~

Tony could not look. He was a passenger at the wheel of his car and was shocked by the loudness of the bang as he and the van smashed into each other and then bounced into the stone wall. The ancient construction gave under the combined force, and the noses of both the Skoda and the van protruded over the fast-flowing river.

Convinced that Audrey had to be dead, Tony opened his door and snow immediately blew in. He pushed against the wind and stepped out of his car. His foot shot out from under him, and he crashed onto his back.

~

Kirill sat at his wheel, not comprehending what had just happened. He'd not been going fast but his van wouldn't stop. The woman, as if connected to a spring, had risen into the air and disappeared. He thought about her thin body and old age and allowed himself a smile. He had changed his mind about killing her, and he had a witness who would back him up that he hadn't, but she would still be out of the way.

The witness! He must talk to him. His brother may think he was lying and still report him to the police. Kirill climbed down from the transit van and felt his heavy boots slide out from under him. He hung onto his door until he regained his balance. Taking baby steps, he walked around the rear of his van and saw the driver of the car lying prostrate. He moved as quickly as the snow and black ice would permit and helped Tony get back on his feet.

'I couldn't stop,' Tony said.

'It is your fault. You were not driving carefully enough for condition. You pay for van.'

'Where is Audrey? The woman? We've got to call an ambulance.'

'She in river. Downstream somewhere.' Kirill tried to keep the elation he felt out of his voice. 'Probably dead, drowned.'

CHAPTER THIRTY-THREE

Following an early viewing, Tina approached Audrey's house and swung into the short driveway. She was surprised to see Malcolm's car with its taped-up side mirror and decided today was not the time to give Audrey her news. She was about to reverse her VW out when she noticed the front door was wide open with snow blowing in.

Debating what to do, she sat with her engine running. Finally, she switched it off and opened the driver's door. She walked past Malcolm's car, through the settling snow, to the open entrance and looked into the house.

'Audrey! It's Tina.'

She stepped into the hallway and searched for the light switch. It was morning, but the sun had not penetrated the thick layer of cloud. She flicked on the light and was immediately disturbed to see Audrey's two suitcases and toiletries scattered across the hall, partially covered by wind-blown snow. She spotted the door keys, picked them up and put them in her pocket then looked up the stairs into the gloom.

'Audrey! It's Tina. The front door's open.'

She listened for an answer. She looked back at the open door and then noticed the torn bits of medical packaging blown to the base of the stairs.

~

Tony moved as quickly as the black ice would allow to the downstream side of the bridge and stared at the rush of water funnelled between its three arches. Audrey's handbag swept past, tossed in the raging flow. Then he saw a head bob up and hands scrape the stone bridge support, seeking purchase – nails clawing at the joins.

'*AUDREY!*'

He hurried as fast as he could on the black ice to the Hawksmead side of the bridge and shouted to Kirill.

'Call the police. Call them *NOW*.'

Kirill took out his phone and followed Tony, who slid down the snow-covered bank to the river's edge.

'Don't do it. You cannot save her!' Kirill yelled.

~

Audrey lost all sense of direction as she was spun uncontrollably. She could not tell which way was up or down. She breathed in water and felt a great stabbing pain in her thin chest. For a brief moment, her toes touched the bottom, and she tried to push up, but the power enveloping her was too great. She saw Bobby sitting in the back of the coach. She heard his scream when the old engine roared. She saw his little friend hold up his hand and speak to the nun. She saw the driver open the door and the nun usher Bobby off the coach. She felt his little arms squeeze her neck as they hugged and hugged. She heard her mother calling them in for tea …and she felt great contentment. She could stop fighting. She was home.

~

Tony did not have a plan. For a moment, he thought a log

was floating downstream and then he realised it was Audrey. He knew if he gave it a second's thought he wouldn't have the courage – so he threw himself into the freezing water – and immediately regretted it.

~

Resting her hand on the banister, Tina walked up the wide wooden stairs to the half-landing. The thought of seeing the pale face again terrified her. She hurried down the long corridor and climbed the stairs to the second floor and on up to the top-floor landing. The faint *thank you* written by a fat forefinger on the window pane was still discernible. To her right was the closed door to Audrey's bedroom. She reached for the old brass knob, pushed the door open and peered into the room. Through the window, snow was coating the bare boughs of the oak tree, casting the dormitory in a colourless glow. She flicked on the centre light.

On the beds and floor were untidy sheets and blankets and discarded clothing. But neatly folded on a far bed were Malcolm's jacket, shirt, tie and trousers.

She walked back onto the landing and was about to go downstairs when a siren caught her attention. She hurried to the window and looked down into the High Street just in time to see a police car, with blue lights flashing, race past.

Out of the corner of her eye she saw something move.

She spun round.

Across the landing was a slim figure.

'Audrey! I was so worried. Is everything okay? I've broken it off with Spartak. I'm so sorry they caused you trouble.' Another siren attracted Tina's attention. She looked down as an ambulance tore up the High Street.

She turned back to Audrey …but she was gone.

~

Audrey's coat snagged a heavy branch that lay half on the bank and half in the water. It gave Tony the chance to save himself. With one hand he grabbed the branch, and with his other hand he grabbed the collar of Audrey's coat. The force of the current was phenomenal and he knew that he could not hold onto her for long.

'You. Take my hand.'

Tony looked at the great hulk sitting astride the branch. He inched his fingers towards Kirill and felt a wave of relief as the man's great paw clamped around his wrist.

'Let the woman go. She is done for,' Kirill shouted above the roar of the fast-flowing water.

'No!' Tony's lips were so numb he could hardly speak.

Kirill pulled Tony's arm and hauled him onto the slippery riverbank.

'Help me,' Tony gasped, and together they pulled Audrey's body fully out of the river. Tony laid her on her back and could see she wasn't breathing. Hands shaking, he undid the zipper on her coat and tilted her head back.

'She's dead,' Kirill said.

'Go up to the street and tell the ambulance where we are.'

'Don't order me!'

'*GO!*'

Kirill stomped off, slipping on the snow-covered riverbank.

Tony did not have any medical training but he'd written an article about cardiopulmonary resuscitation, for his father's newspaper, so he sort of knew what he had to do.

Adrenaline sharpened his mind as he knelt astride Audrey's lifeless body and placed one hand on top of the other on her chest. He locked his elbows and pushed down. He remembered that he was supposed to sing the Bee Gees' hit *Stayin' Alive,* but he couldn't remember quite how it went. He pressed and pressed, and after thirty seconds he gripped Audrey's nose, clamped his mouth over hers and breathed air into her lungs. He saw her chest rise and blew again even harder. He went back to pumping her breastbone and, after about thirty compressions, he gripped her nose again and blew hard into her lungs.

The first person to arrive was a police officer who said he would take over, but Tony refused to stop. He pumped for thirty seconds, blew two big puffs into Audrey's lungs and pumped again.

What seemed like an eternity later, two paramedics slid down the snow-covered bank, dragging medical boxes. 'We'll take it from here, sir.'

~

Tina checked she had the house keys and left the old school boarding house, carefully locking the door behind her. She had definitely seen Audrey. She had spoken to her. And yet, and yet…

She teetered on her high heels through the snow to the end of the drive where she saw Kirill walking past, looking wet and muddy.

'What you do to my brother?' he called.

Tina was unsure how to respond or what to do. The massive man didn't seem to notice the biting cold or that his clothes were soaking wet.

'House up for sale,' he continued. 'She die.'

Tina approached him, warily.

'I pull her out of river, but she not look good. Not breathing. She go to hospital.' A giant hook of a hand grabbed Tina's arm and he hauled her close to him. 'Why you break up with Spartak?'

I broke up with him because his brother is a nutter with an axe, was what she wanted to say. What she did say was, 'I'm very fond of Spartak, but our cultures, our backgrounds are too different.'

Kirill looked into her eyes and let go of her arm. 'He miss you. You give it another try, yes?'

'I'll think about it.'

'Call him. Tell him you think about it.'

Tina watched Kirill walk off down the High Street then hurried as best she could to her VW Golf with its new side mirror. She had moved heaven and earth to get it fixed, but now, her perfect car was nothing more to her than a means of transport. She slid into the driver's seat and started the engine. The nearest accident and emergency unit was in Undermere General Hospital. It was still snowing, but her Golf had good tyres and front-wheel drive, so went well in slippery conditions. If the traffic wasn't too bad, she could get there and back before her next viewing appointment.

~

Tony had no choice but to go in the ambulance with Audrey. He knew he was suffering from hypothermia; his clothes were soaked and had been taken off him, and he had no means of getting home as his car was wrecked. Wrapped in a blanket and shivering almost uncontrollably, he didn't know whether he had saved Audrey's life or simply delayed her death. The small section of her skin he could see had the look of alabaster tinged with blue.

He'd asked Kirill to visit *The Chronicle* newspaper and let his father know what had happened. His phone lay dead amongst his wet clothes and no amount of drying in a bag of rice was likely to bring it back to life. But what about the heating pads distributed around Audrey's inert body? Could they bring her back to life?

CHAPTER THIRTY-FOUR

Audrey had been rushed through Accident & Emergency and was now in the Intensive Care Unit. Although her heart had a weak beat and she was breathing, her core temperature was still extremely low. The consultant physician had requested a haemodialysis machine, usually reserved for people with no kidney function. It was not easy getting the needles into Audrey's thin veins, but after a few worrying minutes her blood started to pump through the machine where it was gently warmed.

~

'She had nowhere to go apart from the river,' Tony said to Andy, who was looking down at his son.

Tony was lying in bed in a bay in Accident & Emergency, also surrounded by warming pads.

'The chilblains are driving me mad. I feel like my skin is on fire. The doctor said it will pass, but it's bloomin' agony.'

Andy lent his phone to Tony so he could call his wife. It took about twenty minutes to assure Eden that his life was not in danger and another twenty minutes listening to her berating him for putting himself at risk in the first place.

'Audrey would rather be dead than have your children grow up without a father,' Eden said, finally pausing to draw breath.

Tony heard Charlie crying in the background so, mercifully, the call was ended. He gave the phone back to his father.

'You scared her,' Andy said, 'but she's also immensely proud of you, as am I. I could not have a more wonderful son.' He turned his back and appeared to examine the *In Case of Fire* notice pinned to the wall.

~

In the hospital car park, Tina stuck the pay-and-display ticket on her windscreen and pressed the fob to lock her Golf. Fortunately, it had stopped snowing but it was still bitterly cold. She walked to the main entrance and went up to the reception desk. A few minutes later, she found herself sitting alone in the intensive care unit visitor area, thinking about Audrey. How could someone so full of life and vigour now be dying or dead?

'Have you come to see Audrey?'

Tina looked up, perplexed.

'My name's Tony Blake. This is my dad, Andy. We're with *The Chronicle*. We did a feature on your agency last year.'

'What's happened? Why are you wearing a bathrobe?'

'My son pulled Audrey out of the river,' Andy interjected.

Tina could not remember when she had last felt this confused. 'The Russian property developer told me *he* pulled her out.'

Andy emitted an ugly grunt.

'Let's say it was a joint effort,' Tony responded.

'If my son hadn't jumped into the river,' Andy said, 'Audrey would now be in the morgue.'

'We'd probably both be there if the Russian hadn't

helped me.'

'Shouldn't you be in bed?' Tina asked. 'You're shivering.'

'I'm fine. I was in A&E, but I was brought over here so the same consultant could keep an eye on both Audrey and me. She may still not make it.' He swallowed hard. 'Fortunately, Malcolm's going to be okay.'

'Malcolm?' Now Tina's confusion was off the scale.

Tony told her about the fall and Malcolm's injuries.

'It's that house. It's cursed.' She looked at Andy. 'Are you going to put all this in your newspaper?'

'Yes. But at the moment, I don't know how the story is going to end.'

~

There was nothing else for Tina to do but go to work. She drove back to Hawksmead and tried to keep her mind focused on the viewings listed for that day, but her thoughts kept returning to Audrey and the old school boarding house.

Following a lacklustre viewing of a flat situated above Merlin's Hardware Store, she entered the estate agency. Without a word to her colleagues, she flopped down at her desk and put her head in her hands, exhausted, bereft of her usual vibrancy.

After a few moments, a mug of coffee was placed in front of her.

'Freshly brewed.'

Tina looked up at Trevor. 'You never make me coffee.'

'Yes I do. I made you coffee when you came for your interview.'

'That was three years ago. I was still in my final term at school.'

'Then I'm sure you're ready for another cup.'

She looked at the steam rising from the brown surface and did something she never allowed herself to do in front of her boss – she wept.

CHAPTER THIRTY-FIVE

Tony was in a quandary: should he tell Malcolm that Audrey was unconscious in the room next door and that she may not survive? Or was it better for Malcolm not to know?

He had been hailed a hero by his father, but he didn't feel one. Yes, there had been black ice and snow was falling but, whichever way he looked at it, his car had blocked Audrey's escape and forced her to jump into the river. And now he had to tell this kindly old man news that would probably kill him.

'Are you ill?' Malcolm asked, as he attempted to rally his hair.

Tony looked down at his towelling dressing gown and smiled. 'I'm fine, thank you, but I do have something to tell you.' He pulled up a chair and explained to Malcolm exactly what had happened earlier that morning. The old man listened, not interrupting at any point. It was only when Tony revealed that Audrey was in the room next door that Malcolm reacted.

~

'Show some spunk.' Her mother's words always inspired her and would invariably galvanise her into action.

'I'm too tired, Mummy.' Audrey opened her eyes and saw a blurred figure standing by her bed. She had no idea where she was or how she'd got into this room. She thought back and the last thing she remembered was Malcolm. She smiled. They had made love and it had felt so right. But how had she ended up here, surrounded by medical equipment? She tried to move but couldn't. Lead flowed through her veins.

'It's Tony, Mrs Willatt. You saved our baby.'

The cogs in her brain ground as she thought back to the Olde Tea Shoppe. 'How is he?'

'He's perfect. Thanks to you. But how are you feeling?'

'What am I doing here?' She heard her voice, and it sounded little better than a death-rattle. She tried to take a deep breath, but her lungs hurt too much.

'You were on the bridge and jumped into the river to avoid being killed by a van …and a car.'

'I don't remember.'

'You don't remember being in the river?'

'Malcolm. I was with Malcolm. Where is he?'

'He was in your house.'

'Yes. We were together.' Audrey felt her lips rise in a smile.

'Do you remember him falling down the stairs?'

Her mouth opened, and a spasm rippled through her body. 'Is he all right? Is he hurt?' She saw Tony swallow as she searched his face.

'Malcolm has broken a few bones but he's all right and will make a full recovery.'

Audrey fought to sit up, but her muscles would not respond. It was as though her nerve connections had been broken.

'I want to see him.'

'I'm sure when you've recovered a bit more, they'll take you to him.'

Audrey took a few pained breaths. 'How did I get out of the river?' She looked at his dressing gown. 'Was it you?'

'Me and one of the Russian property developers pulled you out, but it was the medical staff who saved your life.'

Audrey reached for his hand and squeezed it. 'Thank you.'

'You know, I think Malcolm loves you.'

Audrey smiled. 'And I think, I love him.' She closed her eyes.

'Audrey, Mrs Willatt, why were you standing on the bridge in the freezing cold?'

For a moment, she saw her little brother reaching out for her.

'Audrey?'

'I don't know.' She took a painful breath and felt herself drifting away.

CHAPTER THIRTY-SIX

Eden watched her husband button up his shirt. She could see a slight tremor in his fingertips.

'It's very cold outside. Why not take the doctor's advice and stay a night? For observation. Just to be sure,' she said.

'I'm coming home.'

Eden held onto Tony's arm as they left the hospital, determined never to let him go again. Their car was in the police pound following the accident on the bridge, so she had borrowed her father-in-law's beaten-up Audi. By the time she had driven home to their new-build town house, it was almost eight p.m.

Tony's mother, Maggie, crept down the carpeted stairs in her stockinged feet. Comfortably plump, her chocolate-box smile hid the protective nature of a tigress, which Eden understood and admired.

Maggie had given Eden a hard time when she and Tony first started dating, but it didn't bother her. Eden knew she was clever but she was also proud of her rich, auburn locks and D-cup boobs which attracted much male attention. When she worked as a barmaid in the Falcon pub, as her mother kept reminding her, she had the pick of go-ahead young guys and more than one proposal of marriage – including Tony, who almost popped the question before she'd pulled his second pint.

'Believe it or not Mrs Blake, it's not every woman's ambition to earn squillions of bucks simply to pay for a nanny. I want to care for my future husband, my future home and my future children, should we be so blessed.'

'But Tony told me how well you did at school,' said Maggie. 'For Christ's sake, you got offered a place at Cambridge. I would have given anything to have received that honour.'

'I let somebody else who wanted it more have the privilege.'

'But Newnham College – how could you turn it down?'

'God has given me a great brain, and I'm wasting it. It's like having a Ferrari and using it for the school run.'

'I couldn't have put it better myself.'

The marriage went ahead. Nine months after the honeymoon, exhausted from giving birth to Georgiana, Eden still had enough strength to grip her mother-in-law's hand. The two women, who loved the same young man, locked eyes.

'Maggie,' Eden said. 'This little baby has a mother who is fiercely ambitious. Her mother is going to be the very best mum this world has ever seen. Your beautiful granddaughter is going to have her mummy nurturing her from the moment she wakes to the moment she falls asleep.' She let go of Maggie's hand and reached for a plastic cup of water. She took a sip then fixed her eyes on her mother-in-law. 'I'll read her stories, we'll join other mums at playgroups, we'll go to the park, we'll play games, we'll sing songs, we'll…'

'I get it,' Maggie said. 'I have one child because I was too busy building my pension pot to give Tony a brother or sister. I get it, and I love you for it.'

'I'll pop up and give them a kiss.' Tony peeled off his coat and handed it to Eden.

'They've just gone down.' Maggie kissed her son. 'I told Georgiana you'd see her when she wakes in the morning.'

'I'll be quiet as a mouse.' Tony crept upstairs, and Maggie headed off to the kitchen.

Eden hung their coats in the understairs cupboard and waited in the hall. She could hear her mother-in-law clattering about and Sky News blaring from the sitting room. She sat on the stairs and tears of relief coursed down her freckly cheeks. Their baby son had escaped unscathed from meningitis and now her husband from a watery grave. She knew she should feel blessed, relieved, but her confidence was gone, and all she felt was fear.

She heard Tony coming down the stairs and got up to make way. Immediately, she could see something was wrong. Just as he reached the bottom tread, his knees buckled, and he collapsed into her arms, causing them both to fall in a heap on the carpeted floor.

'Mags, we need you,' Eden shouted as she tried to prevent Tony's head from hitting the newel post at the base of the stairs.

'What's going on?' Andy called from the sitting room.

Maggie was the first to appear and helped Eden place Tony on his side with his face angled towards the floor.

'What happened?' Andy shouted, coming to help.

'Not so loud,' Maggie responded. 'You'll wake the little ones.'

'He's breathing, all right.' Eden tried to appear calm. 'I think he fainted.'

Maggie reached for the landline phone. 'I'll get an ambulance.'

'No,' Tony mumbled. 'I'm all right.'

'You don't look it, son,' Andy said. He turned to Maggie. 'I'll drive him. It'll be quicker.'

Tony struggled in Eden's arms. 'No, I'm fine.' He tried to push himself off the floor. 'I'm all right. Just a bit tired.'

They all helped Tony get off the floor and onto his feet.

'Right, let's get you to a comfy seat.' Andy took the brunt of his son's weight and guided him to an armchair in the sitting room. Eden found a footstool, and Andy placed his son's feet on it. Maggie grabbed the TV remote and turned off the news. For a moment there was silence – then a child-like wail from deep within burst through Tony's shivering lips, and his whole body convulsed in sobs as his hands clawed the air for purchase on an imaginary river bank.

'It's shock – pure and simple,' Andy said. 'I'll make us some tea.'

Eden hugged her husband and made gentle noises to try and soothe him. From upstairs she heard her baby's high-pitched cry and turned to her mother-in-law for help. She saw Maggie was weeping. But another, closer cry, grabbed her attention.

Standing in a nightie holding her bunny was Georgiana, tears coursing down her pink cheeks.

Andy emerged from the kitchen and swiped away his tears. He scooped up his granddaughter.

'We're all playing a game, darling,' Andy explained. 'We're seeing who can cry the loudest. And I think your baby brother is the winner.'

He carried Georgiana out of the sitting room and away from Tony's child-like sobs.

Several minutes passed before Eden was able to calm her husband down. Maggie emerged from the kitchen with a tray of tea which she placed on a side table. She poured a half cup, tipped in some milk and reached for the sugar bowl.

'He doesn't take sugar,' Eden said.

'It will help with the shock.'

Eden held the cup for Tony, and he took a few sips.

'Thank you,' he said, and he closed his eyes.

Maggie poured two more cups and handed one to Eden. She looked at Tony. 'He's exhausted. He'll feel better in the morning.'

'We all will.'

'You know, Eden, there's something about Audrey I find bothersome. She's here on a mission. I can feel it.'

Andy entered from the hallway. 'They're settled – thank God. Any tea left?'

'Mum,' Tony said in a quiet voice. 'Charlie is asleep upstairs thanks to Audrey coming here. Her mission, whatever it is, doesn't matter.'

CHAPTER THIRTY-SEVEN

It took several days before sensation fully returned to Audrey's hands and feet. She felt as though she'd slept for more hours than there were in each day, but she understood from her consultant physician that her body had had to shut down conscious brain activity to martial all its resources to repair damage to nerves caused by hypothermia.

When awake, her thoughts invariably returned to Malcolm.

'We're just keeping an eye on him,' Audrey was told. 'He's had a nasty shock to the system, and we want to monitor him closely for at least a couple of weeks.'

'It may seem odd,' Audrey later explained to Tina, 'but I don't want Malcolm to see me looking like this, like an old lady.'

'Tony says he's completely smitten and worships the ground you walk on. And he's not looking his best, either.'

Audrey had never felt so weak. She could move all her limbs but still needed to rest on an arm to walk to the lavatory.

'What about you?' Audrey asked. 'Who is your beau these days?'

Tina looked shamefaced. 'I don't have one. Spartak keeps bombarding me with messages and Sean doesn't want "soiled goods".' She forced a smile. 'But I like your doctor, Mr Bisterzo.'

Audrey chuckled. 'So do I.'

~

Every day, Tony came to check on Malcolm and, every day, Tina came to check on Audrey.

'Well, fancy meeting you,' Tony said, spotting Tina waiting by reception in the intensive care unit. 'Have you been in to see her, yet?'

'She's with the doctor.'

A door opened and a tall, good-looking Italian emerged. Mr Bisterzo smiled as he approached them. 'She's doing well.' He turned to Tony. 'And how are you feeling?'

Tony looked a bit sheepish. 'I'm fine. Although I don't think I could beat you at tennis yet.'

'What about golf?'

'You're on! There's crazy golf by the kiddies' playground in Solefield Park.'

Mr Bisterzo laughed. 'Not exactly what I had in mind, but I'll be there. To be serious; your actions in the river, and after you pulled Mrs Willatt out, saved her life. No bones about it.'

'It was the least I could do.'

The consultant nodded. 'Well, as testament to how brave you are, Mrs Willatt will be released to a general ward tomorrow.'

'Great news,' Tony and Tina said in tandem.

Mr Bisterzo turned to go then looked back at Tony. 'Pound a hole? Or we could make it ten pounds if you want more excitement.'

'Bring it on. Ten pounds it is.'

Mr Bisterzo laughed again and walked away.

Tony turned to Tina. 'How many holes are there at the

crazy golf?'
  'Eighteen, I think.'
  'Shit. I'd better get practising.'

CHAPTER THIRTY-EIGHT

Audrey was reluctant to let her sons know what had happened to her, but she was worried that they would try and call her mobile phone, which she no longer had.

'I saw your handbag in the river,' Tony said, sitting by Tina on one of their daily visits.

'What a nuisance – I liked that bag!' She smiled. 'I also liked my phone, purse and debit card.'

'We have a spare iPhone at the office,' Tina said. 'I'll bring it in so you can take your time going through emails. Can you remember your password?'

'I think so. Fortunately, not everything got washed away.'

What are you going to do about your house?'

Audrey looked at Tina, a bit puzzled. 'Malcolm and I are going to turn it into a hostel. Of course, it needs loads of renovation, new plumbing and wiring, but I have the financial resources. Since the school closed, the town has fewer visitors, so I'm hoping that the hostel will encourage people to return.'

'I think it's a brilliant idea,' Tony said. 'If we don't keep refreshing Hawksmead, all the enterprising people will leave.' He kissed Audrey on her cheek. 'I can tell you're definitely on the mend.'

Audrey smiled and looked up at her handsome saviour. 'How is Charlie?'

'Up to his usual tricks and fit as a fiddle, thanks to you.

I'll see you again soon.' Tony smiled and left the unit.

Tina turned a serious-looking face to Audrey. 'I saw you.'

'You saw me – when?'

'On the morning you nearly drowned. I was up on the top landing in your house, and you were there. I spoke to you.'

Audrey stared at Tina as the wisp of a memory floated into her mind. 'I thought it was a dream. You were looking out of the window.'

'Let me sell the house.' Tina grasped Audrey's hand. 'Too many bad things have happened there.'

Audrey felt herself smiling. 'I found love in that house. I found a man with whom I want to share the rest of how many days, months, years, we have together.'

'But he fell down the stairs,' pressed Tina.

'He probably tripped on the same raised board that I tripped on when I first arrived. A hammer and a few nails should sort it out.'

CHAPTER THIRTY-NINE

Spartak Dryomov hesitated for a moment. So far, he had a clean record in England, and although human rights legislation would make it hard for the British authorities to deport him and his brother back to Russia, and even harder to prevent them returning to England, he did not want the inconvenience of being arrested. He switched on his heavy, long-handled Mag-Lite torch and pointed the beam at the door so that his brother could see where to place the jemmy. In summer, at this time of the early morning, it would be daylight, and more people would be about, but the cold and wind and impenetrable darkness would keep snooping eyes away.

He smiled when he saw the lock had not been changed since Kirill broke in to retrieve the axe, so the jemmy was redundant. They stepped across the threshold into the laundry room. In Spartak's left hand was a 1950s' electric fire he'd seen tossed into a skip and had kept for just such an occasion as this. Around his waist was his tool belt with an assorted selection of screwdrivers and pliers, a short extension cord and socket with a programmable timer, and a coil of copper wiring.

Spartak had begun his working life as an electrician and his brother as a bricklayer and plasterer. They had come to England to get rich but had found the English unpredictable and difficult to bribe. Even physical threats had proved to be of limited value, which was why their plan for the old school boarding house was the simple, smart solution, especially as the owner was safely tucked up in a hospital bed. They'd locate the main electrical fuse box and swap the thin circuit-breaking copper wires with much thicker eighteen-gauge wire that would not easily break with a power surge. He hoped the old house did not have modern trip switches; if it did, he would have to resort to Kirill's plan and splash around the petrol they had in cans sitting in the back of their van. Either way, the house would be destroyed and the land put up for sale. The old widow owed her life to Kirill so, with a bit of pressure, he was sure she would sell to them.

They found the electrical circuit board in the understairs cupboard and, as expected, it had the old style ceramic fuses with thin copper wiring. But what really caught Spartak's attention, behind an assortment of old Hoover upright vacuum cleaners, was a pile of at least a dozen electric fires, similar to the one he'd brought.

'Christmas has come early,' Spartak said.

'You have brought coals to Newcastle,' Kirill responded, laughing at his own joke.

Spartak turned off the main power supply and pulled out all the ceramic fuses. Kirill held the torch while he cut the thin copper wires and replaced them with the thick wire. He then selected five of the old electric fires.

Carrying their booty, they wandered around the old school boarding house, deciding where to place the fires. Spartak was particularly pleased to see that each room had the small old-fashioned Bakelite sockets that were specifically designed to power table lamps. He cut off the plugs from the fires and inserted the wires into the sockets, which would become live when the room light was switched on. To keep the wires in place, he rammed nails into the sockets. If there was a cupboard nearby, he hid the fire inside, facing it towards the dusty, dry wood panelling. If there wasn't a cupboard, he hid the fire behind an item of old furniture or curtains.

They reached the top dormitory room, and Spartak looked for the small-sized lighting socket. He tore off the plug from the end of the extension cord and pushed in the wires, securing them with two nails. Next, he cut the coiled filaments within the electric fire and made a new connection with the eighteen-gauge thick copper wire.

'Just to make sure,' Spartak said to himself more than to his brother. 'This will definitely cause a ring of fire throughout the whole lighting circuit.' He used a screwdriver to force the old copper wires into the timer socket, secured them with two nails, then hid the fire and extension cord under one of the unused beds.

Through the window, they saw the first signs of dawn. Spartak loosened the bulb from the centre light and flicked on the light switch.

'For how many hours have you set the timer?' Kirill asked.

'Relax. We'll be drinking Moskovskaya in the Falcon long before this place goes up.'

Back in the understairs cupboard, Spartak turned on the mains power.

CHAPTER FORTY

Jessica Bassett had been in the police service for twenty-five years and was still surprised by how often people… well, surprised her. Audrey was a legend in Hawksmead and so Jessica had expected to see quite a few get-well cards but not the bundles that were stacked up on the windowsill by Audrey's bed, one of four in the side ward. Two of the other beds were occupied – one old patient in her nineties looked asleep and the other, a young woman who'd crashed on the Old Military Road whilst talking on her phone, had earbuds in and, from the jangly noise leaking out, was listening to Tinie Tempah.

'We've taken statements from Anthony Blake and Kirill Dryomov with regard to what happened on the bridge, but we would very much like to hear your thoughts. Are you still having problems remembering?'

'I've slept on it for quite a few nights. All I can remember is being with Malcolm Cadwallader, following a lovely day out, and then waking up in this hospital. I do recall a few dreams, mostly childhood memories, but nothing that will confirm exactly what happened. I have no idea why I was on the bridge and absolutely no memory of being in the river. All I can say is, without Tony Blake's brave actions, I wouldn't be here.'

'He feels partly responsible.'

'Really? I don't even blame that wretched Russian,'

Audrey laughed. 'I know about black ice; my brother wrote about it in his…'

'You've remembered something?'

'No, it's nothing.'

'It might be something. Don't force it. There's no hurry.'

'No, it's gone. Thank you for coming. You have a perfect bedside manner, and if anyone could tease out the truth, I'm sure you could.'

'You mentioned your brother. Could you give me his contact details? He may be able to fill in the blanks.'

Audrey closed her eyes, and Jessica saw tears trickle from the corners.

She leant across and gently squeezed Audrey's arm. 'I am so sorry to have caused you distress.'

'Tissue, please.'

Jessica reached across for a box on the bedside unit and pulled out a couple. Audrey mopped her eyes.

'I'm sorry. Fifty years ago, my brother attended Hawksmead College. He didn't return home.'

Jessica stiffened.

'I'm very tired,' Audrey whispered.

There were a dozen questions Jessica wanted to ask. She waited for Audrey to open her eyes, but Audrey appeared to be asleep. Her questions would have to wait for another day.

Audrey heard the door open and close. She had to get back to the house and retrieve the diary. The door opened again, and she felt the kiss of an angel on her forehead.

She opened her eyes.

Tina lurched back.

'Tina!'

'It's good to see you looking better.'

'It's lovely to see you. I didn't mean to frighten you.'

'I thought you were asleep.'

'I've done enough sleeping. What I need now is a shower, some clothes, and some money. I managed to persuade my bank to deliver a new debit card here, and not to my home in Sevenoaks, but until I get it, I do not have a brass farthing.'

Although she felt weak, the shower made Audrey feel good. She could see she was skinny but, as she smiled to herself, her former model agency would probably say she still had more to lose.

CHAPTER FORTY-ONE

The planned meeting with Audrey meant a great deal to the old, broken man. He had undergone an operation to relocate his shoulder and to screw a plate to secure his fractured hip. He also had a plaster cast to set his arm and wrist.

'You know, I have it on good authority that Audrey Willatt really cares about you,' Tony said. 'She wants you two to be together and to turn the old school boarding house into a hostel for ramblers.'

'Are you sure?' Malcolm asked. 'When did she tell you that?'

'She's been chatting to Tina whilst I've been here with you. Tina's been filling me in.'

'But I don't understand. After what happened, I felt sure she'd want to be shot of the place. She has no reason to stay.'

'Perhaps it's fortunate she has no memory of your fall. Her time in the river seems to have washed it away.'

'She can't remember …anything?'

'Nothing bad. According to Tina, her last memory is of a very happy time with you.'

Malcolm nodded. *What about my confession? Did that get washed away too? What if she regains her memory in the coming days?*

~

Tina stopped her car behind Malcolm's, which was still parked in Audrey's drive. She took a deep breath and forced herself to open the door. She climbed out and pushed back her hair as she walked up to the front entrance. She removed Audrey's house keys from her shoulder bag and, feeling more than a little trepidatious, unlocked the heavy oak door.

Fortunately, Audrey had abandoned her suitcases in the hallway, so she wouldn't have to climb the creaking stairs up to the top of the house. The hallway appeared as she had last seen it, although some of the toiletry containers looked cracked and crushed. She switched on the feeble light and opened one of the suitcases. Audrey had given her explicit instructions, but finding the right clothes and underwear took a bit of time.

As quickly as she could, she put together three outfits and hoped that Audrey would approve. Despite leaving the front door open and switching on the hall light, she still had to use the torch in her phone to help her select items of make-up scattered across the floor that were still usable.

Clothes draped over her arm, and a pair of shoes in her hand, Tina switched off the light, locked the door and rejoiced in getting out of the house and back into her car.

~

Tony held a mirror for Malcolm as he used his right hand to comb his hair and smarten up his pyjamas. He got Tony to place his dressing gown on the side of the bed so that when it hung down, it hid the yellow urine collecting in a plastic bag.

The spring in the door handle squeaked. Tony hurried away from the bed and stood by the window.

Malcolm, tense, excited, nervous, watched the door open and was momentarily disappointed to see Tina enter the room.

'Mr Cadwallader. There is somebody here to see you.' She held the door open and Malcolm saw Audrey standing in the corridor wearing a patterned turtle-neck sweater, and a plain-coloured woollen skirt that came to just below her knee. His first impression was how thin she looked, but he was thrilled to see the amazing sparkle in her eyes.

'May I come in?' Audrey asked. Her voice was weaker than he remembered. He beckoned with his good arm.

Audrey smiled and walked in. She leaned over the bed and kissed his cheek. 'I've missed you.'

'We'll leave you to it,' Tony said. 'Tina's got houses to sell, and I've got a ninetieth birthday party to photograph.'

Audrey blew them a kiss. When the door was closed, she pulled up a chair and sat as close to the bedside as her chair would allow. Malcolm clasped her hand in his. Fortunately, he was the only patient currently residing in the small side ward.

'I have something to tell you,' Malcolm said, trying to instil some youth into his gravelly voice. 'It's a confession which you've heard before but don't remember.'

'What I do remember was absolutely lovely.'

'It was. It was.' Malcolm's resolve began to waiver.

She squeezed his hand. 'We're together. That's all that matters.'

Malcolm licked his dry lips. He had to get this right. 'When I came down from Oxford, I was twenty-one; the first generation not to have to put on a uniform and fight a war, or do national service. It was before The Beatles; Cliff Richard was the young star at the time. I had a first in English and no job and no idea of what I wanted to do. I heard that Hawksmead College was looking for an English master, and I applied. It was easy for someone like me to get a job teaching – educated and from a respectable family. I quite enjoyed my time at the school, although the boys were often challenging. They mostly came from troubled backgrounds, sent to be physically educated in the hope that it would improve their minds. The school had almost no admissions criteria apart from being able to afford the fees. Unfortunately, some boys destined for reform school could elect to come to us, if the courts approved and their parents could afford it. We provided a tough environment, designed to straighten out the troublemakers, but it didn't work. There were fights, and serious physical injury often resulted. For the more sensitive boys, there were the arts; a place of safety away from violence, but there was no drama group. I wanted to change that, and although Mr Gibbs, the headmaster, was not at all cultured, he was persuaded to allow me to form a dramatic society.'

He felt Audrey stiffen but kept a firm grip on her hand. 'In September, fifty years ago, your brother arrived. He was brilliant at English; he could write an essay on any subject and give it a unique viewpoint, and he was kind to other boys. He had a dreadful stutter, not helped by the harsh regime and the brutal violence. I didn't think he'd last a term. But then he walked on stage to audition for Roxane in *Cyrano de Bergerac*, and I saw something magical.'

Audrey pulled her hand away.

'May I have a drink of water?' Malcolm asked.

She looked at the side table and poured a small quantity of water into a plastic cup.

He took a few sips and handed the cup back to her. 'Do you remember when we were in bed together?'

She nodded.

'Do you remember what I told you prior to my falling down the stairs?'

'Lying with you in my narrow bed is the last thing I remember, until I woke up here, in hospital.'

He should quit now, he thought. Even telling this wonderful woman half the truth would probably drive her away.

'You were his English master?'

'Yes.'

'You were the Mr C in his diary?'

Malcolm's stomach heaved. Diary? This was the first he'd heard of a diary. What had the boy said? He took a breath and continued. 'The Sunday morning, after the final performance of *Cyrano*, I drove to the boarding house to congratulate Bobby on his mesmerising Roxane. We chatted, and I offered him a lift in my motorcar to avoid him being late for Sunday chapel. He ran down the stairs ahead of me, full of youthful exuberance. I tried to keep up and arrived at the top of the stairs in the hallway in time to see him tumbling down, head over heels.'

He could not look at her.

'Why did you lie to the police?'

Malcolm was shocked by her question. 'How do you mean?'

'I read a newspaper article in which it stated that when you arrived at the boarding house you found Bobby lying on the floor in the hallway.'

'I… I was foolish. I thought that if I told the police I'd gone up to the dormitory, it could imply that I had acted inappropriately in some way and was responsible for him rushing down the stairs.'

'But you were responsible. You had already acted inappropriately when you took him back to your cottage.'

The knife blade slipped between his ribs and found his heart. He felt her eyes on him. He took a moment to breathe. He could still smell the shampoo in Bobby's blond hair when he'd wrapped his arms around the boy. To this day, he did not know what he had wanted to do other than hold Roxane.

'Did he run down the stairs in youthful exuberance, or was he desperate to get away from you?'

'I did nothing. Nothing to harm him. I would never have harmed him.' Malcolm knew he had to look her in the eyes. 'Perhaps it was the wrong time, the wrong place, but I told Bobby he was so good in the role of Roxane, he could become a professional actor. He was excited by his achievement after suffering so much from other boys. Despite his stammer, he knew he had the skill, the talent, to make an audience believe. Full of confidence, he rushed ahead of me down the stairs and must have tripped when he reached the half-landing. It was an accident. A terrible, terrible, tragic accident.'

He waited for her to say something.

'Did you touch him?'

Malcolm was shocked by the directness of her question. 'Good God no!'

'But he ran away from you?'

'I told you, he was excited about the play and was looking forward to having a ride in my car.'

'He had a bicycle.'

'It was cold. Bitterly cold that morning. Icy.' He closed his eyes and tried to erase the memory of what happened. He heard Audrey draw a deep breath and get up from the chair.

Malcolm opened his eyes and looked up at her.

'Is that it?' Audrey asked.

He felt himself shrivel before her eyes. 'Earlier that dreadful term, I had driven into a boy on the bridge and killed him.'

Audrey's hand shot up to her mouth.

'There was black ice,' he continued. 'I couldn't stop.'

'You were the schoolmaster driving the car?'

Malcolm nodded. 'I lost control and crushed a young life. I nearly killed Bobby, too. The shock of the accident affected me badly, and from then on I was desperate to protect your brother.'

He felt the heat of Audrey's penetrating gaze. A few seconds later, she left without saying another word.

Malcolm looked at the ceiling in his side ward. For a few brief moments, he had believed it possible that he could spend his final days in the company of the most wonderful woman he'd ever met. He had been drawn to Audrey as soon as he saw her. Why had he not connected her to Robert Oakes? Now he knew the relationship, the similarity between Bobby's Roxane and Audrey was undeniable.

CHAPTER FORTY-TWO

Audrey returned to her ward and retrieved five twenty-pound notes that Tina had withdrawn from an ATM and Audrey had hidden in her pillow slip. In the bedside cabinet, she found her house keys. Why they had been discarded on the floor in her hallway she had not the least idea, but the fact that Tina had also found her suitcases packed and in the hallway told their own story. She knew she was not yet strong enough to be officially discharged from hospital, but she had to get Bobby's diary. That was all that mattered to her now; that – and leaving Hawksmead for good.

Audrey paid the taxi driver and walked to the front entrance of the old school boarding house, past Malcolm's Honda with its battered side mirror. It was one of those bleak days when it never really gets light, and the coat she'd borrowed from a receptionist she'd befriended in the intensive care unit was not really up to the job.

She pushed open the heavy door, flicked on the hall light, and looked at her two suitcases lying on the floor. Stepping around them, she walked to the base of the stairs, kicking aside various toiletry items. She was too weak to hurry, so took her time climbing to the half-landing. At the top, she took a few deep breaths into her weakened lungs and headed up the short flight to the first floor corridor. She switched on the light, walked to the end and headed up to the second floor, flicking more old light switches as she went.

By the time Audrey reached the top floor landing she was exhausted, and slumped down on the wooden floorboards to catch her breath. She looked across to the dormitory that had been her bedroom for what seemed an eternity, and could not help but think of lying in bed with Malcolm. Something about the man was still alight within her. She hoped, once she had left Hawksmead, her feelings for him would fade.

Audrey struggled to her feet. She pushed open the dormitory door and looked at the mess of sheets and blankets and discarded clothing, including Malcolm's jacket and trousers. Out of pride she felt she should tidy up, but she simply wanted to retrieve Bobby's diary and get on the train, south.

She looked at the rotted shelf then spotted the encyclopaedia lying on a bed, and opened it. The cut-out section was empty – no diary.

Had someone been in the house and stolen it?

No, she must have hidden it somewhere else; probably under her pillow.

She went to switch the light on and saw the switch was already down. She looked at the bulb, took a pained breath, and in the dim daylight searched her bed, throwing all her bed clothes on the floor.

Hot and emotionally exhausted, realisation finally dawned. She had lost her handbag when she fell in the river, and together with her wallet and phone must have been Bobby's diary.

She sat on her bed and wept. She had lost her only thread to Bobby and betrayed his memory. How she wished the river had swept her away, too. Her brother was dead; her mother was dead; her husband was dead and… her heart yearned for Malcolm. How could she ever confess to her father, aged eighty-nine, that she was in love with the man responsible for killing his only son, even if it had been a tragic accident?

'Audrey, get up, wash your face and show some spunk. Stop feeling sorry for yourself.'

She smiled as she remembered her mother's stern words. She pushed herself back onto her feet and walked out of the dormitory and down the creaking stairs to the half-landing. She looked into the hall and continued on, along the dark corridor to the washroom. She pushed open the door and switched on the lights.

There was an almighty bang as one of the bulbs blew. For a moment, Audrey was taken aback – shocked.

Then she smiled. 'Yes. You're right – time to go.'

She entered a cubicle and slumped down on the old wooden seat. She didn't bother to flush and went to one of the many washbasins. She splashed water on her face, looked in the mirror, grimaced and took a deep, resigned, breath – and coughed.

She coughed again.

CHAPTER FORTY-THREE

The electrical lighting circuit had heated up as Spartak Dryomov planned. Within the walls, hot wires burned through insulating sleeves, causing wood panelling, baked dry over one hundred and fifty years, to catch fire. Helped by paraffin fire-lighters stacked around the fuse box, the cupboard under the stairs was soon ablaze and the main hallway thick with smoke.

In the washroom, Audrey coughed every time she took a breath.

She opened the door to the corridor and was engulfed by hot, acrid smoke. She slammed the door shut and hurried to a washbasin to flush out her mouth. She was in trouble; five minutes earlier she had wanted to curl up and die, but now, she absolutely did not.

She looked across at the windows on the far side of the washroom. They were more like high-level vents, horizontally hinged with opaque glass, and way too high to reach. Even if she had a stepladder and could open them or break the reinforced glass, the gap was too small for her to crawl through.

There was only one way out and that was through the main entrance hallway. What were her choices? She could stay where she was, keep the door shut and wait for help, or she could make a dash for it.

Audrey leant over the washbasin, full of indecision. The

tiles through her shoes were heating up. It was only a matter of minutes before the washroom would succumb to the fire. She was trapped without a phone and nobody knew she was in the house. How ironic that she should nearly die by drowning and now was about to die by fire.

Water. The one thing she had was water. Audrey grabbed the towels and her bathrobe hanging on a hook and rushed to the shower area. She hoped the fire had not yet destroyed the water flow. She turned on the cold tap and allowed the increasingly hot water to drench her clothes, towels and bathrobe.

She put the soaking robe over her borrowed coat and the wet towels over her head and hurried to the closed door.

The remaining lights went out.

The floor almost glowed with heat. To protect her feet, she had to jump from one foot to the other.

She was frightened, very frightened, but she had no choice. She took a few deep breaths, filtered through a wet towel, and opened the door, hiding behind it as scorching, caustic smoke roared into the washroom. She hurried through the doorway and was immediately engulfed by the noxious killer.

Her head covered, Audrey edged her way along the corridor to the top of the stairs. She could feel flames scorching her legs as the wet towels rapidly dried.

The crackle of the flames consuming the wooden staircase that led down to the hall was truly terrifying, and she was tempted to rush back to the temporary respite of the washroom.

'Show some spunk, girl,' she said to herself as she launched into the flames that were burning up the tinder-like stairs. The old oak planks, their life's work done, held her weight, but flames licked with gusto through the gaps in the joins, barbecuing her calves. She knew that taking a breath could be fatal, but she was desperate for air. It was a relief to reach the tiles in the hallway, and she aimed for where she knew was the front door and salvation. But her foot caught one of her suitcases lying open on the floor and she lost her balance, landing hard. She heard a bone break and felt stabbing pain in her right forearm. How easy it would be to give up and slip away into blessed oblivion.

Ten feet, girl. She could only be ten feet from the door. With her good arm, she dragged herself along the floor and came to the base of the front door. She reached up for the latch, but it was too high. She had to get to her feet, but her legs were screaming with pain and refused to respond to the command from her neurons. She was inches from cool, fresh air but couldn't move. Even with layers of towel over her mouth, every breath she took was thick with burning smoke. Her head felt as though it was about to burst, and her eyes, though screwed shut, were being stabbed with a thousand skewers. Worst of all was the sound – the incessant roar of a furnace as flames consumed the wood panelling.

Audrey almost laughed. She had told her sons that when it was her time, she was to be cremated.

'Well, be careful what you wish for, girl,' said her inner scared voice.

CHAPTER FORTY-FOUR

'Audrey's house is on fire!'

Tina heard Tony's voice on her hands-free speaker as she drove along the Old Military Road. She was on her way to a viewing of a modern townhouse at the southern end of Hawksmead, and had decided to avoid the inevitable traffic by taking the longer route across the moor.

'Did you notice anything wrong when you went to collect her clothes?' Tony continued.

'I didn't smell any smoke, or burning. Have you called the fire brigade?'

'Someone rushed into *The Chronicle* to tell my dad, and Dad called me as he wants me to take pictures. I'm on my way there now but the traffic is terrible. I presume the emergency services have been called. At least we know Audrey and Malcolm are safely tucked up together in hospital.'

~

But Audrey wasn't safely tucked up in hospital. She was a skinny little ballerina in a tutu who had attempted an arabesque by raising a straight leg behind her and had toppled over onto the floor.

"Get up girl!" said Miss Bush. The headmistress in Audrey's ballet school was never to be disobeyed. Even the

girls' parents followed her instructions to the letter.

Audrey forced her agonised body to move and stretched up for the door latch. The metal seared her hand and her skin fused to the hot surface. Whimpering with pain, she protected her fingers with her towel, reached up again and managed to pull the door open. Wind off the moor blew ice cold air into her face and she staggered through the open gap.

Burned and broken-boned, she stumbled down her drive, bumping into Malcolm's car, as oxygen, sucked in through the front door, fed the fire. Victorian panes shattered throughout the boarding house, hurling molten glass and debris into the air as voracious tongues licked up the sides of the building.

~

Tina blasted her horn to clear a way through onlookers who were blocking the end of the short drive. Through her windscreen she spotted Audrey's frail figure hobbling towards her; bare skin showing through burnt clothes and black soot around her mouth and nose. Leaving her door open and her treasured car unlocked, Tina rushed to help Audrey and was astounded by the blast of heat from the roaring flames.

'Audrey, it's Tina.' She placed her arm carefully around Audrey's shoulder and guided her to the Golf. She opened the passenger door and eased Audrey in, not bothering with the seat belt, anxious not to inflict further pain.

Tina slipped into the driver's seat and grimaced at the smell of Audrey's scorched skin. She fired up the engine, tooted her horn several times to clear a path and reversed into the High Street, expertly spinning her steering wheel so her car was pointed in the right direction.

Headlights on full beam, despite the sun not yet setting, Tina hared south through Hawksmead, her manicured thumb stabbing the horn on her steering wheel whenever another vehicle looked likely to block her route.

'Call Tony Blake,' she barked at her hands-free phone, and within two rings Tony answered.

'I'm on the way to Undermere Hospital with Audrey. She's badly hurt. Can you call and let them know? I should be there within ten minutes. Tell them she has burns, smoke inhalation and is in a critical condition.'

Tina drove with great precision and as fast as she dared, oblivious to flashing speed cameras. Red traffic lights she used simply as a guide. Even a Ford Fiesta's sharp-blue roof lights reflecting into her eyes from her rear-view mirror did not cause her foot to lift from the accelerator.

The Ford Fiesta police patrol car kept pace with the Golf and added the wail of its siren to the flashing roof lights and full-beam headlights.

'Shit!' Tina felt the natural fear of authority stir her gut. She stole a glance at Audrey, who was either unconscious or asleep.

A Range Rover Sport pulled out of a side turning ahead of the Golf and Tina was forced to slam her foot on the brake. Audrey slid forward and hit the dashboard. The police car behind swerved and took the opportunity to accelerate and pull up alongside Tina's door. She mouthed, *'Help'* at the police officer in the passenger seat and pointed at Audrey who had slumped back at an angle.

The police car pulled in front of her and forced Tina to slow to jogging speed. Ahead was a lay-by with a bus stop and the Ford Fiesta's rear light signalled left, indicating for her to follow.

Tina looked at Audrey and couldn't tell whether she was asleep, unconscious or dead. All she knew was that wasting time talking to the police was not going to help. She saw the officers open their car doors, glanced into her recently replaced side mirror, saw that it was sort of clear behind and pumped her accelerator. The turbocharged stratified injection VW Golf engine spun the front wheels, and she shot off, almost hitting the police car's open door. The driver of a Lexus Hybrid braked hard behind and blasted his horn. Tina gave him an apologetic wave before indicating she was turning right. Ahead was the entrance to the hospital.

NO ENTRY
AUTHORISED VEHICLES ONLY

Tina took a chance and swerved across the on-coming traffic, ignoring the horn and flashing lights of a silver Mercedes C-Class Coupé, a car she normally would have taken time to admire. Ahead was a curved drive, lined with conifer trees, which she fervently hoped was one-way only as she injected copious quantities of fuel into her engine. A quick glance in her rear-view mirror reminded her that the police were hot on her rear bumper so now was not the moment to falter. She rounded the next bend, saw the ambulance entrance for Accident & Emergency, pressed her thumb down on the horn button and slid to an untidy halt. The tailgating police car almost rear-ended her as Tina leapt out and ran around the nose to open Audrey's door. A male doctor and two female nurses, all wearing green scrubs, came through the main entrance, wheeling a stretcher.

'She's badly burned!' Tina shouted, standing back to let the doctor lean into the car to examine Audrey slumped in the passenger seat.

'Hello, my name is Dr Chaudri – can you hear me?'

Audrey nodded. 'I think my right arm is broken.' The doctor had to lean in to hear her raspy words. 'My lungs are painful. And I think I'm a bit burnt – my legs hurt like hell.'

'We need to get you out of the car and onto the stretcher,' Dr Chaudri said, his tone gentle.

Tina watched anxiously. Every time the doctor touched Audrey she whimpered in pain. 'Let me try myself,' Audrey croaked.

Tina, the doctor and the nurses watched as Audrey eased her blackened clothes and roasted body out of the VW. She staggered like a child taking its first steps to the wheeled stretcher and screamed as she eased herself onto it.

Tina wanted to stay with Audrey but was persuaded by the police officer driving the patrol car to move her Golf first.

'Nice driving by the way.'

She smiled at the compliment.

'With luck, you should only get a six-month ban.'

'What?' Tina was shocked.

'It's all the cameras. Here's my card,' he said. 'I'm PC Gary Burton. Let me know when your case is heard, and I'll put in a good word. And if you want a chat or fancy a meal out, you've got my number.'

He winked and headed back to his patrol car.

Tina called after him. 'A little unprofessional under the circumstances, don't you think?'

'I wish your grandma all the best,' he called back as he opened his car door.

Tina got into her Golf and negotiated her way past various No Entry signs to the hospital's extortionate pay-and-display public car park. She was standing by the machine, waiting for her ticket to be printed when she saw Tony pulling in, driving his father's Audi. Ticket in hand, she went over to him.

'The fire has all but destroyed the house,' Tony said, using the electronic key fob to lock his car. 'It went up like a tinder-box. Another Grade II building destroyed.' He looked at Tina. 'How is she?'

'Not good.'

After sticking the parking tickets to their windscreens, Tina accompanied Tony to the hospital's main entrance.

In Accident & Emergency, they saw Audrey on the trolley, breathing with an oxygen mask, and a woman wearing a white coat over her green scrubs, taking her pulse.

As they approached, Tina heard her say, 'Mrs Willatt. I am Miss Caringi, a consultant physician. You have first and second-degree burns, which are exceedingly painful, but they will heal. The treatment involves bandaging to prevent infection. At this stage, I don't think you need skin grafts, but it may become necessary in coming days. Our main concern is the damage to your trachea and lungs. We'll do a blood test to determine how much oxygen your lungs are currently able to absorb.'

~

After much discussion, Tina and Tony agreed that Malcolm should be told about Audrey's fire and subsequent injuries. They entered his side ward and Tony approached the bed. Tina waited near the door.

'When she's up to visitors, would you like us to arrange a wheelchair for you to go and see her?' Tony asked.

Malcolm looked up at him and took a deep breath. 'No. It's over between us. I'm the last person she wants to see, but I think her sons should be told. She won't want to worry them, but they ought to know. Tell me the truth. Please. How serious is it?'

'Well, Tina drove like the clappers to get her here as quickly as possible. She gave no quarter. Even outran the police.'

'I can believe that.' Malcolm looked at Tina. 'Thank you.'

'She is hurt,' Tony continued, 'but they've told us she will heal. It's bad, but it could have been a lot worse.'

Tina walked a few paces towards the bed. 'Her lungs have suffered a bit.'

'Do you know what caused the fire?' Malcolm asked.

Tony looked at Tina. 'Any ideas?'

She blew out her cheeks and shrugged. 'I expect there'll be an investigation.'

'And it's destroyed the whole house?' Malcolm wrinkled his brow.

'It can be rebuilt, of course,' Tony said. 'I'm sure Audrey was insured.'

Tina turned to Tony. 'What about Malcolm's car? It's parked in the drive.'

He looked puzzled. 'The drive was blocked by fallen rubble. I'm sorry, Malcolm, I didn't see your car.'

'Alas poor, Honda, I knew it well.' Malcolm shook his head and offered a wintry smile. 'At least it saves me the bother of getting the side mirror fixed.'

CHAPTER FORTY-FIVE

Audrey did not want any fanfare. As soon as her consultant told her that she could leave hospital and go home to plenty of rest, she sought out the clothes that Tina had brought weeks ago, before the fire, and carefully put on a lightweight dress. Her skin still felt tender, but she was healing well, and her broken arm was now in a supportive bandage.

She went to the hospital shop and bought a pack of envelopes, using a second replacement debit card delivered by the bank a few days earlier. On her way back to the side ward, she removed her maximum daily allowance from the hospital ATM. In her room, she wrote the names of nursing staff and junior doctors on the envelopes, and enclosed several twenty-pound notes in each. Her writing arm still felt weak, but the broken bone had fused well, and she was confident that some gentle tennis, when summer came, would strengthen her muscles.

Hoping she had left no one out, she went to the unit reception and gave the envelopes to Amy, one of the receptionists.

'Your hospital, your colleagues have saved my life, twice. This is a small thank-you to you all.'

'Why have you included me? You've already replaced my coat with a much more expensive one.'

'It's for you to spend on your little ones this Christmas.'

Amy came out from behind the reception area and gave Audrey a gentle hug.

~

Wearing a dark blue raincoat Tina had picked up for her from Marks & Spencer in Undermere, Audrey took it easy as she walked down the corridor to the main entrance. She saw a taxi waiting and a man leaning against the front passenger door.

'Mrs Willatt?'

Audrey smiled. 'Is it that obvious?'

'You're a celebrity!'

For several weeks, *The Hawksmead Chronicle* had run stories about Audrey and her little brother. The mix of tragedy, ghostly sightings, and a conflagration linked to rumours of arson, kept readers hooked from week to week.

Online, fake news abounded, with superimposed images of spooky schoolboys turning old photos of the boarding house into MSN clickbait.

Producers from reality TV shows had zoomed in on Tina's beauty and youth, and offered her increasing sums of money to appear on *Love Island,* or fly to Australia to join the cast of *I'm A Celebrity... Get Me Out of Here!*

'As tempted as I am by the money,' Tina had told Audrey, 'I am a home-girl, and I do not want a brief moment of fame to come between me and my plans to build a business empire.'

CHAPTER FORTY-SIX

The train pulled out of Undermere railway station, and Audrey sat back in the first class carriage. She had chosen a table seat as she didn't want people to see her sitting with her legs not quite touching. Tender skin rubbing against tender skin was still painful, so keeping cool air circulating was essential.

As the train headed south, the view through the window of the bleak and beautiful moorland countryside brought tears to her eyes, which surprised her. She leaned back against the seat, resting her head, and tried to clear her mind. Instinctively, she went to feel for her wedding ring and remembered it had come off and dropped between the floorboards in the boarding house – now gone for good.

The gentle movement of the high-speed train lulled her into the twilight zone between being awake and asleep. It had been when she was dummy at a bridge tea with her lady friends that the idea to investigate her brother's death had first taken hold. She was still amazed that the old school boarding house had actually been up for sale, and how quickly it had given up its tragic secret. What surprised her most of all was how much she had fallen for Hawksmead and its wonderful residents. She loved Tina – during her weeks of recovery, she had become the daughter Audrey never had; and she thought of Tony as a favourite nephew, with a lovely wife and two beautiful children.

Malcolm's face entered her mind uninvited, and she snapped her eyes open to wipe the image. A tall man was standing by her table.

'Good morning, ma'am. May I take your order for lunch?' asked the liveried waiter.

'I'll have the salmon, please.'

'Anything to drink?'

Audrey looked at the menu and selected a quarter bottle of Sauvignon Blanc. Whilst waiting for her food, she tried not to think about Malcolm and their wonderful meal at the Rorty Crankle. But when a gentleman walked past her seat who looked like him from behind, her heart skipped a beat and she hastily turned away. She was not wearing a scrap of make-up; her hair was long over-due for a colour and her exposed upper chest was decidedly blotchy. Not a pretty sight, for sure.

Why was she even thinking about Malcolm? It was over. Finished. Every mile, she was excising him a bit more from her life.

She arrived at Euston Station and took the Circle Line to Liverpool Street Station. Joshua, Audrey's elder son, had wanted to meet her, but she had kept quiet about when she would be arriving as she wanted more time for her body to heal and, more importantly, to regain her equilibrium.

She bought a rail ticket to Wivenhoe, a village situated on the River Colne, near the old Roman city of Colchester. Sitting at a table, she tried to read the free London Evening Standard newspaper but her thoughts kept wandering back to the people she had left behind. Audrey had always made friends easily, but the friends she had made in Hawksmead were completely different to her friends in Sevenoaks. Perhaps it was their youth she loved, but there was more to it than that. Both Tony and Tina had gone way beyond what most good people would do to help an older person. Why had she left them without saying goodbye? Of course, she knew why.

Audrey looked out at the River Colne as her train approached Wivenhoe Railway Station. Once a ship building and fishing village, it still retained its industrial charm despite the prolific growth of new housing. Stepping onto the platform, it felt odd not having a handbag; she carried a supermarket plastic bag containing a couple of items of clothing, a toothbrush, toothpaste, bits of make-up and an almost empty bottle of mineral water. In her coat pockets were her return ticket to London, her bank card, and a small packet of tissues.

The air was damp and cold, and the light was fading fast as Audrey made her way to the water's edge. She took a few moments to breathe in the fresh, salty air and to martial her thoughts. She walked up Quay Street and knocked on the blue stable-style front door to a small two up, two down cottage. Within a few seconds, a bolt was drawn and the door opened. It was quite a while since she'd last seen Richard Oakes and her father, at the age of eighty-nine, did look a bit older.

'Hi, Daddy. Sorry to arrive unannounced. May I come in for a cup of tea?'

She saw his brow furrow with surprise and then his eyebrows almost join as concern, laced with anger, took precedence.

CHAPTER FORTY-SEVEN

Tina had three more days before her appearance in the magistrates' court to face a charge of speeding and driving without due care and attention, and the inevitable loss of her licence. She decided to take a couple of hours off and drove in her VW to the hospital. She liked Malcolm and had hoped that he and Audrey would get back together.

Malcolm leant on Tina's arm, looking frail, bent and old. A metal walking stick, supplied by the hospital, and a profound limp had removed the last vestiges of his youth.

She looked at his baggy clothes. 'I should have bought you a size smaller.'

'Marks & Spencer usually fit me like a glove, a glove that fits of course, but I've lost a bit of weight. Oh, I nearly forgot. I must pick up my wallet and mobile phone from reception. They've been keeping them safe for me.'

'What about your keys?'

'My car is no longer with us, of course, but my house keys would have been handy. Best guess, they were consumed by the fire, along with my favourite suit.'

'Forgive me for asking the obvious, but how are we going to get in? I'm already up on one charge for speeding, I don't want to add breaking and entering.'

Malcolm laughed. 'Perfect Locks should be at the property when we get home. Tony organised it for me.'

'Heating? It's been really cold.'

'The boiler is on a timer, so the cottage should've remained warm.'

'It's funny,' Tina said. 'We've had many chats over the last few weeks, but I've never thought to ask you about your boiler.'

Malcolm laughed. 'I'm grateful for all you've done. Your visits gave me great comfort. I'm a lucky man.'

'Who needs to build up his strength.'

'Food,' Malcolm said. 'Would it be possible… ?'

'I've bought a few essentials to tide you over for a couple of days. If you text me a list, I'll do a much bigger shop.'

'I would very much appreciate your company for tea rather than waste your time in a supermarket. I can order goods online and have them delivered.'

Tina, who liked to go everywhere fast, found Malcolm's walking pace painfully slow. It was a great relief to leave the hospital's recycled air and head to her car.

'When are you up before the beak?' Malcolm asked.

For a moment, Tina was completely puzzled. 'The beak? Oh, you mean, when do I go to court?'

'Yes. I'm going to speak to the magistrate. Let the court know how your driving saved Audrey's life.'

~

At that very moment, in the county of Essex, Audrey's father looked at her with a mix of love and disapproval. 'Where is the diary now?'

She examined the scarred skin on the backs of her hands. 'I lost it when I fell in the river. That is what I presume happened. All I remember is lying in bed in the old school boarding house and then waking up in hospital.'

'That was the first time you were in hospital?' Rosemary asked, a slim, attractive, dark-haired woman, far removed from the fair looks of Audrey's mother, her father's late first wife. 'You were admitted again, after the fire?'

Audrey took a long breath. Her lungs felt better, thanks to the damp river air, but were nowhere near as good as new. She was very fond of her stepmother and realised that Rosemary and her father would be celebrating their fortieth wedding anniversary in a few months. Following the death of Audrey's mother, her father had been bereft of company until, through correspondence initiated by a letter he wrote to a sailing magazine, he met and fell in love with Rosemary.

'Yes,' Audrey replied. 'I was in the house when it caught fire and became trapped.'

'What are you going to do now?' her father asked.

'I plan to give the property to the people of Hawksmead.'

He nodded. 'And with your life?'

She looked at her father and her stepmother. The bond of love, forged over forty years, was evident in every aspect of their life together.

'I don't know,' Audrey answered. She really didn't know. Her life felt empty.

'When did you last see Freddie and Belle?'

Audrey looked at her father and smiled. 'I hope to see them very soon.'

'Joshua brought them to see us,' her father added. 'He was very worried about you.'

Audrey had been so wrapped up in another world, she knew she had neglected her living family. She had achieved what she set out to do and must now get on with being a good grandmother, a good mother and good daughter.

'Have you made plans for Christmas?' Rosemary asked. 'You know, you're always welcome here.'

Audrey smiled. Her family needed her. She had to accept that she was no longer a wife, a partner ...a lover.

CHAPTER FORTY-EIGHT

Audrey booked a room at the Royal Oak Hotel at the southern end of Sevenoaks. Within a day, she had selected a furnished cottage to rent in Bosville Road, a short walk from the railway station and near the town's former cattle market. She didn't want to disrupt the family renting her home so close to Christmas and, in truth, she didn't even want to visit the house her husband's firm had built.

She kept her eyes closed and allowed the taxi to lull her into a soporific state. Memories of happy years raising her boys, sharing school runs, meeting friends, hosting dinners and helping her husband deal with local authorities and investment bankers crowded her thoughts. Duncan always said that she was his secret weapon. She didn't want today's reality to supplant so many happy memories.

They turned left into her drive and she marvelled, as she always did, at the way her husband had created the effect of a winding road blasted out of a stone quarry, now shaded by mature deciduous trees. She remembered the day when the giant rocks were delivered and positioned, and the saplings first planted. The next day, she had given birth to her younger son, Benjamin.

In a spacious, three-car garage, she saw her Skoda Estate and was surprised to see how the paintwork shone. She paid the taxi driver and turned to approach the front door when it was opened by a slim, stylish woman, mid-thirties, whose figure belied the fact she had given birth to three boys over four years. Quite a production line, smiled Audrey to herself.

Lucy held out a long, slim arm that was complemented by fine-boned fingers.

'You cleaned my car,' Audrey said, shaking Lucy's hand.

'Mike insisted on giving it a thorough going over,' Lucy replied, standing aside to let Audrey into her home.

Did she want to go in? It would be rude not to. Audrey crossed the threshold and was hit by a massive surprise. Where Louis van Staaten paintings of Dutch barges had once hung, there were now beautiful painted portraits, signed by Lucy, of her husband and their three sons.

Audrey felt overwhelming relief. This was not her home. Yes, it was her house, but it was Lucy's family home, and Audrey felt nothing more than a welcome visitor. There were no ghosts from the past; just bricks and mortar, for which Lucy and Mike were paying a substantial rent. Her life in this house was locked away in her albums and in her memories. People make a home, and without those she loved, this big house with its picture windows was just a building to be let for other families to enjoy.

For the first time since returning to Sevenoaks, she felt confident she could find a new kind of contentment living in the old market town.

CHAPTER FORTY-NINE

A Widow's Retreat

Following the death of her husband, long-time Sevenoaks resident Audrey Willatt wished to start afresh in a new town, with new people and in an old school boarding house with a reputation for being haunted.

'I wasn't rejecting Sevenoaks,' explained Audrey to *The Chronicle*. 'I simply couldn't live with all the memories. Everywhere I looked, I was reminded of my dear husband, Duncan, and the wonderful times we shared with our sons. I suppose you could say I needed a rest from grieving.'

That rest involved moving to Hawksmead – a small town on the edge of a vast moor – crossing swords with the Russian mafia, nearly drowning in a flooded river and just escaping with her life when her haunted house was destroyed by fire.

We caught up with Mrs Willatt on her return to Sevenoaks and asked her how she feels about our town after all she has been through.

'I can now move on. I needed to make a break with the past, but my life was, and is, and always will be in the beautiful town of Sevenoaks. And the weather's much warmer down here!'

Scars clearly evident on her hands and legs, we ventured to ask the wanderer returned one last question. Did she see any ghosts in the old school boarding house?

'Not that I recall,' said Mrs Willatt, although her smile conveyed to our reporter a different story.

~

After getting through a second Christmas without her darling Duncan, but with the joyous company of her grandchildren, Audrey settled back into life in Sevenoaks. She occupied her days as best she could with bridge, long walks with fellow ramblers, and visits with girlfriends to West End musicals but, no matter how hard she worked to live in the present, the recent past still woke her in the small hours.

When summer finally arrived, the weather was mixed including heavy downpours and a heatwave in mid-July. She was pleased she'd kept up her membership of the local country club as she started almost every day with an early morning swim in the open-air swimming pool. Often on Saturdays, her elder son would give his wife a break and bring her grandchildren to visit for picnics and swimming.

Her younger son would ring for a long chat most weeks, but there were too many hours for her to fill to keep the deep pain of loneliness at bay.

It was late summer when the invitation came via email as the sender did not know her current postal address. For several minutes, Audrey stared at the screen on her new tablet. On the one hand, she was settled in her cottage and didn't want the upheaval; on the other hand, how could she say no?

CHAPTER FIFTY

Audrey sat back in her first-class train seat and watched England's lush countryside pass her window. There were a few marks on her legs from the fire, but they were no longer tender.

The train pulled into Undermere Station, and she took a taxi to the White Hart Hotel. She had arrived a day early as she wanted time to rest, unpack, and to let the creases drop out of her dress and coat. In truth, she was nervous and wished to look her best for the people who had once meant, for a short while, a great deal to her.

She ate a light supper in the hotel and woke up to a beautiful September morning, feeling rested. She went down for breakfast and was surprised by the butterflies she felt in her stomach. Back up in her room, a local hairdresser washed, dried and styled her hair. She would have liked a professional make-up artist to sort out her face, but a light base, a little rouge on the lips and a few flicks with a mascara brush would have to do.

'I've seen you looking worse,' she said to her reflection in the dressing table mirror.

The bedroom phone rang and the hotel's reception informed Audrey that her taxi was waiting. She took a last look in a full-length mirror, grabbed her handbag, bought especially for the event, and took the lift to the ground floor. Normally she would have walked, but she didn't want to risk tripping on the stairs in her heels.

~

It had not been a great year for the Dryomov brothers. Both had been summoned to the crown court charged with VAT fraud and the misappropriation of council subsidies. Bribery had secured the original contract to build new homes to the south of Hawksmead but they had been caught in a police sting handing over dirty money to the director of planning when tendering to extend the housing development. There was a risk they could be deported, although their solicitor had told them that deportation orders are rarely carried out. Despite the threat, they continued their lucrative sideline dealing in smuggled caviar, vodka, cigarettes, counterfeit icons, forged paintings and fake Fabergé eggs.

You can't always get what you want – Mick Jagger's voice blared from the white transit van's radio as Spartak pulled over at the top of Hawksmead High Street. How ironic, he thought, turning up the volume. Even he, with his handsome face, lean body, charisma and cash could not get what he wanted more than anything in the world. His brother had offered to kill the competition, but he knew that would not work. There had to be a smarter way.

CHAPTER FIFTY-ONE

Audrey paid the taxi driver and got out at the southern end of Hawksmead High Street. More than eight months had passed since she had last stood in the former mill town and almost a year since she had arrived at the old school boarding house, hoping to discover more about the circumstances surrounding her brother's death. Of course, it was impossible to think about Bobby without thinking about Malcolm. She hoped he was well, that his bones had healed and that he could look forward to a few happy years. She adjusted her coat and placed her purse in her matching handbag.

The weather had held, and Audrey grew warm as she walked up the High Street. She came to the Olde Tea Shoppe and was surprised to see the Closed sign on the door. Below, stuck to the glass, was a handwritten note which brought a smile to her face.

Audrey continued on up the High Street. The library came into view, and she thought about Shirley and her young love for Edward Holden. She checked the time on her watch and crossed the road to the library on the off-chance that Shirley may be working. She pushed the door but it was locked. In the window was a neatly printed note. Audrey read it and laughed out loud. There was clearly a pattern forming. She walked past the Falcon pub and tested the door. Surprisingly, it opened, and she looked into the gloom.

'Sorry love, just about to close,' Ted said, wearing a smart suit and tie, complemented by a yellow rose in his button hole.

'I'll see you there,' Audrey replied letting the door close behind her. She continued on. The Methodist Church, both plain and imposing, came into sight and beyond it was an uncluttered view, through trees still in leaf, across the river to the moor.

Where was her house? She had expected to see something, but there was just the garden wall and an empty space where the old school boarding house had once stood. She didn't know what to feel, but as she walked towards the entrance to her driveway she could never have imagined the incredible sight that graced her eyes. Spilling out onto the pavement from her drive was a great crowd of people dressed in their Sunday best.

'Audrey!'

She tried to locate the source of the voice.

'Audrey! Audrey Willatt!'

Finally, she clapped eyes on Heather wearing a beautiful, simple dress, far removed from the utilitarian attire she invariably wore in the Falcon.

'Look! It's Audrey Willatt,' came another voice.

She could hear a hum of voices speaking her name as dozens of pairs of eyes turned towards her.

Audrey smiled – she was home. She was with the people she had come to know and love.

'How wonderful to see you,' Maggie said, kissing Audrey on each cheek, taking care not to clash their wide-brimmed hats.

'Andy's borrowed Tony's camera and is taking the pictures,' Maggie continued. 'Needless to say, the wedding of the year is going to make *The Chronicle*'s front page.'

'Mrs Willatt!'

Audrey recognised Colin Turner, a local councillor, who was with his wife, Penny. 'How lovely that you're here on this special day. As you can see, they took a leaf out of your book.'

'Really?' Audrey wondered what leaf that could be.

'They invited the whole town to their wedding – as you did for your housewarming.'

Several others came up to welcome Audrey back to Hawksmead, telling her how much she had been missed and how they wished she would make the little town her home again.

'I'm coming to the end of my time,' Vivian said, the September sun reflecting in her mayoral chain. 'Next month, I have to pass on the chain of office to Malcolm Cadwallader. He's our new mayor. After what he's done here, we persuaded him to stand and then couldn't get anyone to stand against him.'

Audrey's heart flipped. 'Malcolm?'

'Follow me.' Vivian took Audrey's arm and led her down the short drive, past wedding guests who applauded or held out their hands to shake Audrey's. People parted to make way for her, and she was able to see what had happened to her former home. Where there had once been an imposing oak door and a giant red-brick edifice, only the stone foundations remained. Amongst the ruins were newly planted shrubs, trees in tubs, and wild flowers. Beyond was a vision of breathtaking beauty.

'I call it the Garden of Eden,' Amy said, 'as I love to come here and sit while my children play.' Audrey recognised her as one of the receptionists in Undermere's intensive care unit whose coat she had borrowed and replaced.

Audrey walked on, shaking hands and kissing, with a growing following of wedding guests and excited children running around.

'Malcolm came to the council and we agreed his plan,' Colin Turner said. 'This is entirely his vision and his money. For years people had crossed the road to avoid the old school boarding house but Malcolm wanted to change that by creating a memorial garden. The council helped sort out the removal of all the rubble and make the ruin safe for visitors.'

'Audrey!' She turned as Andy Blake came up to her, smartly dressed in a suit and tie, with a white rose in his lapel, and gripping his son's long lens camera. 'Have you seen the memorial? Follow me.'

He took Audrey's arm and, joined by Maggie, and more than a dozen wedding guests, he led her to where the oil-fired boiler had once stood. In its place was a large memorial stone.

This garden is dedicated to the memory of five schoolboys who were taken from their families: Edward Holden, Christopher Wilkins, David Turnbull, Mark Small and Robert Oakes. Please relax, enjoy and love each other in their memory.

'Malcolm planned for the garden to be dedicated to your brother and Mark Small, a boy he knew from when he was a teacher up at the school,' Andy explained. 'And to two boys who drowned in the River Hawk by the bridge as you nearly did. When news of the memorial spread, he was told about the suicide of Edward Holden a few years earlier.'

Audrey read and reread the names carved into the memorial stone and then looked at the garden, resplendent with colour.

'Malcolm did all this?' Her voice cracked as she spoke.

'He got professionals in to help him and loads of volunteers – me included,' Andy said.

'It's beautiful,' Audrey whispered.

'Audrey.' Andy spoke as close to her ear as her hat would allow. 'Malcolm told me what happened to your brother and his involvement; and also the incident on the bridge with black ice. My son nearly killed you in the same way.'

Audrey gave Andy a little nod and called out to Colin Turner. 'Does the council intend to rebuild the house?'

'The insurance money you kindly donated,' Colin called back, 'we are using to help finance genuinely affordable homes for young people who have grown up in Hawksmead. We have no plans to rebuild the boarding house.'

'Perfect.' She gave him a thumbs-up, much to the councillor's evident pleasure.

Beyond him was Malcolm, standing tall and looking very dapper in his formal suit. He was chatting to Maureen, an elegant widow and bridge fanatic whom Audrey had met at her housewarming party.

'Everything all right?' Andy asked.

She looked up at him and smiled. 'Yes, thank you. And thank you for helping to create this wonderful garden. I am so grateful for what you and others have done.'

She walked away as casually as she could and pretended to enjoy the gentle majesty of the garden. Every now and then, she stole a look in Malcolm's direction and was not sure whether she was relieved to see him still chatting to Maureen or annoyed. She felt her pulse quickening and knew her cheeks were flushed. She understood why Malcolm as a young man had fallen for her brother. Bobby had the kind of adorable looks that made people want to hug him. He and Audrey had always looked very much alike when they were children. As Roxane, standing centre stage in the *Cyrano de Bergerac* cast photograph hanging in the Falcon pub, Robert looked beautiful. Malcolm, as a young, inexperienced man, had confused emotions. He had fallen in love with Roxane and, fifty years on, Audrey had rekindled those buried emotions. But what about now? Was she looking old? Did the scars on her legs show? He looked wonderful. She loved his posture, his slim physique, his fine cheekbones and defined jaw. His work, producing this magical experience, had clearly rejuvenated him, and she wished she'd been here to help.

Eleanor sidled up beside Audrey. 'Maureen has had the hots for Malcolm long before she became a very merry widow.'

Audrey looked at Eleanor, and the two women hugged as best their two hats would allow.

'What a wonderful day, and what glorious weather,' Eleanor continued. 'The whole town will never forget this wedding.'

'I'm so looking forward to seeing Tina. I know she'll look stunning. Have you seen the lucky groom?'

'I think he's hiding behind the wall, practising his speech, together with his best man, Tony Blake. Over the last few months, the two couples have been almost inseparable. Tina is an honorary aunt to Georgiana and Charlie.'

'Where is Charlie?'

'He's being looked after by Shirley – you know, from the library. On Saturday afternoons, she often meets up with the two couples and the little ones at my tea shop, and they usually stay long after I put up the closed sign. Malcolm often joins them, following a hard day working here in the garden.'

Audrey blinked back tears. 'I don't know what to do.'

Holding Audrey's hand between both of hers, Eleanor looked squarely into Audrey's eyes. 'I regret one thing in my life. I had a chance to fulfil a dream, but I convinced myself that it wasn't the right thing to do. You know what? Sometimes the right thing is the wrong thing and vice-versa, if that makes any sense.'

Audrey laughed and licked her dry lips. She was on the fast track to old age. But standing twenty metres away was a man who complemented all that she was and loved. For the first time in her life, she felt a tsunami of heat spread throughout her entire body, and her breathing became short, almost painful, as her damaged lungs sucked in the warm air.

'Are you all right?' Eleanor asked.

Black sheets flapped in front of Audrey's eyes as she fell backwards down a long tunnel... fainting like a teenager at her first Beatles concert.

CHAPTER FIFTY-TWO

Malcolm had been aware of Audrey from the moment she had arrived in the garden. When he saw her faint, he wanted to rush to her side. Now he was acutely aware that she was back on her feet and coming closer. Every sinew in his body stiffened. She was almost upon him before he could politely interrupt Maureen's flow. She smiled encouragingly and stepped away.

The gabble of chat and laughter quietened as the two people who were responsible for giving the memorial garden to the townsfolk of Hawksmead came to meet again for the first time since the old school boarding house had been consumed by flames.

Malcolm looked into Audrey's eyes. He felt his knees go and wished he still had his hospital walking stick.

Silence.

His heart was pounding.

What was she going to say to him?

Audrey wrapped her arms around Malcolm's neck and kissed him gently on the lips. A cheer went up, accompanied by spontaneous applause.

Hawksmead's Brass Band blasted out Mendelssohn's *The Wedding March* and the guests, almost as one, stretched their necks to see Tina and her father, John Small, riding in the rear of an open-top vintage Rolls-Royce Silver Ghost.

A black Daimler came to a halt behind the Rolls, and the liveried chauffeur got out before the car had fully stopped. He opened the rear passenger door and Eden, Tina's chief bridesmaid, dressed in pale peach, stepped out of the car, followed by Georgiana, in a mini version of the same dress. Taking her daughter's hand, Eden walked towards the rear of the Rolls and stood back as the chauffeur opened the tiny side door and offered his gloved hand to the bride.

Eden straightened out Tina's ivory wedding dress and veil. The bride's father, resplendent in a dove grey morning suit, came to offer his arm. Eden and Georgiana picked up Tina's train as the stunning bride was escorted down the red-carpeted driveway.

The music played on. The splendour of the setting, the warmth of the September sun and the natural scents from the memorial garden were intoxicating, and many guests, before a vow had been spoken, reached for lace-trimmed handkerchiefs, or used the tip of a finger to wipe away an escaping tear. Even tough old journo Andy blinked back tears as he looked upon his daughter, Eden, and his little granddaughter, Georgiana, undertaking bridesmaid duties.

Tina walked slowly with her father down the carpeted path to a flower entwined pergola. Waiting to greet her, with the Holy Book open in his hand, was the tall figure of William Longden, the Methodist minister. Standing before him, watching his beautiful bride approach, was her husband-to-be, PC Gary Burton, supported by his Best Man, Tony Blake.

Audrey kept a firm grip on Malcolm's arm. 'Where would you like us to be married?'

He looked into her eyes. 'It's the bride's right to choose.'

'Welcome,' Reverend Longden announced, 'to a very

special day in the history of Hawksmead. We are here in this beautiful memorial garden to bear witness and to celebrate the marriage of Christina Louise Small to Gary Simon Burton.'

Audrey heard the eighty-six-year-old minister's words as her mind swam in a sea of happiness. She looked at Tina and a great wave of love washed over her. For a few seconds, she had felt guilty for abandoning her friends in Sevenoaks – it had been a wonderful summer catching up whilst her body healed, but Hawksmead felt like home.

'The ceremony was to be in the Methodist church,' Malcolm said, quietly. 'But as the weather was so good, Reverend Longden was more than happy to agree to officiate in the garden so the whole town could come. I think our lovely mayoress sorted out the licence.'

Following the ceremony, champagne corks popped every few seconds. Trestle tables, adorned with white tablecloths, were resplendent with finger food on silver-effect platters, together with a three-tiered, iced wedding cake with two figures standing on top. The atmosphere of joy and love, bathed in a sun that was dipping to the horizon way too quickly, was like nothing Audrey had ever experienced.

Tina and Gary were honoured by a speech from her proud and emotional father. 'Finally, I would like to thank Malcolm Cadwallader whose concept it was to create this memorial garden and for including the name of my big brother, Mark Small, who was killed on the bridge, aged thirteen, when a car skidded on black ice.'

Audrey whispered to Malcolm. 'Does he know?'

Malcolm shook his head. 'I confessed all to Andy Blake. I thought he would print it in his paper, but he said that it served no purpose.'

A voice shouted from the back of the crowd, 'I know

who was driving that car!' It was Vincent, whom Audrey had met in the Falcon on her first evening in Hawksmead. The garden went quiet. 'It was the same person who killed my beautiful Roxane,' declaimed the former Cyrano de Bergerac.

Everyone looked at Vincent who was wearing a smart suit and appeared stone cold sober.

From within the throng, Ted shouted, 'Vincent! Keep your mouth shut.'

Audrey squeezed Malcolm's arm then stepped forward to the dais. 'May I speak?'

John Small nodded and offered her the microphone, which Audrey accepted.

'Almost a year ago, I came to Hawksmead in the hope that I would uncover the truth behind my brother's death in the old school boarding house fifty-one years ago. I discovered that in one term, two boys drowned in the river and that one boy was killed on the bridge by a car skidding on black ice. Those three deaths traumatised a young teacher who reached out to protect my brother. That same teacher subsequently suffered a further agony when my brother died falling down the boarding house stairs.'

'He killed my Roxane,' Vincent shouted.

'No he didn't,' responded Audrey, her voice soft but firm. 'He was a young man who witnessed a tragic accident that affected his entire life.'

Silence.

Audrey stepped off the dais and handed the microphone to PC Gary Burton.

'You're looking a bit better than when I last saw you, Mrs Willatt.'

'Many congratulations.' She kissed him on the cheek.

John Small, Tina's father and Mark Small's younger brother, walked up to Malcolm. Audrey hurried to be by his side.

'My mother received a letter from Robert Oakes,' John Small said. 'The boy wrote in precise detail what happened on the bridge. He made it clear, you were not to blame.' He offered his hand to Malcolm.

Gary Burton cleared his throat into the microphone.

'Ladies and gentlemen, I would like to thank you all for your generous gifts but, more importantly, for your presence on this, our very special day. My wife and I…'

He was interrupted by cheers of approval.

'My wife and I would like to propose a toast to two people whose kindness and generosity have given our wonderful town this memorial garden. Ladies and gentlemen – I present the arresting…' He paused for the inevitable laugh. 'I present… the amazing Audrey Willatt and Malcolm Cadwallader.'

The guests repeated the names and John Small was the first to applaud the couple.

'Finally,' Gary continued, 'I would like to propose a toast to my wife's beautiful bridesmaids.'

As the sun lost its brilliance, torches planted around the garden were lit by Malcolm. The cake was cut and Tony, who had relieved his father of the camera, took lots of photos.

Audrey and Malcolm were chatting to Eleanor when Tina, accompanied by her new husband, came to say goodbye. Audrey hugged the young estate agent. As the two women, more than forty years apart in age, looked upon each other, Audrey knew that she would spend the rest of her days in Hawksmead.

Tina and Gary headed for the Rolls Royce as copious quantities of confetti petals were thrown from all angles. The chauffeur opened the rear door and Tina slipped onto the Silver Ghost's soft leather seat. Eden and Georgiana made great play of ensuring that her wedding dress did not get trapped in the door. Gary got in the far side and slid across the seat to his beaming bride.

The chauffeur backed the car out into the High Street as guests, tears streaming down their faces, waved goodbye.

'Gary! Be warned,' Tony bellowed. 'This is the last time Tina will not be in the driving seat!'

With smiles as broad as Hawksmead High Street, the happy couple waved goodbye and blew countless kisses as their luxury carriage pulled away, escorted by two BMW police motorcycles, with blue and yellow livery and flashing blue lights.

Most of the wedding guests had departed when the Reverend William Longden walked, in the growing darkness, along the carpeted pathway to where Audrey and Malcolm were chatting to Andy and Maggie. Staff from the catering company were clearing up the last of the debris, and folding away trestle tables and chairs.

'I've married a lot of young couples,' the reverend said, 'but I am hard pushed to recall a happier wedding or one in a more beautiful setting. You have absolutely worked wonders, Malcolm.'

'It was a labour of love and, of course, I had a lot of help,' Malcolm replied.

Reverend Longden turned his keen eyes to Audrey. 'The town has missed you Mrs Willatt. We all hope that we can persuade you to linger a little longer this time.'

'I intend to linger for the rest of my days.' Audrey gently

squeezed Malcolm's arm.

She heard a whisper in the mighty oak tree and looked up to see the leaves rustling in the late summer breeze.

CHAPTER FIFTY-THREE

'Mum, listen to me… It's too quick… We don't know him… We've not even met him… Don't do this to us… You belong here… With your family… We've lost Dad, we nearly lost you, and now you're forsaking us for some old man who's probably just desperate to have you cook and wash for him.'

Audrey listened as her elder son tried his best to reason with her. Although she was disappointed that both her boys had declined the wedding invitation, in some respects she was relieved.

~

Undermere Town Hall provided a classic Victorian setting for the smartly dressed couple. Accompanied by their witnesses – Andy from *The Chronicle* and his wife, Maggie – and Ted and Heather from *The Falcon* – Audrey and Malcolm celebrated their marriage on another glorious September day followed by a wedding reception at the Rorty Crankle Inn overlooking the Ridgeway. Harry and Cathy had taken on extra staff so they, too, could join in the celebrations.

'It's unusual for a former pupil to be friends with a teacher once school days are over,' Audrey commented to Ted.

'You know I played Christian in *Cyrano de Bergerac* up at the old school? Your brother played Roxane. Well, the boys that drowned in the river were two of my best friends. They weren't in the play, so they had to go out camping on the moor for three days with the rest of the school – outward-bound training in its rawest form. For some reason, they were allowed to canoe on the river when it was in full flood without life jackets, and that's how they came to drown. My parents were abroad in the Far East, and I had no way of expressing my grief. Malcolm recognised how I felt and helped me through a very difficult time. A few years later, we ran into each other and became firm friends.' Ted paused. 'He told me what happened to your brother. I did my best to help him, but the burden he's carried all these years is considerable. Today is the first time I have seen him looking genuinely happy.'

~

Audrey was surprised by how quickly she settled into married life with Malcolm. His cottage was small but she came with nothing apart from her favourite van Staaten painting, transported from her house in Sevenoaks. Looking for a place to hang it, Malcolm removed the photograph of his first wife, Mary.

'No, Malcolm,' protested Audrey. 'This is still her home.'

'Mary's niece, Rosie, has always loved this photo of her aunt and asked me to leave it for her when I shuffle off this mortal coil. I think she would be thrilled to have it now.'

~

It was a Sunday morning, and Audrey and Malcolm were

sitting in bed listening to *Love Songs* on Radio 2. Malcolm was reading the latest Peter James' thriller and Audrey was trying to learn lines. She'd joined Hawksmead Amateur Dramatic Society, and their last play before the Christmas pantomime was a supernatural thriller called *The Widow*. Audrey had been cast as an American, determined to go to any lengths to save the life of her sickly son.

'Any good?' Malcolm asked.

'Ssshh.' Audrey sighed and put the play down. 'You're going to have to help me. At the moment, my memory is like Teflon.'

'Nothing sticking? Ha-ha... I know what will help. Let's go out on the moor and tackle the Ridgeway while the weather is still fine.'

'Great idea. We could park your shiny new motor by the memorial garden, walk over the bridge and set off for the moor. We could take a picnic.'

'I have a better idea. Why don't we drive, not walk, over the bridge and park the car in the grounds of the old school? There's a public path that leads to the Ridgeway.'

'On the other hand, we could drive to the Rorty Crankle Inn, have a drink and walk from there.'

Malcolm laughed. 'That's a stroll, not a walk!'

Hawksmead was quiet, apart from the cheerful calling to prayer of church bells. Malcolm parked his snazzy-looking, silver Honda Civic hatchback across the road from the memorial garden.

'Why are we stopping?' Audrey asked.

'I want to take a quick look at the garden – make sure that the gardeners are doing a good job.'

They both got out of the car, and Malcolm retrieved a beech-wood walking stick from the boot.

'Alarm?'

He pressed the car fob and saw the hazard lights flash as he and Audrey crossed the High Street.

'What a glorious wedding,' she said. 'Tina looked so happy.'

Audrey's phone beeped and she opened her bag to take it out. She swiped the screen and read a text message. 'It's Tina! What timing. She's asked if we're free for Sunday lunch.'

'What about our picnic?' Malcolm's eyebrows, knitted.

'What about my clothes? I'm dressed for walking, not a smart lunch.'

'Tell you what, let's invite Tina and Gary to lunch up at the Rorty Crankle, then we can see them and also have our walk.'

Audrey tapped out their reply and was thrilled to receive a thumbs-up and a smiley face. She slipped her arm through Malcolm's, and they walked down the drive to the place where Audrey's oak front door had opened and closed for more than one hundred and fifty years.

'Who's that?' Malcolm pointed with his free arm through the trees to a figure.

Audrey put her finger to her lips and then gestured to Malcolm. Even without her spectacles and despite the person's back being towards them, Audrey recognised who it was, kneeling by the memorial stone.

Treading carefully, they walked around the foundations of the destroyed building and along the perimeter wall.

After almost a minute, the person got to her feet and turned towards them. She waited for Audrey and Malcolm to approach her.

'Thank you,' Shirley said to Malcolm. 'His parents must be dead by now but Eddie has a sister, somewhere.'

'I'll call by at the library in the morning,' Audrey said, 'and we'll work out a plan of action to find her.'

'It's beautiful, Malcolm.' Tears sparkled Shirley's eyes. 'I must go.' She headed towards the entrance to the drive.

Audrey called after her. 'Shirley. I still owe you tea and cake.'

'I've not forgotten!' She blew Audrey a kiss.

They watched Shirley walk through the young trees and then, as one, turned and looked at the five engraved names on the memorial stone. For a moment, neither spoke.

Audrey stepped away from Malcolm and touched her fingers to her lips and rested her hand on top of the memorial. 'Be at peace, my love.'

For a moment, she allowed memories of her brother to course through her mind.

'Come on,' Audrey said, resolutely. 'Let's conquer the heights of the Ridgeway.' She turned, but Malcolm was nowhere to be seen. Rising panic set in as her eyes scanned the garden.

'Over here!' he called.

Looking through the trees, she saw Malcolm standing in the driveway. She hurried over to him, surprised by her stressed reaction. In his hand was a bunch of white and pink dahlias.

'For the love of my life.'

Audrey took the flowers and put the blooms to her nose. 'I have an idea,' she said.

CHAPTER FIFTY-FOUR

'Tina's policeman is becoming nuisance,' growled Kirill. 'Because of you, he's destroying our business, our lives. If he tries trick again, leave him to me.' Kirill was at the wheel of the van as they raced down the Old Military Road. It was Sunday morning so there weren't many cars around. 'We have bad smell since arrest. He think he can screw us.'

'At least the road is clear,' Spartak observed from the passenger seat. But even a clear road could not lift his gloom since all hope was lost, following Tina's marriage. Perhaps he should go online and find a Russian bride? He gave the thought a hollow laugh.

~

'They've done a good job repairing it,' Audrey said as she and Malcolm walked towards the humpback bridge, with its three arches and gently flowing river.

'I understand they managed to retrieve the lost stones from the river bed,' he replied. 'It's not quite invisible mending but it's pretty good.'

'I still think the council could do something about making the bridge safer.'

'Hm, yes. Traffic lights to make it single file and a separate footbridge would be a start. Perhaps I could put my new mayoral status to good use?'

She squeezed his arm.

~

Spartak saw they were exceeding sixty miles per hour. 'Slow down.'

'Don't tell me how to drive.' Kirill spat phlegm out of his side window. They passed the end of the road that led to Hawksmead College. 'We should buy old school.'

'And set it on fire, too?' Spartak shook his head. 'All we did was make the whole town happy.'

~

'Please can we not live dangerously?' Malcolm strived to see over the brow of the humpback bridge.

Audrey took a deep smell of the dahlias and threw them over the stone parapet into the river. She watched as they fluttered down to the rippling water and disappeared under the arch. 'Sleep well, my angels.'

~

Kirill heard the blast of cannons from Tchaikovsky's 1812 Overture and he reached into his top pocket. The text was in Russian and he took his eyes off the road for a few seconds to read it, despite the van's high speed. He grunted and handed the phone to his brother.

Spartak read the message and looked up. Ahead was the humpback bridge. 'You're going too fast.'

There was another blast of cannon fire and both men took their eyes off the road to look at the phone's screen:

A warrant has been executed to search your properties, currently being enforced. See you in court. Regards, Gary Burton.

'Watch out!' Spartak jabbed his finger at the windscreen.

Kirill could not believe what he was seeing. A few seconds ago the road leading to the bridge had been clear, but now two people were standing in the middle of the road, holding hands. It was too late to brake. He had no choice but to drive into them. Time seemed to slow as the van bore down. Why were they not leaping out of the way? Why were they making no attempt to save themselves?

Spartak dropped the phone and grabbed the wheel with his right hand. He jerked it down and the van swerved away from the mouth of the bridge.

But it was too late.

The two boys, wearing corduroy shorts, were doomed. Kirill braced himself for the thud. But there was no impact. No thud.

The van veered off the road and shot like an arrow through the beech hedgerow.

~

From the apex of the bridge, Audrey and Malcolm watched as the van hit a low, dry-stone wall and flipped into the air. It landed with a metal crunching *humph* and rolled and rolled again, slamming into the base of a mature oak tree.

~

William Longden shook hands with each member of his congregation, which had swelled since he had officiated at Tina and Gary's wedding. There was a sudden change in air pressure before he heard a mighty *whoomp* carried on the breeze.

Everyone stopped to look.

They waited.

A second even louder explosion was accompanied by a warm glow in the sky.

CHAPTER FIFTY-FIVE

'Next spring,' Audrey said, as she and Malcolm shared a pot of tea the following Wednesday. They were with Eden, who had popped into the Olde Tea Shoppe with her children.

Eleanor entered from the kitchen with a tiered display stand bedecked with cakes.

'Next spring, I promise,' Audrey repeated, placing her hand on Malcolm's arm.

'Wee-wee, Mummy,' Georgiana announced.

'I'll take her.' Eleanor lifted the former bridesmaid off her chair, and held her little hand as they hurried to the rear of the tea room.

'Next spring – what?' Eden asked as she offered a forkful of sponge cake to her son.

'Next spring, Malcolm and I are going to walk the Ridgeway.'

Eden looked at Malcolm.

'God willing,' he said, with a smile creasing his handsome face. 'Please excuse me.' He eased out of his chair and winced. 'My hip, my joints, my muscles seize up if I sit around too long, especially if they know I'm enjoying myself. They like to remind me of my great age.' He headed for the lavatory, holding the door for Eleanor, who emerged with Georgiana.

Shirley entered the Olde Tea Shoppe and smiled at Audrey. 'A very happy newly-married gentleman popped by the library this morning and told me you would be here.'

Audrey got up from her chair and kissed Shirley on the cheek. 'Black Forest gateau?'

The toot-toot of a car's horn attracted their attention. Audrey looked out of the window and saw a white VW Golf reverse into a parking space.

'It's Tina!' She hurried out to greet the young estate agent, but it was a man who got out of the similar-looking car.

Embarrassed by her mistake, Audrey turned and did a quick check of her hair in the tea shop's window. But the face that looked back wasn't hers. In the reflection, she saw a young woman – a woman she'd only seen in a photograph hanging in Malcolm's cottage.

Audrey re-entered the tea shop, slightly disturbed by what she thought she had just seen.

Eden spotted Audrey's puzzled expression as she sat back down at the table. 'Are you all right?'

'For a moment, I thought I saw Mary, Malcolm's first wife. She was smiling. It's given me quite a shock.'

'I knew her a little,' Shirley said. 'Very sad. But in her final days, I think she and Malcolm found the love for each other that was missing for so much of their marriage.'

'She had a very kind face. I would like to have met her.'

'Perhaps you just have.' Shirley rested her hand on Audrey's. 'She's buried in the Methodist churchyard, next to your memorial garden.'

Audrey's phone beeped and she took it out of her bag. 'It's a text from my son, Joshua. He's booked a family room in the Falcon pub for half term.' She heard another beep coming from the rear of the tea shop and glowed with pride as her new husband weaved his way between the chairs towards her.

'I've received a text. It's from your younger son,' Malcolm said. 'He was wondering whether it's okay for him and his wife to stay for a couple of nights at the cottage. I hope you don't mind but I've texted back a smiley face and a thumbs up.'

Audrey's smile turned into a big grin.

ACKNOWLEDGEMENTS

Thank you to Chris Jones, of The London Screenwriters' Festival, who devised the Twisted50 short-story competition, inspiring me to become an author.

Thank you to fellow writer Ali Loconte for sharing her wisdom, experience and considerable talent.

Thank you to Brian Edwards for freely imparting his electrical expertise.

Thank you to Miranda Summers-Pritchard for her sublime editing and proofreading.

Thank you to my son, Harry, for a brilliant final polish.

…and thank *you* for reading my first novel.
If you have a moment, please leave a review online. Your help to spread the word is very much appreciated.

ABOUT THE AUTHOR

Romola Farr first trod the boards on the West End stage aged sixteen and continued to work for the next eighteen years in theatre, TV and film, and as a photographic model. A trip to Hollywood led to the sale of her first screenplay and a successful change of direction as a screenwriter and playwright. *Bridge to Eternity* is her debut novel.

As Roxane would say in *Cyrano de Bergerac*, Romola Farr is a nom de plume.

romolafarr@gmail.com

@RomolaFarr

www.wildmoorpress.com

Hawksmead Amateur Dramatic Society

is pleased to announce that newly married Audrey Cadwallader is
to play Elizabeth in our production of *The Widow* opposite newly
married estate agent, Tina Burton who is to play Catherine.

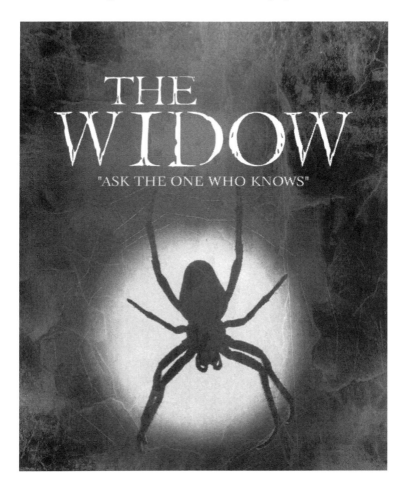

ACT ONE

Lights up in a baronial entrance hall that is adorned with faded portraits. Upstage left is Joshua's bedroom and downstage right is Catherine's bedroom .

Centre stage and downstage left is where most of the action takes place. An old clock chimes the hour at various times.

Scene 1

The doorbell tinkles followed by banging on the main entrance door. No one comes. The bell tinkles again followed by more banging on the door. No one comes. The door opens and a man enters carrying a heavy bag which he puts down with a thud. It is Dewi, a taxi driver.

Dewi   Mrs Hinkley! *(He turns to the open door).* I suggest you come in. You'll catch your death standing out there.

314

Catherine Long enters; she is in her 20s, graceful and beautiful.

Catherine	I didn't think it'd be as cold as this.
Dewi	We're not in Chelsea, Miss. You have to take care of yourself out here. The Brecon Beacons are very unforgiving. *(Catherine looks around at the austere entrance hall).* Feeling a bit nervous are you?
Catherine	Nervous about what?
Dewi	Longden Hall. *(He does a sweep of his hand taking in the stuffed birds under glass domes and a flea-bitten stuffed fox that has definitely seen better days).* It's been empty for years. Even the vandals kept away until Mrs Hinkley bought it.
Catherine	Why's that?
Dewi	It's haunted.
Catherine	Perfect - better than a guard dog - and ghosts don't need feeding.
Dewi	I admire your bravery.
Catherine	I'm not brave. Dead people can't harm you, it's when they're alive you've got to worry about them.
Dewi	Well, rather you than me.
Catherine	How much do I owe you?
Dewi	Don't worry, love… it's on Mrs Hinkley's account.
Catherine	Do you have a business card?

Elizabeth Hinkley enters from the corridor, stage left.

Elizabeth	Catherine! How delightful to see you. *(She is in her late 40s or 50s and is a fine looking woman who speaks with a Manhattan accent. She approaches Catherine and kisses her on each cheek).* Welcome to Longden Hall.

Catherine	Thank you Mrs Hinkley.
Elizabeth	Leave your bag - I'll show you to your room.
Dewi	Miss! My card for the return journey. *(He holds out his business card).*
Elizabeth	I have your number, Dewi.
Dewi	Right then. I'll be off.
Catherine	Thank you for the ride. I'll let you know if I see any ghosts.
Dewi	I'd rather you didn't! *(He exits).*
Catherine	*(To Elizabeth).* You have an amazing house.
Elizabeth	We don't use it all. Far too expensive to heat.
Catherine	It's not exactly the ideal weather for a photo shoot.
Elizabeth	I fear you're right, although the weather is very changeable in this part of the world. One minute it is lashing down and then the sun breaks through and it's glorious.
Catherine	Well I hope I do a good job for you.
Elizabeth	As soon as I saw your photos on the agency website, I knew you were the perfect model.
Catherine	Thank you. *(Beat).* When are the others arriving?
Elizabeth	Later today. *(Mrs O'Brien, a leathery woman, stout and strong, enters from the corridor, stage left. She picks up Catherine's bag).* Mrs O'Brien helps out with the running of the house and is a marvellous cook. *(Mrs O'Brien puts the bag down in the bedroom stage right).* After you.

Elizabeth follows Catherine into the bedroom.

Catherine	*(Gesturing to the old portraits).* Family members?
Elizabeth	They came with the house. I don't have the heart to take them down.
Mrs O'Brien	I'll get on with dinner, Mrs Hinkley.
Elizabeth	Thank you, Mrs O'Brien. *(Mrs O'Brien exits stage right).* I hope you'll be comfortable here. The timbers creak and groan but it is a friendly old place.

Lights down. Elizabeth exits. SFX: the clock strikes the 6 o'clock hour. Upstage left the lights come up in Joshua's bedroom where a young man sits on his bed looking through a family album. He is Joshua Hinkley, mid-twenties, pale and sickly looking. Elizabeth enters carrying a mug.

Elizabeth	I've brought you your milk.
Joshua	Thank you. *(She puts the milk down on the side table).* Have the others arrived yet?
Elizabeth	Yes, they are freshening up.
Joshua	Mrs O'Brien should not have stolen Catherine's family album.
Elizabeth	She thought you'd like to see how beautiful Catherine is.
Joshua	Why are we doing this, mom?
Elizabeth	You know why, Joshua; she is the correct lineage and the perfect age. You'll see that mommy's made the right choice.
Joshua	But to set up a whole fake photo shoot; well, it's embarrassing.
Elizabeth	What choice did we have? She is a photographic model - it was the only way to get her here, you know that.

The lights come up downstage right in Catherine's bedroom. She is talking on her mobile phone.

Catherine	Sam, you have to get me out of this job. It's freezing cold and I'm miles from anywhere. And there's something very odd about Mrs Hinkley. I don't like her at all.
Sammy	*(Voice Off)*. For thirty thousand, you don't have to like her, Cathy. Just do your stuff and smile.
Catherine	Has she paid the money, yet?
Sammy	*(Voice Off)*. Yes.
Catherine	In full?
Sammy	*(Voice Off)*. Yes, and we've already transferred twenty-two thousand and a few hundred to your account.
Catherine	Oh… I suppose I'll have to stay then.
Elizabeth	*(Entering)*. Dinner is ready, Catherine.
Catherine	*(Surprised by the intrusion)*. Thank you.
Elizabeth	I thought I'd escort you and make the introductions. My son hoped to join us, but he's not well and will be dining in his room.
Catherine	I'm sorry to hear that. What's your son's name?
Elizabeth	Joshua. He's looking forward to meeting you.

Lights fade down.

Scene 2

Fade up lights in the entrance hall. Joanne enters from the corridor, downstage left. She is the make-up/stylist for the photo shoot and aged about 32. In her hand is a glass of red wine.

Jean-Claude enters stage left, also holding a glass of red wine. He is a photographer, also in his 30s. He sneaks up behind Jo and says "boo" in her ear, giving Jo a shock.

Jo	Don't do that, I'm spooked enough by this place already.
Jean-Claude	I took a photo of a ghost once.
Jo	Really? Well, you'll be in your element here.
Jean-Claude	My belief is that no matter how good the technology, it's the human contribution that brings a photograph to life.
Jo	The ghost wasn't a good model then?
Jean-Claude	I've known worse! *(They both laugh).* Photography is all about timing. Choosing the right moment to get the perfect shot.
Jo	I was on a shoot once, and while the photographer was taking a comfort break, the sun came out and created the most marvellous effect on the water behind the model. I grabbed the camera and rattled off a few shots, and they were the ones the client used!
Jean-Claude	Exactly my point. The photographer had chosen the right location; composed the scene; framed the shot, but would have missed the perfect moment if you hadn't been there to snap it. As I say, it's all about timing.

Elizabeth and Catherine enter to join them.

Elizabeth	I would like to introduce you to our model, Catherine Long. This is Jean-Claude, our photographer.
Jean-Claude	Hello Catherine. *(He takes Catherine's hand and kisses it).*
Elizabeth	And Jo who is looking after wardrobe and make-up.
Catherine	Hi, Jo. *(She gives Jo a hug).*
Jo	It's great to see you again.

Catherine	In the land that time forgot.
Jo	It's nice to get away from London.
Elizabeth	Within a week, Catherine, I predict that Longden Hall will be your spiritual home. *(She picks up a glass of wine from the bureau).*
Jo	Spirits being the operative word. Jean-Claude just mentioned that he once took a photo of a ghost.
Jean-Claude	Perhaps I should save it for the morning. I don't want to spook you on the first night.
Catherine	I don't believe in ghosts. You die and that's it. Why can't people accept it?
Jean-Claude	Well, don't blame me if you have nightmares.
Catherine	Nothing keeps me awake… certainly not clanking chains. *(Elizabeth hands the glass of wine to Catherine).* Thank you.
Jean-Claude	OK, if you're sure but those of a nervous disposition… Jo, may wish to block their ears!
Catherine	You survived, so I think we will.
Jean-Claude	*(Taking a sip of wine).* I was once staying in an old house when away on a shoot, much like this one. At night, I would hear noises outside my bedroom door. I decided to set up my camera with the shutter open in the corridor so that it would capture anything that moved. Early the next morning I checked my camera and you can clearly see the image of a young man looking into the lens. The same young man I'd seen in an old wedding photo hanging on my bedroom wall… dated 1936. *(He throws back some of his wine).* You have a good cellar, Mrs Hinkley.

Elizabeth	Thank you. You have a good eye for detail.
Jean-Claude	Mrs Hinkley, I've been checking out some locations and Longden Hall is a fascinating place. Do you know its history?
Elizabeth	It was built by William Longden as a wedding gift for his wife Lillian, and then sold to Alfred Hinkley.
Catherine	*(Surprised).* Hinkley?
Elizabeth	My son was researching his late father's family roots and saw that a branch of the family had once lived in this house. Joshua says that coming here is like coming home. It feels right.
Jo	Don't you find the house a bit spooky?
Elizabeth	I like the feeling that others have lived here before; walked the same corridors.
Catherine	May I ask how old your son is?
Elizabeth	He was born almost two years before you, Catherine. He's vulnerable to infection. We have to be careful.
Mrs O'Brien	*(Entering downstage left).* Dinner is served, ma'am.
Elizabeth	Thank you, Mrs O'Brien.
Mrs O'Brien	Mrs Hinkley, may I speak with you?
Elizabeth	*(Turning to her guests).* Please go through to the dining room. *(She gestures to the exit, downstage left).* I'll join you shortly.

Still holding their glasses of wine, Catherine, Jo and Jean Claude exit. Mrs O'Brien pulls a British passport out of her pocket.

Mrs O'Brien	When I broke into the young lady's flat, amongst the items that I took, I found her passport. *(Elizabeth takes the passport and flicks*

it open). I can always mail it to her flat, anonymously, or we can destroy it.

Upstage, Joshua enters the main playing area from his bedroom.

Elizabeth	Let me think about it. Once this is over, I shall arrange for everything to be returned to her. In the meantime, we have a job to do – and this could prove useful.
Mrs O'Brien	Yes, ma'am.
Elizabeth	You have unerring instincts, Mrs O'Brien.
Mrs O'Brien	Thank you.
Joshua	*(Approaching the two women)*. What have you got there, mom?
Elizabeth	I was just looking at an old passport.
Joshua	It's red. American passports are blue. I bet you a dime to a nickel that it's Catherine's.
Elizabeth	Yes it is and she looks divine, even in her passport photo. *(She offers the passport to Joshua who makes no move to take it)*.
Joshua	No doubt this is your handiwork, Mrs O'Brien.
Mrs O'Brien	I'm just trying to be of assistance, Master Joshua.
Joshua	Was planting another model's portfolio in Catherine's flat, together with some explicit photos also trying to be of assistance?
Mrs O'Brien	I was simply doing what had to be done. It's for the best, Master Joshua.
Elizabeth	*(To Joshua)*. You look tired, sweetheart. I think you should go back to bed.
Joshua	I don't want to do this, mom.
Elizabeth	See how you feel in the morning.

The lights flicker and then there is almost darkness.

Mrs O'Brien   That'll be the fuse. I'll sort it out.

SFX: the sound of heavy rain. They all exit.

When the lights come up it is morning and a weak sun reveals an empty hallway. The front door bursts open and Catherine, Jo and Jean-Claude rush into the hall. Catherine is wearing Victorian night attire, Jo is laden with a stylist's bag and Jean-Claude is carrying camera equipment.

Jean-Claude   Come on, get in before her hair is completely ruined.
Catherine   It <u>is</u> Wales... I suppose it's what we should expect.
Jo   One minute it was brilliant sunshine and then we're being drenched.

A mobile phone starts ringing.

Jean-Claude   We'll have to do a few shots here. *(He sets up his camera as Jo tries to sort out Catherine).*
Catherine   Is that my phone? *(Jo hunts around for the ringing mobile).* If it's Sean tell him it's too late.
Jo   Have you broken up?
Catherine   I found another model's portfolio under our bed. Need I say more?

The mobile phone continues to ring.

Jean-Claude   Someone answer the damn phone!
Jo   *(To Catherine).* He's getting stressed because he doesn't have an assistant.
Jean-Claude   There wasn't enough in the budget to pay for one!
Catherine   That surprises me. I thought Elizabeth was very generous.
Jean-Claude   Not to me.

Jo	*(Looking at the screen on the phone).* It says anonymous. *(She hands the phone to Catherine; it stops ringing).*
Catherine	I hate that.
Jean-Claude	Jo, let's do a few shots here. Catherine can you stand on the stairs and do your stuff.
Jo	Yeah, it'll look really good. *(Jean-Claude sets up the shot, moving the camera about to get the right angle whilst Jo attends to Catherine's hair. Then, to Catherine).* You know you have an admirer.
Catherine	Jean-Claude?
Jo	*(Moving closer to Catherine).* No! Mrs Hinkley's son.
Catherine	What? I've not even met him.
Jo	I saw him watching you from his bedroom window. For someone who's ill, he looked pretty fit.
Catherine	*(Her phone chirps and she checks the screen).* It's a text… from Mrs Hinkley's son. He's inviting me to dinner, in his… huh! …bedroom.
Jo	Very mysterious and slightly worrying. How did he get your number?
Catherine	The agency must've given it to Elizabeth.
Jo	What are you going to do?
Catherine	Accept, of course. After what you've just said, I'm way too curious to turn him down.
Jo	Do you want a chaperone?
Catherine	*(Ignoring Jo's question).* Although, I hope whatever disease he's got isn't catching.
Jo	For God's sake, don't do anything… physical!
Catherine	I wasn't referring to <u>that</u>, Jo!
Jo	Oh.

They both burst out laughing. Jean-Claude snaps his fingers to get their attention.

Jean-Claude   Come on girls, let's get on with this. We've a lot to get through.

Fade down lights. They all exit.

Lights up on Upstage left in Joshua's bedroom. Joshua is getting dressed for dinner. His mother enters Upstage left carrying a bottle of red wine and two glasses, which she places on the side table.

Elizabeth   Let me have a look at you, my handsome son. *(She fusses around him like a mother hen).*

Joshua   What if she doesn't like me, mom?

Elizabeth   She'll love you, with all her heart. How could she not?

Joshua   I wish I had your confidence. I also wish I had your confidence in what we're doing, mom.

Elizabeth   Sweetheart. You must have faith.

Joshua   In God?

Elizabeth   In your future.

Joshua   Have I got one?

Elizabeth   Yes.

Joshua   I hope you're right, mom.

Lights down.

Lights up in Catherine's bedroom. Jo is sitting on the bed waiting for Catherine, who emerges from the bathroom in a dress that is simple and stunning.

Jo   Perfect.

Catherine sits on the upright chair and looks out at the audience as though looking in a mirror.

Catherine   Not bad. Eat your heart out, Sean.

Jo	*(Brushing Catherine's hair).* Trust you to get a dinner date in the middle of nowhere.
Catherine	What about you and Jean-Claude? I think he likes you.
Jo	Another week and in the right light, I could be tempted! *(Catherine laughs. Jo kisses Catherine on her hair).* Enjoy your dinner-a-deux. I want to hear all about it. See you in the morning.
Catherine	Thank you, Jo.

Jo exits. Catherine gets up from her chair and picks up her phone. She adjusts the chair, sits down and, holding the phone at arm's length, is about to take a shot when the lights flicker. Blackout.

The lights flicker on revealing the haunting presence of Mary Longden standing right behind Catherine, who takes a photograph. The lights flicker again. When they come back on, Mary Longden has gone. Catherine touches the screen on her phone and then puts it to her ear.

Sean	*(Voice Off).* Hello.
Catherine	Sean, I've sent you a photo to remind you of what you once had. *(She cuts the connection).*
Elizabeth	*(Entering).* I thought I'd show you the way to Joshua's room.
Catherine	You're very kind. It's such a big house, I was sure to get lost.
Elizabeth	Thank you for accepting Joshua's invitation to dinner. He's not up to mixing with the others at the moment, but he is very keen to meet you.
Catherine	I hope I won't tire him.

Blackout.

Scene 3

SFX: the clock chimes the hour.

Mary Longden *(Ghostly Voice)*. Ask the one who knows.

Lights up in Joshua's bedroom. Joshua is sitting on his bed when Elizabeth enters followed by Catherine.

Elizabeth Joshua, I would like to introduce you to Catherine.

Catherine steps forward and offers her hand to Joshua, who gets to his feet.

Catherine It's a pleasure to meet you.
Joshua The pleasure is all mine, I assure you.

Catherine sits on the upright chair and Joshua sits on his bed. They are separated by the bedside table.

Elizabeth Would you like a glass of wine, Catherine?
Catherine Thank you.

Elizabeth pours two glasses of red wine.

Joshua How is the photography coming along?
Catherine It's going well, I think.
Joshua Do you enjoy it?
Catherine Mostly, but it can be tough.
Elizabeth I'll inform Mrs O'Brien that you're ready for dinner.
Joshua Thank you mother. *(He raises his glass in a toast to Catherine).* To your future.
Catherine To your good health.
Joshua I'm feeling better already.
Elizabeth I'll leave you two to get to know each other. *(She exits).*
Joshua This has to be the strangest place for a first date.
Catherine Is that what this is? A first date?

Joshua	I would have liked to have taken you somewhere nice, somewhere special, but I'm not quite up to it.
Catherine	No, this is great. Memorable.
Joshua	Just so that you know you're not at risk of catching some deadly disease… I've got a brain tumour with a fancy name that I choose to forget.
Catherine	I'm sorry.
Joshua	Don't be, this is the best time I've had in months.
Catherine	Are you having treatment?
Joshua	I've had the works… surgery, radiation, chemo… I've got one more option left.
Catherine	What's that?
Joshua	My mom has put her faith in an old wives' tale passed down through my family about the restorative powers of this ancient house. *(Catherine's eyes take in the room)*. I know it's crazy but what have I to lose?
Catherine	I wish I could do something to help.
Joshua	You're already helping me more than you can imagine.
Catherine	*(Picking up her glass)*. To the present.
Joshua	*(Raising his glass)*. To the present.

Lights down.

The lights come up in Catherine's bedroom. Elizabeth is searching through Catherine's handbag. Catherine's mobile phone starts ringing on the dressing table. Elizabeth hesitates and picks it up. She looks at the phone then puts it back. It stops ringing. She exits, stage right. Lights down and then up in Joshua's bedroom. Time has clearly passed and is shown by two empty wine bottles on the table.

Joshua	I'll see if Mrs O'Brien can rustle us up some coffee.
Catherine	I'd love to talk all night, but your mother did not hire me with dark rings and blood-shot eyes. I must get my beauty sleep.
Joshua	Then allow me to walk you home.

They both laugh.

| Catherine | I accept. |

Joshua gets up from the table; he pulls back Catherine's chair as she gets up. She slips her hand through his offered arm and they cross to centre stage.

Joshua	My ancestors from my mother's side of the family, were God-fearing, church people; they believed in abstinence, a trait I have definitely not inherited.
Catherine	Do you believe in God?
Joshua	I'll let you know in a few weeks.

They stop outside Catherine's bedroom.

Catherine	Thank you for a lovely evening.
Joshua	Sleep well, Catherine. *(He turns but she reaches out and touches his arm).*
Catherine	Joshua. I am so pleased to have met you.

They gaze into one another's eyes and look as though they are about to kiss. Catherine's mobile phone starts ringing, breaking the moment.

| Joshua | Good night, Catherine. |

Joshua leaves and Catherine watches him until he is lost from view. Her phone continues to ring. Catherine enters her bedroom and picks up the phone. She checks the screen and sighs.

Catherine	Hello Sean.
Sean	*(Voice Off).* Did you see the woman?

Catherine	What woman?
Sean	*(Voice Off)*. The one in the photo wearing the widow's weeds.
Catherine	Widow's weeds? I'll have a look and call you back in the morning. Bye. *(She cuts the connection)*.
Elizabeth	*(Entering, carrying a large mug)*. Everything all right?
Catherine	Yes, fine, thank you.
Elizabeth	*(Placing the mug on the bedside table)*. Hot milk and honey, to help you sleep. *(Beat)*. I have never seen my son so happy.
Catherine	Isn't there anything that can be done?
Elizabeth	We're doing what we can. He takes steroids to reduce the pressure and to alleviate headaches.
Catherine	I wish I could do something.
Elizabeth	You've already done wonders, Catherine. I'll see you in the morning.
Catherine	Goodnight, thank you for the milk.

Elizabeth exits and Catherine takes a sip of milk. She puts the mug down and picks up her phone. She presses a few buttons and looks at the screen. Something on the phone bothers her. She makes a call.

Sean	*(Voice Off)*. Hello.
Catherine	Very clever, Sean. What is she supposed to be? The ghost of Longden Hall? Ooh, I almost felt a chill. Where did you find her? Central casting?
Sean	*(Voice Off)*. That's exactly the photo you sent me. I've not done anything to it.
Catherine	Please Sean… I may be an idiot for going out with you but I'm not a fool. Now go

	back to your little girlfriend and leave me alone.
Sean	*(Voice Off)*. Catherine, you've got to get out of that house. There's something evil there.

She terminates the call. Beat. Her phone rings again.

Catherine	Sean… if you call again I'll change my number.
Margaret	*(Voice Off)*. It's mummy, not Sean. I take it things aren't too good between you?
Catherine	Mum, can I call you in the morning? It's been a very long day.
Margaret	*(Voice Off)*. It would've been nice to have had a call before you left. Even a text. Something, just so that I know where you are.
Catherine	I'm in Wales, mum… not the other side of the world.
Margaret	*(Voice Off)*. When you have a child, Katy, you'll understand. I'll say goodnight. Try to keep warm. Big kiss.
Catherine	Bye mum. *(Beat)*. I love you.

Blackout.

Scene 4

The lights come up in Joshua's room. Elizabeth enters carrying a mug of milk.

Joshua	*(Referring to the milk)*. Thanks, mom. I'll have sweet dreams, tonight. She is beautiful.
Elizabeth	She is perfect in every way.
Joshua	And that's why I can't do it to her, mom.
Elizabeth	She must bear your child.
Joshua	I like her too much. It's not right.
Elizabeth	We've been planning this for months.

Joshua	It's a legend, an old wives' tale.
Elizabeth	We have to give it a go, Joshua. We've come too far to simply give up.
Joshua	There's something special about Cathy, mom. I can't betray her trust.
Elizabeth	I've given her Rohypnol. She won't feel or remember a thing. She's not exactly a virgin!
Joshua	No mom. It's wrong. I'm sorry. I won't do it.
Elizabeth	Josh we've planned for this moment. I've had her watched. I know every intimate, personal, detail of her cycle. It's now or never, sweetheart.
Joshua	I must go to the bathroom.
Elizabeth	I'll wait to say goodnight.
Joshua	I'm not a child.
Elizabeth	I know you're not, sweetheart. *(Joshua exits upstage. She sighs and takes a small phial out of her pocket and puts a few drops of liquid in the mug of milk).* Please forgive me.
Joshua	*(Re-appearing and surprising Elizabeth).* There's nothing to forgive, mom. You're doing what any mother would do for her son.
Elizabeth	Drink your milk and I'll take the cup back down.

Joshua picks up the mug of milk and gulps down the contents. He smiles and gives his mother the empty mug.

Joshua	Do I have a moustache?
Elizabeth	Like Salvador Dali. *(She wipes it away with her thumbs).* I'll see you in the morning.
Joshua	I love you, mom.
Elizabeth	And I love you… more than you'll ever know.

Lights down.

Lights up in Catherine's bedroom. She enters wearing a nightdress and picks up the mug of milk from the dressing table. Just as she is about to take a drink her phone chirps. She puts down the mug of milk and checks the message on her phone. As she reads the message, she smiles and chuckles and then quickly thumbs a reply. She replaces the phone on the dressing table and picks up the mug of milk. She drinks the milk, puts the empty mug on the side table and gets into bed. Lights down.

Lights up in the main hallway and Mrs O'Brien approaches Elizabeth who is carrying Joshua's empty mug of milk.

Mrs O'Brien	Would you like me to check on the young woman before Joshua goes to her?
Elizabeth	He won't do it, Mrs O'Brien.
Mrs O'Brien	He must. It is his only hope.
Elizabeth	He's fallen for her. I don't think I can persuade him to change his mind.
Mrs O'Brien	What will you do?
Elizabeth	What any mother would do in my situation.
Mrs O'Brien	Let me handle it. It is not… natural for a mother to undertake such a task with her own son.
Elizabeth	Thank you, but it's something I must do.
Mrs O'Brien	Well, if you're sure. And the young woman?
Elizabeth	You know what we need. *(Mrs O'Brien exits stage left. She turns and approaches Joshua's room. Lights up as she enters. He is asleep in bed. She looks down at him).* It's a pity. You could have had so much fun. *(She pulls back the bed sheet).*

Lights down.

<u>Scene 5</u>

Morning, in Catherine's bedroom. Catherine is lying in bed fast asleep. Jo enters dressed for the day, carrying her hair and make-up bag and a glass of water.

Jo	Hey, sleepy-head. We've got work to do. *(Catherine groans)*. Drank too much, did you?
Catherine	I don't feel well. *(She sits up slowly and takes the glass of water).*
Jo	So, how did it go?
Catherine	He's dying.
Jo	Joshua?
Catherine	He's got a brain tumour. *(Beat)*. He walked me back to my room and if Sean hadn't phoned at that moment, who knows?
Jo	That's the trouble with mobiles… always interrupting.
Catherine	I feel wrecked. I had a dream… no, my mind's gone blank.
Jo	You'll feel better after a shower. We're shooting by the lake.
Catherine	*(Sighing)*. My head.
Jo	I've got some Ibuprofen. I'll go and get them. It'll help with the hangover.
Catherine	Thanks. *(Jo turns to go)*. Jo. *(Jo looks at her)*. I think I've fallen in love.
Jo	That's a bit sudden, even for you.
Catherine	I'm serious, Jo. There's something about him. I can't explain it.
Jo	Look, you're a long way from home and that can play havoc with your hormones… just like a holiday romance.
Catherine	No. There's something different about Joshua. *(She slowly gets out of the bed and exits stage right).*

| Jo | There's certainly something different about this place! |

Lights down.

Lights up in Joshua's bedroom. Elizabeth enters carrying a breakfast tray; she looks down at Joshua sleeping in bed.

Elizabeth	Good morning, sweetheart.
Joshua	Mom, I don't feel so good.
Elizabeth	It's the French wine. Probably a bit too heavy.
Joshua	I had the weirdest dream.
Elizabeth	Really? Well, you should never tell dreams before breakfast. *(She places the tray on Joshua's lap)*.
Joshua	It's the kinda dream I'm never gonna tell.
Elizabeth	Did it involve Catherine?
Joshua	No mom… sadly not.
Elizabeth	Sounds intriguing.
Joshua	I don't think I'm really ready for breakfast.
Elizabeth	It's important to keep up your strength.
Joshua	Maybe later. *(Elizabeth picks up the tray)*. I'm sorry, mom.
Elizabeth	It's OK, I'll eat it.
Joshua	I meant, about, not going through with our plans last night.
Elizabeth	All I want is what's best for you.
Joshua	I know you do, mom, and I love you for it but we must both accept the inevitable.
Elizabeth	Don't give up the fight, Joshua.
Joshua	I haven't, but sometimes the power of positive thought… is not enough. Sometimes, we just have to let go. *(Elizabeth turns away to hide her emotions)*. I'm sorry for

	doing this to you, mom. You deserve better.
Elizabeth	They say that it's pain that tells us we're alive.
Joshua	No mom, it's not pain… it's love.

Lights down.

Scene 6

The clock chimes the midday hour. SFX: a crash of thunder and torrential rain. Lights up in the Entrance Hall. Catherine is modelling a beautiful white Victorian nightdress. Jean-Claude is on his knees shooting Catherine; and Jo is checking that the nightdress falls correctly.

Jean-Claude	OK, Cathy; I think that's a wrap. Thank you for agreeing to stay the extra couple of weeks. I've never known a client so picky as Mrs Hinkley. Talk about re-shoots of re-shoots. I began to think we'd never get out of here.
Catherine	I don't mind. I've been having fun.
Jean-Claude	Well, it's been great working with you.
Catherine	You made it very easy.
Jean-Claude	Jo, can you double-check that we really have finished?
Jo	*(Examining her clipboard)*. Yup, we've done everything. Yeh! We can all go home.
Jean-Claude	Great, because I'm ready to take my money and run. But, before we get too excited, Elizabeth still has to check the shots, so watch your weight, Catherine.
Catherine	Cheeky! *(A mobile phone starts chirping. Jo takes a phone out of her bag and gives it to Catherine who looks at the screen)*. It's Joshua. He wants to see me. I'd better get changed.

Jo	I don't think he'll mind seeing you as you are.
Catherine	Then I'd better freshen up. *(She smiles and hurries off, stage right).*
Jean-Claude	If I didn't know better, I'd say she was pregnant.
Jo	*(Looking at him).* Pregnant?
Jean-Claude	Every time my wife conceived, I knew.
Jo	That's because you may've had something to do with it!
Jean-Claude	Oh, yeah, you're right. *(He chuckles and exits stage left).*
Jo	Pregnant. *(Beat).* I think it's time we all went home… especially Catherine. *(She exits stage left).*

Lights down.

Lights up in Joshua's room. Catherine enters in her Victorian nightdress. Joshua enters from upstage.

Joshua	Wow. You look… beautiful.

They kiss.

Catherine	How about a walk? Clear the cobwebs?
Joshua	In your nightdress?
Catherine	Who's to see? *(She curls up on his bed; a familiar place).*
Joshua	When are you leaving?
Catherine	I'm not. I'm staying until you kick me out. *(She takes his hand and he sits beside her).*
Joshua	What about the others? Have they gone?
Catherine	Not yet… but I miss them already, especially Jo.
Joshua	Do they live in London?

Catherine	It's where the work is. You can live elsewhere but all the main agencies are based in London.
Joshua	Tell me about your boyfriend.
Catherine	My boyfriend? What do you want to know?
Joshua	What's he like? What does he do? How long have you been together?
Catherine	*(Moving her face closer to Joshua).* That's a lot of questions.
Joshua	I want to be sure he deserves you.
Catherine	*(Moving closer to Joshua).* Well… he's handsome, but he doesn't know it. He's clever, witty and charming, but…
Joshua	But?

Catherine kisses him on the lips as Elizabeth enters.

Elizabeth	Hello, sweetheart.
Joshua	Hi, mom.
Elizabeth	Catherine, you look stunning.
Catherine	Thank you. May I keep this? *(She gestures to her nightdress).*
Elizabeth	Absolutely.
Catherine	*(To Joshua).* If we're going for a walk, perhaps I'd better get changed. *(She kisses him on the lips and exits).*

Before speaking, Elizabeth makes sure that Catherine is not within earshot.

Elizabeth	The others will be gone soon and then she'll be all alone. Once we know for sure that she's pregnant, we can…
Joshua	*(Interrupting).* I told you, I'm not going to make her pregnant. It's not fair.
Elizabeth	What's not fair is that you are dying.

Lights down.

Mary Longden *(Ghostly Voice).* Ask the one who knows. *(Lights up in main hall).* Catherine…

Catherine enters. She heads for the main entrance, the door suddenly swings open. Catherine is transfixed. Her eyes follow someone we cannot see as the lights flicker. There is a crash of thunder then darkness. The lights flicker and we see a woman, Mary Longden, dressed in black Victorian clothes, by the entrance to the corridor, stage left. Blackout. The lights flicker on and Jean-Claude enters stage left, making Catherine jump.

Jean-Claude I hear you're staying on?
Catherine Did you see her?
Jean-Claude See who?
Catherine A woman. A Victorian woman. I think I've just seen a ghost!
Jean-Claude A ghost? What happened to: "I don't believe in ghosts. You die and that's it. Why can't people accept it?"
Catherine She said… never mind. Have you seen Jo?

Lights down.

Scene 7

Lights up in Catherine's bedroom where Jo has packed Catherine's bag and is preparing to leave. Catherine enters and Jo is momentarily shocked.

Catherine What are you doing?
Jo You can always return but I want you to come with us now.
Catherine I'm not leaving. I don't know how long he's got and I want to be here for him. I love him. Nothing's going to make me leave.

Jo	*(Approaching Catherine).* Do you remember when we were in Morocco and I'd met that Italian?
Catherine	This is different.
Jo	Listen to me. I was in love and would have done anything he wanted as long as I could be with him. But you saved me.
Catherine	This is not the same. *(She breaks away).* If it's a mistake then let me make the mistake. Joshua's dying. What harm can come to me?
Jo	*(Crossing to Catherine, she takes hold of her arms).* I have a bad feeling about this place, sweetheart. Elizabeth… I can't put my finger on it, but she bothers me. She really bothers me.
Catherine	Her only child is dying and if I can make his last days a bit happier, then that's what I'm going to do. *(She tries to hide her tears).*
Jo	Oh, Cathy, I'm so sorry. *(She hugs Catherine).* I'll stay with you. At least for a few days.
Catherine	*(Regaining some control of herself).* I'll be fine. And I can always talk to you on my phone.
Elizabeth	*(Entering. To Jo).* Your taxi's here.
Jo	Look after my friend, Mrs Hinkley.
Elizabeth	Like a daughter. *(To Catherine).* I have shopping to do, so I'm leaving you and Joshua in the capable hands of Mrs O'Brien. She'll get you some lunch.
Catherine	Did I see a car tucked away somewhere? Josh and I could go for a drive. Have a change of scene.
Elizabeth	It's Mrs O'Brien's. I can't cope with driving on the left-hand side of the road so I just use taxis. I'll see you later.

Jo	Goodbye, Mrs Hinkley.
Elizabeth	Goodbye, Jo.
Jo	Thank you for the job.
Elizabeth	My pleasure. *(She exits).*

Jo turns to Catherine and they hug.

Jo	Keep in touch. You've got my number.
Catherine	I know I'm crazy. I just can't help it.
Jo	If you can't be crazy when you're young, when can you?
Catherine	I'll see you to the taxi.

Jo exits through the front door and Catherine follows her and stands by the entrance. SFX: a taxi leaving. Catherine closes the door. SFX: a young man's chuckle echoes through the hallway. Catherine sees something approaching her and backs up until her back is against the door. SFX: the young man's cruel laughter is heard again. Lights down.

Lights up in Joshua's room. Catherine enters. The room is empty.

Joshua	Catherine.
Catherine	*(Spinning round as he enters upstage).* You want to know what the problem is with my boyfriend?
Joshua	He lives with his mother?
Catherine	No. Your mother I can live with. *(She sits on the bed and Joshua kneels before her).*
Joshua	You've seen the ghost? Mary Longden.
Catherine	Yes, and someone else.
Joshua	That will be her son, Gilbert.
Catherine	A really horrible looking man.
Joshua	He killed Mary and now I think she's waiting for me.
Catherine	What do you mean?

Joshua	*(Getting up)*. I keep seeing her. Sometimes it's just a glimpse, a slight movement, a sound; sometimes I wake in the night and feel her looking down at me; sometimes I just feel a chill.
Catherine	*(Standing)*. What are you saying? That I'm competing with a ghost?
Joshua	No you're not! *(He reaches out for Catherine)*. She's for the next life but I've still got a lot of living to do in this one. *(Catherine's phone chirps. She glances at the screen)*. Your boyfriend?
Catherine	Yes. NO! You're my boyfriend.
Joshua	Take the call but treat him gently. You may want to go back to him.
Catherine	*(Taking Joshua's hand)*. No, I've made my decision. I'm with you.
Joshua	That's lovely but, unfortunately, it's a temporary arrangement.
Catherine	Not in my eyes.
Joshua	That's very flattering. *(Catherine's phone chirps again)*. Take the call.
Catherine	It's a voice message.
Joshua	I have to use the bathroom. *(He exits upstage)*.

Catherine dials a number and we hear the voice mail message.

Sean	*(Voice Off)*. Cathy, it's me, Sean. Look, I keep finding stuff on the internet about Longden Hall and it's not good. Can you call me? You know I love you. I always will.

Catherine cuts the connection and dials a number.

Catherine	Sammy, it's Catherine.

Sammy	*(Voice Off)*. I was just about to call you. I've got another job for you starting Monday. It's a commercial, shooting in Morocco. Great money.
Catherine	Oh.
Sammy	*(Voice Off)*. What's the problem? You should be pleased. This is turning out to be your best year ever.
Catherine	I can't do the commercial.
Sammy	*(Voice Off)*. Not another reshoot?
Catherine	No, the shoot went well, it's just that I've met a guy... and can't leave him.
Sammy	*(Voice Off)*. Don't be ridiculous. He'll still be there when you get back. *(Catherine doesn't respond)*. Catherine?
Catherine	There's something else.
Sammy	*(Voice Off)*. I don't want to hear it. Come back to London and sort yourself out. Be professional.
Catherine	I think I'm pregnant. *(Silence from Sammy)*. Hello?
Sammy	*(Voice Off)*. This better be a joke.
Catherine	No, it's not a joke and we were careful but, clearly, not careful enough.
Sammy	*(Voice Off)*. Oh Catherine, why do you always have to screw things up? So who is the Lothario? Jean-Claude?
Catherine	His name's Joshua. He's Elizabeth's son and he's a really great guy. *(Beat)*. Maybe I can model maternity wear? *(She laughs)*. Anyway, I wanted to thank you for making me take this job. It's changed my life.
Sammy	*(Voice Off)*. You can't have the baby. Get rid of it. Is Jo there? Perhaps she can talk some sense into you.

Catherine	They've all gone. Bye, Sammy.
Sammy	*(Voice Off).* Catherine!

Catherine cuts the connection. Blackout.

Scene 8

Lights up on the Dining Area upstage, right. Elizabeth enters and sits down. Mrs O'Brien enters carrying a tray with some crockery, which she places on the table.

Mrs O'Brien	Your son and his young lady will be down shortly. Would you like me to serve dinner?
Elizabeth	Thank you, Mrs O'Brien, but I would like to wait.
Mrs O'Brien	I take it that everything is going to plan?
Elizabeth	We can but hope, Mrs O'Brien, although I believe that we have grounds for optimism.
Mrs O'Brien	Your son certainly has a spring in his step.
Elizabeth	Yes he does and it gladdens my heart.
Mrs O'Brien	You are a wonderful mother.
Elizabeth	Thank you. *(Catherine and Joshua enter holding hands. She gets to her feet to greet her son).* How lovely to see you up, sweetheart. The walk clearly did you a world of good. *(Catherine sits down to the right of her and Joshua sits on her left).* As you can tell from the delightful aroma, Mrs O'Brien has been busy in the kitchen.
Catherine	It smells delicious, Mrs O'Brien.

Mrs O'Brien gives a brief nod.

Elizabeth	Where did you go for your walk?

Catherine and Joshua look at each other.

Joshua	We didn't quite make the walk.
Elizabeth	Oh, I see.

Mrs O'Brien	Would you like me to serve you, ma'am?
Elizabeth	That's quite all right, Mrs O'Brien. We can look after ourselves.
Mrs O'Brien	I'll say goodnight then.
Catherine	Goodnight, Mrs O'Brien.
Mrs O'Brien	I hope you enjoy your dinner.
Elizabeth	I'm sure we will, Mrs O'Brien. *(Mrs O'Brien exits)*. Catherine, you're glowing tonight.
Catherine	Thank you.
Elizabeth	Please forgive my… my nosiness, but my instinct as a doctor tells me that you are carrying a baby.

Joshua is shocked and Catherine is momentarily surprised.

Catherine	I didn't know you were a doctor.
Elizabeth	Technically, I'm not. I married Joshua's father shortly before I was due to qualify and abandoned my medical career to be a good wife and mother.
Joshua	My father died last fall.

Silence.

Catherine	Yes. I think I may be pregnant.
Elizabeth	Wonderful!
Joshua	Is it… my baby?
Catherine	I wasn't pregnant when I came here, if that's what you mean?
Joshua	But I was careful. It shouldn't have happened. How can it have happened? *(He looks at his mother; she is barely able to disguise her glee)*.
Elizabeth	*(To Joshua)*. This is wonderful news, sweetheart.
Catherine	*(To Joshua)*. Is it wonderful news, Joshua?
Elizabeth	Of course it is. It's what we all want.

Catherine looks at Elizabeth, surprised by her comment.

Catherine   Is it? Anyway, it's early days.

Elizabeth   Which is why I'll look after you during your
                 confinement. *(She picks up her glass of wine).*
                 Joshua Hinkley Junior… it has such a classy
                 ring.

A ghostly scream is heard offstage.

Catherine   Did you hear that?
Joshua   Hear what?
Catherine   A scream. I'm sure I heard a scream.
Elizabeth   It's an old house with lots of creaks and
                 groans. *(Beat).* Will you return to modelling
                 after the baby's born?
Catherine   I'm not sure. I do have a degree in fine art
                 and graphic design so I could always get a
                 job in a studio.
Elizabeth   I think you should marry, Joshua.
Joshua   Mom, it's generally accepted that the man
                 proposes to the woman, not his mother!
Elizabeth   We don't necessarily have all the time in the
                 world, sweetheart.

Joshua gets up from the table and approaches Catherine. He
gets down on one knee and takes her hand.

Joshua   Catherine, would you do me the greatest
                 honour and marry me?
Catherine   *(Blinking back her tears).* Yes.

They hug.

Elizabeth   I'll ask the Reverend Shepherd to arrange a
                 special licence.

Blackout. The ringing tone of someone calling a mobile phone is heard.

Catherine   *(Voice Off)*. Hi, this is Catherine, please leave a message and if I like it, you'll hear back from me.

SFX: Beep.

Sean   *(Voice Off)*. Cathy, it's me, Sean. I spoke to Jo and she told me that you're getting married. Are you insane? You don't even know the guy. Why are you doing this to me? You know I didn't have an affair. I don't know how that portfolio got there. Probably one of your model friends left it. All I do know is that I love you and I would never cheat on you. If you get this message in time, then please cancel the wedding and come home. *(Beat)*. Please come home, sweetheart. I miss you. *(Beat)*. Bye.

SFX: Organ music. A white cross is lowered.

Scene 9

Lights up as a Curate enters carrying a large brass candlestick with a lit candle. Over his arm is a tippet (the Vicar's preaching scarf). The Curate places the candlestick in a suitable location as the Reverend Shepherd enters upstage dressed in a cassock and surplice.

The Curate approaches Shepherd and they bow. Shepherd takes the scarf, kisses it reverently, and places it over his head and around his neck so that it hangs down evenly. The Curate exits upstage as Jo, Elizabeth and Mrs O'Brien enter and take up positions to the side of the stage.

Catherine, wearing a white wedding dress with veil, enters with Joshua, who is dressed in a dark suit. They stop in front of the Reverend Shepherd, and Joshua takes Catherine's left hand.

Catherine   With my body I honour you, all that I am I give to you, and all that I have I share with you, within the love of God, Father, Son and Holy Spirit.

Rev Shepherd   *(Giving the sign of the cross above the young couple).* Now that Joshua and Catherine have given themselves to each other by solemn vows, with the joining of hands and the giving of a ring, I pronounce that they are husband and wife, in the Name of the Father, and of the Son, and of the Holy Spirit. *(Beat).* Those whom God has joined together let no one put asunder. *(He smiles).* You may kiss the bride. *(Joshua carefully lifts Catherine's veil and they kiss tenderly on the lips. After a few seconds, Joshua cries out and sinks to his knees, holding his head).* I'll call for an ambulance.

Joshua   I'm OK. I'm OK. Just give me a minute.

Catherine   *(Cradling Joshua's head).* We must get him home.

Rev Shepherd   Catherine, you do realise that you are not yet married in the eyes of the law.

Elizabeth   *(Rushing forward).* What?

Rev Shepherd   Joshua and Catherine were married before God, but for it to be lawful, they must both sign the marriage certificate and have their signatures witnessed.

Joshua   I can sign.

Catherine	*(To Rev Shepherd).* Do you have a handkerchief? *(Rev Shepherd gives her a pristine red handkerchief).* Thank you.
Mrs O'Brien	*(Offering Elizabeth a silver hip flask).* A few drops of brandy may help.

Elizabeth takes the flask and gives it to Catherine.

Catherine	Thank you, Mrs O'Brien. *(She puts the flask to Joshua's lips).*
Joshua	I'm sorry.
Elizabeth	Joshua, let's do what we have to do with the marriage certificate and then go home.
Joshua	I have felt better, Cathy, but I've never been happier.
Catherine	I love you so much.
Rev Shepherd	I'll get the register.

The Curate enters with a large, bound book which he gives to Rev Shepherd and then exits. Catherine hands the flask back to Elizabeth.

Joshua	*(To Catherine).* I don't think I've got long. I feel life's being squeezed out of me.

Elizabeth turns to Mrs O'Brien and gives her the flask.

Elizabeth	Mrs O'Brien, would you kindly see if the taxi's outside?

Mrs O'Brien nods and exits.

Rev Shepherd	It's all filled in apart from the signatures.

Catherine rests the register on Joshua's knee and accepts a fountain pen from Rev Shepherd, which she places in Joshua's hand. He signs the register.

Joshua	Not my usual flourish. *(Catherine takes the book and pen and signs her name. Suddenly, he*

cries out and grabs his head). God, it's like a
vice!!

Elizabeth   We must get him home. Would you witness
Catherine's signature, Joanna?

Catherine hands the register to Jo and then helps Joshua to his
feet. Mrs O'Brien enters.

Mrs O'Brien   Mrs Hinkley, the taxi is waiting.
Elizabeth   Thank you.
Jo   Catherine, why have you signed the register
Mary Charlotte Longden? *(She shows
Catherine the register).*
Mrs O'Brien   Sign it again!

Catherine hastily signs again then gives the pen and register to
Rev Shepherd.

Rev Shepherd   Yes, that's good, I'll be the second witness.
(He scrawls in the book).

Catherine and Elizabeth get Joshua to his feet.

Elizabeth   Thank you very much, Reverend.
Rev Shepherd   It was a privilege.
Elizabeth   Coming, Catherine?
Catherine   I'll be out in a minute.

Elizabeth looks reluctant to go without Catherine.

Rev Shepherd   *(To Elizabeth).* Allow me to walk you to
your car.

Elizabeth and Mrs O'Brien support Joshua as they leave the
church, followed by Shepherd.

Jo   I must go, Cathy.
Catherine   Thank you for coming. I wish you could
stay a bit longer.

Jo	I wish I could too, but I've a job in the Lake District and I'm already a day late. *(Beat)*. You look beautiful. Your mother would be very proud of you.
Catherine	I couldn't invite her. It's not what she planned for me… pregnant and a dying groom.
Jo	*(Hugging Catherine)*. I must go. Any problems, you promise you'll give me a call? *(Catherine nods as the Rev Shepherd enters)*. It was a lovely service.
Rev Shepherd	Yes, it was.

Catherine follows Jo and shakes Shepherd's hand.

Catherine	Thank you very much.
Rev Shepherd	Mind how you go, Catherine. *(Catherine exits. He picks up the register and reads the name)*. Mary Charlotte Longden.
Mary Longden	*(Ghostly Voice)*. Ask the one who knows.
Rev Shepherd	Oh, dear Lord. *(He follows someone with his eyes who we cannot see)*.
Mrs O'Brien	*(Entering)*. Reverend Shepherd. *(Rev Shepherd jumps, clearly disturbed)*. Mrs Hinkley was wondering whether you would care to join us up at Longden Hall for the wedding breakfast?
Rev Shepherd	Did you just pass a young woman, Mrs O'Brien?
Mrs O'Brien	Is there a problem, sir?
Rev Shepherd	There was a woman. She was wearing 19th century clothes, and she had the most pleading, desperate look on her face.
Mrs O'Brien	*(Looking around)*. She appears to have gone now, sir.

Rev Shepherd	*(Suddenly remembering).* Mary Charlotte Longden… I know that name. *(He hurries over to a suitable section of scenery).* Look. The wood's been carved: 'In Memory of Mary Charlotte Hinkley, nee Longden, 1807 to 1844.'
Mrs O'Brien	Not a long life.
Rev Shepherd	'Wife of Alfred Hinkley and Mother of Gilbert Hinkley.' Catherine signed her name in the register: Mary Charlotte Longden. What made her do that?
Mrs O'Brien	I do not have the least idea.
Rev Shepherd	Wait! I remember, now… I read an article about the Hinkley family in an old copy of the parish gazette. I've got it, somewhere. If I remember correctly, the article described a satanic ritual… and a murder. Matricide. *(Mrs O'Brien picks up the candlestick)* … and there was a curse that affected the male line of the Hinkley family. I'm worried, Mrs O'Brien. I fear that Catherine may be in danger. We must warn her.

Mrs O'Brien removes the candle, lifts the candlestick above her head, blows out the candle, and… black out.

END OF ACT ONE

If you would like to read Act Two, please contact Stagescripts Ltd, Lantern House, 84 Littlehaven Lane, Horsham, West Sussex, RH12 4JB, UK
Tel (UK) : 0345 686 0611 or +44 (0)700 581 0581
sales@stagescripts.com / www. stagescripts.com
Registered in England and Wales No. 06155216

This play is a work of fiction. The characters are entirely the product of the author's imagination and any resemblance to actual persons, living or dead, is entirely coincidental.

Printed in Great Britain
by Amazon

54472190R00210